"In a first novel that is guaranteed to please Fannie Flagg and Bailey White fans, Gillespie introduces the Bottom Dollar Girls with a flair for timing and a cheeky southern turn of phrase...Brace for a wild ride chock-full of Southern wit and down-home advice from a clutch of quirky characters you will hope to see again soon."

– Booklist

"Use your very last bottom dollar, if you have to. Just BUY THIS BOOK. You will laugh yourself sick and love every minute of it."

– Jill Conner Browne, The Sweet Potato Queen

"A winner of a first novel, filled with Southern-style zingers and funny folks."

– Kirkus Reviews (starred review)

"The characters are the kind of steel magnolias who would make Scarlett O'Hara envious."

– The Atlanta Journal-Constitution

"Laugh out loud... this perfect summer read [will] find permanent beach-house residence."

– Richmond Times-Dispatch

A DOLLAR SHORT (#2)

"Those plain-speaking, cheeky Bottom Dollar gals (*Bet Your Bottom Dollar*) return with more rollicking adventures in Cayboo Creek, South Carolina...Never a dull moment...this fast-paced screamer of a romance begs a giggle, if not a guffaw."

– Booklist

"Laugh-out-loud antics as...Gillespie continues her entertaining Bottom Dollar Girls series...Certain to please women's fiction fans of all ages."

– Romantic Times (Top Pick)

"As tart and delectable as lemon meringue pie...a pure delight."

– Jennifer Weiner, Author of Good in Bed and In Her Shoes

"A fine romp of a book, well-written and thoroughly entertaining."

– The Winston-Salem Journal

"*A Dollar Short* is meant to entertain, and it does. It takes talent to sustain this level of comic writing for over 300 pages. Gillespie keeps the ball in the air, spinning madly, until the end."

– The Boston Globe

DOLLAR DAZE (#3)

"Each character is lovingly crafted in Gillespie's hilarious, heartwarming, and often irreverent look at senior living in small-town America. The third book in the Bottom Dollar Girls series (*Bet Your Bottom Dollar*; *A Dollar Short*) can also be enjoyed as a stand-alone."

– Booklist (starred review)

"Hilarious and endearing...Gillespie's humorous style will have readers hooting out loud, and her cheeky characters will have them coming back for more!"

– Janean Nusz, The Road to Romance

"Readers will be chuckling over crazy man-getting antics, sighing at the complexity of life, love and matrimony and maybe even shedding a tear over the heartbreak and tragedy. This novel is charismatic and replete with poignancy."

– Romantic Times

Girl Meets Class

Books by Karin Gillespie

GIRL MEETS CLASS

The Bottom Dollar Series

BET YOUR BOTTOM DOLLAR (#1)

A DOLLAR SHORT (#2)

DOLLAR DAZE (#3)

Girl Meets Class

Karin Gillespie

HENERY PRESS

GIRL MEETS CLASS
Part of the Henery Press Chick Lit Collection

First Edition
Trade paperback edition | September 2015

Henery Press
www.henerypress.com

ISBN-13: 978-1-941962-85-5

Printed in the United States of America

To Julie Cannon.
I miss you every day.

ACKNOWLEDGMENTS

Thanks so much to the superlative team at Henery Press. Particular thanks goes to Kendel Lynn, Art C. Molinares, Erin George, and Rachel Jackson who are always accessible, cheerful and kind.

A great debt of gratitude is due to Anne Bohner, who is one of the loveliest people on the planet and who I can't thank enough. Thanks also to my wonderful early readers: Magda Newland, Ed Gillespie, Jackie Miles and Jo Ann Appleton. Thanks also to the Converse MFA program.

One

The unspooling of my Tiffany and Wild Turkey lifestyle began with a trip to the Luckett County Jail. It was mid-July in Rose Hill, Georgia, and I was trapped in the backseat of a police car. The air inside was close and thick like sawmill gravy. Up front the radio crackled and hissed with static as the dispatcher announced the city's Thursday night dark doings: a mugging, a domestic disturbance, and a pit bull fight.

"Don't you people have an armed robbery or a murder to go to?"

No response from behind the mesh barrier. Might as well have been a mute mosquito.

The law enforcement center loomed over the hill, a tombstone-colored tower leaking a sickly, yellow light. First time I laid eyes on the place I scared myself silly, imagining strip searches, filthy cells, and sadistic wardens. This time the sight barely made me flinch.

Here we go again, I thought.

We arrived, and the cops hustled me out of the car and into a processing room. It contained a haphazard collection of utilitarian desks and smelled like dirty feet. A stout policewoman lumbered toward me. She had a gray front tooth and a sprig of hair creeping out of her nostril. I wasn't her typical customer, and she was sizing me up.

I tried to see myself through her eyes: A twenty-one-year-old blonde, blinking and stumbling in the harsh fluorescent lights, wearing a strapless pink party dress, gold gladiator sandals, and diamond drop earrings.

Maybe she was imagining what kind of car I drove—a cherry-red Porsche Boxster convertible—or who my people were. Likely she'd heard of my family's company and probably had a few cans of Cornelia's Southern-Style lima beans or black-eyed peas collecting dust in her pantry. Most everyone in America did.

I was photographed and fingerprinted. The cop confiscated my python clutch and peered at the contents, a lipstick in a plum shade called Promiscuous and a Platinum Visa in the name of Toni Lee Wells. If only I could give her that card and make my latest blunder go away.

She glanced up from my clutch and gave me a look that could freeze vodka. It seemed to say, "I don't care who you are, princess. Now you belong to me."

The cop gestured for me to follow her. We were headed in the opposite direction of the holding cells. For a brief panicky moment I wondered if she was taking me to some secret dark room where repeat offenders were taught a lesson with a rubber hose. Instead I was led to a dank narrow hallway with a stone bench. "Sit," she said. "Someone's on the way to pick you up."

I was relieved, naturally, but also curious. *Who was coming?* It's not like I'd called anyone. After a few minutes my father approached, wearing a pair of wrinkled camouflage pants and a John Deere cap.

Daddy hugged me with his meaty arms, wrapping me in his scent, oak chips mixed with perspiration. The embrace went on for more than a minute. It was as if I'd been released from a ten-year stay in a Turkish prison instead of a brief jaunt to jail.

"Let's get out of here," he said.

Outside bloated clouds scudded overhead; the sky seemed close enough to touch. A jacked-up, emerald-green Cadillac roared past us, its frame shimmying with the bass from a rap song. I climbed into the refuge of my daddy's Land Rover. His yellow Lab, Beau, pounced on my lap and bathed my cheeks with warm, liver-snap scented saliva.

"How'd you know I was here?"

My daddy's freckled scalp shone through his thinning red hair. "Sibbie Stevens saw you being put into the back of a police car outside Bistro 91. Public intoxication, Toni Lee? What did you do?"

"Nothing. Just fell asleep. That's not a crime."

Not unless you were operating heavy equipment, which I wasn't. Just my iPhone a few minutes before I passed out.

"Fell asleep where?"

"In the bar. It was just a little catnap. Don't know why they felt they had to call the law."

That wasn't the whole story, but no need to share all the damning details. Before I hit the ground, I'd been singing along to a Katy Perry song on my phone, maybe a little too loudly and probably off-key. The usual bartender, Rita, was out sick and a snippy substitute was working in her place. The sub asked me to cut out the singing, and I tried to loosen her up by asking her to dance with me. Somehow I ended up knocking over a couple of highball glasses on the bar. Then I got dizzy and the next thing I remember was a cop pulling me up from the floor.

It'd have never happened if Rita had been on duty. Whenever I got a little wobbly in my shoes, she always took good care of me. In exchange I made sure she went home with a nice fat tip tucked into her pocketbook.

No more shots of Cuervo Gold, I thought. I'd only started drinking heavily a few months ago and was still learning the ins and outs of alcohol. Tequila was in a class by itself. No wonder they called it to-kill-ya.

On the way home, my father's silence was so loud he might as well have been yelling at me. I was grateful when his Land Rover sailed through the security checkpoint at the entrance of Country Club Hills. The car came to a stop in front of my condo, and he gripped the steering wheel so hard his knuckles were white.

I broke the silence between us. "I don't know what got into me tonight, but it was a one-time thing. It'll never happen again."

By then I felt completely sober. A trip to jail was a guaranteed buzzkill.

Daddy gave me a hard look. "One-time thing, huh?"

I nodded vigorously.

"That's odd because according to one of the officers you're practically a regular at the jail. Few more trips and they'll be naming a cell after you."

"Two trips hardly makes me a—"

"It's not just that," he continued. "You've been out of control for months. I'm still getting calls about that terrible thing you did to Baby Bowen at Lois Atkins' funeral."

I'd never live that stunt down. Ten years from now people would probably still be talking about what I'd done to Baby Bowen at that funeral.

"Maybe you ought to give that Dr. Lyons another try."

I wrinkled my nose. Dr. Lyons had white carpet in his office and made me take off my shoes before I was given permission to enter. During our visit, he kept squirting Purell into his hands. He seemed crazier than I could ever aspire to be.

Daddy was scratching Beau's ears, waiting for me to speak.

"Forget Dr. Lyons."

He let out a heavy exhale of air.

"I understand why you're acting out like this. Anyone in your situation probably would, and I'm the first to sympathize. But here's the thing—"

"I'm tired. Can we talk about this another time?"

"Toni Lee."

"It's really late. You should get back to bed." I patted his arm. That's when I noticed a faded yellow bruise on his bicep.

"What did you do to yourself this time?" My father was the most accident-prone man I'd ever met. He was forever running into doors or tripping on loose stones. If there was a banana peel within a ten-mile radius he'd find it and slip on it.

"Don't try to change the subject."

I kissed his cheek. "Goodnight, Daddy."

"This is serious."

I mussed his wispy hair and flounced out of the car.

"Toni Lee!"

I ignored him and sprinted to my condo, a replica of a three-story Italianate villa divided into six residences.

Inside it was bright and noisy. As usual I'd left on every light, and the television blared with a commercial advertising a Chevy Truck Blow-Out sale. I hurried to the kitchen and popped open a bottle of Zin Your Face, a California Zinfandel. I chose wines with funny names; it made alcohol seem tame and friendly, like Hi-C with a kick. One glass, I thought. I surveyed the contents of my cupboards and chose a brandy snifter the size of a baby's head.

I filled the glass to the brim and moved to the living room, plunked down in front of the large-screen TV, and shoved *Texas Chainsaw Massacre* into the Blu-ray player. I was addicted to horror movies, the gorier the better. They helped put problems into their proper perspective. Yes, my life might have recently taken an unlucky turn, but at least I wasn't being chased by a chainsaw-wielding maniac. In fact, if I was a shrink and one of my patients was having a meltdown, my advice would be to watch *Evil Dead 2* and call me in the morning.

The next day I cracked open one eye. The sharp pain behind my temple told me it was going to be another Goody's Powder morning. I'd fallen asleep on the couch; the clock on my Blu-ray player said it was almost twelve. I'd have liked to stay asleep for a couple more hours but someone was banging on my back door.

"Toni Lee! Are you in there?"

I carefully got up from the couch so as to not disturb the delicate condition of my head. It felt like it was full of broken glass.

The back door was cracked, and a hand was fumbling with the chain. The door swung open, and my best friend Joelle burst inside. Her eyes narrowed into sharp green shards. I was in trouble. How did I mess up this time?

"How much did you drink last night?" she said.

The stripes of her dress looked like they were moving. She had a penchant for animal prints, and today she was passing herself off as a zebra.

"Who says I was drinking?" I peeked into my ceramic coffee jar and found only a pile of crumbs.

"You smell like you took a swan dive into a wine vat...And you forgot to pick me up from the oral surgeon this morning."

She glared at me. Joelle was just under five feet tall with long, frizzy hair the bright red color of Cheerwine.

"Was that today?"

"There I sat waiting. Lips blown up to the size of a raft. In so much pain I felt like cutting off my head. The nurse kept asking, 'Are you sure someone's coming to get you?' 'Oh yes,' I said. 'Toni Lee might not be the most reliable girl but she would never let me down in my moment of greatest need.'"

I had a good excuse for forgetting Joelle's appointment but decided not to tell her about last night's debauchery. Used to be I'd share everything with her. Lately I'd been doing a lot of editing.

I tried to hang my head but it made me dizzy. "I'm so sorry. Don't know how it slipped my mind but I'll make it up to you."

"How so?" Joelle leaned against a granite island littered with a flotilla of empty Chinese food cartons.

"I could give you my new Prada clutch." I smiled weakly. There were more clutches where that one came from. If I wanted, I could buy a new clutch each month.

"You're blatantly exploiting my pathological weakness for pricey pocketbooks."

"Guilty."

She plucked at the strap of her own bag, a small and battered Coach from an outlet mall near Commerce, Georgia.

"Much as I love Prada, I'd rather you keep your promises instead of trying to buy me off."

"I'll work on it."

I was glad she seemed to be in a forgiving mood. To placate her further I suggested lunch at the Rose Hill Country Club. My treat, of course, since Joelle wasn't a member.

* * *

We arrived at the country club ladies' grill, a viciously sunny room with picture windows overlooking the deep greens of the golf course. The grill was nearly deserted except for a table of elderly women, and a young couple with a toddler in a sailor suit.

Joelle wagged her fingers at the child and said, "Ahoy matey." She came from a big family—six brothers—and had the motherly instincts of a grizzly bear.

My instincts, on the other hand, were more like a cuckoo bird's. The females trick other species of birds into raising their babies by laying eggs in their nests. Then they fly off, single and unencumbered.

Once seated, the waitress arrived at our table, and I ordered a patty melt and a bloody Mary.

Joelle raised a fiery eyebrow. "Tossing gasoline on the bonfire, are we?"

I smiled, even though facial movement was painful. "I'm in training for spring break."

"That's a long time from now."

"No harm in getting started early."

Joelle's eyes widened, distracted by something behind me. "What is it?"

"Oh Jesus. You won't believe who just came in."

"Who?"

"Baby Bowen."

I sunk down low in my seat. I hadn't run into Baby since the infamous incident at Lois Atkins' funeral.

"Is she armed?"

"Doesn't need to be. She could take you down with one hand tied behind her back."

True enough. Despite her nickname, Baby was over six feet tall and likely wore an F-cup bra. She was huge but had no extraneous adipose tissue. The girl was pure muscle.

"She's headed over here," Joelle said.

"Has she spotted me?" I was tempted to duck under the white linen tablecloth and hide myself.

"I think so. Her face is turning red and there's a violent gleam in her eye."

The air molecules seemed to quiver as Baby headed in our direction. I hoped she was going to stalk past us without speaking, but no such luck. She reached our table and trained a pair of bulging blue eyes on me.

"You."

"Listen, Baby, I'm really sorry. I—"

She pointed a cigar-sized finger at me. "You!" she said again.

"Did you get my note of apology? And of course, I'll be happy to pay—"

Baby loomed over me, her face wide as a planet. I shrank away, fearing she'd grab me by the roots of my hair and toss me across the room. Certainly she was entitled. "Everyone's sorry about what happened to you, but maybe it's time you got yourself some professional help." She straightened her spine, pivoted on her schooner-sized shoes and left the grill.

"That was a close one," I said.

I expected Joelle to be quivering with laughter. Instead she was solemnly shaking her head.

"What?"

"If you don't know, I feel sorry for you."

"You don't even like Baby."

Joelle and Baby had been in the same class at Rose Hill Prep, three grades above me. Joelle was a scholarship student, and Baby never let her forget it.

The sun had lit the strands of Joelle's red hair; it looked as if sparks might fly from her scalp at any moment. "One day you'll go too far. One day something really bad is going to happen to you."

I met her gaze and, in a very soft voice, I said, "Hate to tell you, but the worst has already happened. From here on out everything else is anti-climactic."

An uncomfortable moment of silence followed, and I was

grateful when Henrietta—Henry for short—appeared at our table. She was the club's dining room manager. "Ms. Wells, could I have a moment of your time?"

"Sure thing. What can I do you for?"

Henry glanced at Joelle. "Maybe it would be best if we went into the hallway and had a private talk."

"You can talk in front of Joelle. She's like family."

It took Henry a moment to speak. She kept glancing down at her white work clogs and touching a bun pulled so tight I imagined it smarted. She said, "I'm sorry. You no longer have club privileges here."

"I don't understand."

"It's your father," Henry said in a low voice.

"Is he behind on dues?"

Daddy spent wads of money on gambling and sometimes came up short at the end of the month. Usually all he had to do was call my aunt and she'd cover any outstanding debts.

"It's not the dues." Henry blinked rapidly, clearly uneasy with her task. "Earlier this morning your father called to cut off your membership."

"You're joking."

"I'm afraid not."

"I don't get it. Why would he...?"

I thought about last night and how uptight Daddy had been, but to cancel my club membership...That wasn't like him. He'd never been a strict parent and had always acted more like a buddy than a dad. Then again, until several months ago, I'd been the ideal child.

Was he trying to get my attention? Fine. So long as he didn't involve Aunt Cornelia. That'd be a mistake of mythical proportions.

Henry fidgeted with the collar of her starched white uniform, waiting. I'd always liked her and regretted she had to get mixed up in my family's dramas.

"I'm sorry, Henry. I have no idea why my father would do such a thing but I'll leave right now."

She nodded and returned to the kitchen.

"What was that all about?" Joelle said.

I rifled through my bag for some more Goody's Powder. In the last few seconds my headache had gone from irritating to kill-me-now.

"It's just a misunderstanding. After I drop you at your car, I'll go over to Tranquility Hall and find out what's going on."

Two

My tires squealed as I negotiated the turns of the winding driveway that led to my father's house. Tranquility Hall was an ivory-shrouded Tudor that hulked in the shadows of several oversized magnolia trees and meandered on for an entire block. When people first saw the house they always commented on its size. At eighteen thousand square feet it was the biggest home in Rose Hill. Back in the 1800s, it was a school for wayward young ladies. One of the bedroom walls still bore marks where some young charge had scratched off the passing days.

I parked the car and grabbed a bottle of forty-year-old, single-malt scotch I'd purchased as a peace offering. The saying "you can catch more flies with honey" was so common in Georgia the legislature should write it into the state law books. I was determined to sweeten Daddy up before he did something more drastic than cutting off my club membership.

I let myself into the house and traveled down a long, hushed hall to my father's study. On the way, I passed an oversized gold-framed portrait of my mother. We favored each other: same fair complexion, same sprawling limbs, and same confusion of burnished blond curls tumbling down our shoulders. The sight of the painting always gave me a chill at the back of my neck. She'd died of a brain aneurysm when I was four.

I almost reached the study when I smelled the familiar reek of Elizabeth Arden's Red Door.

"Daddy," I whispered. "Tell me you didn't."

But he had. No mistaking the cloying stench of Aunt Cornelia's perfume. If I was smart, I'd sneak out the door and get back to my car before I was spotted.

"Do I hear the pitter-patter of little feet?"

Too late. I had no choice but to go inside. I rounded the corner and almost collided with Aunt Cornelia. She wore a pastel pink St. John's suit, matching Ferragamo pumps and a ruffled blouse. Her ensemble and diminutive stature made her seem initially harmless, but closer examination revealed a narrow, humorless mouth and platinum blonde hair cut into a pageboy so sharp-edged it could draw blood.

As usual two assistants accompanied her. A harried young man and woman sat in twin leather club chairs, furiously tapping on laptops, as if racing each other. I recognized neither. My aunt's assistants lasted as long as fruit flies.

"What a nice surprise," I fibbed. Ever since I was a little girl I'd been leery of Cornelia. Used to hide in the closet during her infrequent visits.

My aunt's arms were open wide, waiting for me to fall into them. I trudged to her embrace as if walking to the gallows. The smell of her Red Door wasn't doing anything to help my pounding temples.

"It's been far too long." She released me after nearly cracking my ribs with her signature power hug.

Cornelia was CEO of Cornelia's Southern Foods. Fifty years ago her late mother and father began the company in their kitchen in Pinch Gut, a rundown area of Rose Hill and so-called because the earliest residents were so poor, their guts looked pinched. When my grandparents died in a car accident, my aunt—who'd only been twenty-one at the time—took over the business. Now it was a *Forbes* 2000 company headquartered in Atlanta, and it produced a variety of Southern-style canned goods that were distributed all over the world.

"What brings you to Rose Hill?" I said. Maybe I'd jumped to conclusions, and she wasn't here because of me. Maybe there was some other reason.

"Do I need an excuse to see my darling niece?"

"Of course not."

That's when I knew I might as well snap on a collar and join Beau in his doghouse. She'd *never* make a special trip just for an ordinary visit. Cornelia was a workaholic, and I usually only saw her twice a year, if that.

"Bringing your father a little bribe, are you?" She pointed at the bottle in my hands.

I bristled with indignation. "This isn't a bribe. It's a very late Fathers' Day present."

"Your father's not here. But he wanted me to tell you goodbye. Says he loves you, and he'll see you as soon as he gets back."

"Where did he go?

"Abroad. For a month. Maybe longer. I needed him to check on our international divisions."

"A month? I just saw him yesterday and he didn't say a word about leaving."

"It was a quickie decision."

She nuzzled my cheek. Cornelia was sneaking up on sixty but had the alabaster skin and defined jawline of a woman at least fifteen years younger. Whenever she traveled, she brought a separate Louis Vuitton suitcase that contained a collection of skin creams with exotic ingredients like ovine placenta and seaweed extract.

"In the meantime, I've come here to deal with you and your recent adventures in lawlessness."

My palms dampened with sweat. Why had my father told her about my arrest? He must have been really miffed to do that. When it came to my high-strung aunt, my father and I *always* operated on the mushroom principle: Keep her in the dark and feed her...well, everyone knows what mushrooms grow in.

"Why don't you have a seat?" Aunt Cornelia said. "Kelly, Jason, vamoose please. My niece and I need to have a little tête-à-tête."

The two assistants skittered out of the study like bugs being shooed with a broom. Cornelia smoothed her skirt and took a seat in a burgundy wing chair that clashed with her all-pink outfit.

I meekly sat across from her.

"A little bird told me you've been a busy girl lately," she said. "Two arrests over the course of six months. Not very ladylike. And what about your last credit card bill? When my accountant showed it to me, it was so thick I mistook it for a telephone book."

I squirmed in my chair. I had been spending more recently but it wasn't as if my aunt couldn't afford it. Besides, she'd never said anything about my spending habits before.

"I hate to say this, my dear niece, but you've become an embarrassment to this family."

Cornelia hadn't lived in Rose Hill for years and even had a certain amount of disdain for the place and its inhabitants, but she was fiercely protective of our family's standing in the town. It was only because of her success with Cornelia's Southern Foods that we had gone from being Pinch Gut nobodies to one of the richest families in town, a fact she loved to flaunt.

"I'm sorry. It won't happen again."

"No, it most certainly won't."

I didn't care for her ominous tone. No telling what she had in mind. I knew she was hard on employees who disappointed her. Up until recently I'd always been a source of pride to her and had never experienced her wrath.

"Your father and I have been looking the other way too long. It's been almost eight months since your unfortunate incident and—"

"Six months."

"This aimlessness of yours has gone on too long. Time to do something purposeful."

I had an inkling of what was coming next. Twice in the last few months Cornelia had sent me some graduate school brochures with a Post-it saying, "Look into this."

"Sorry but there's no way I'm going to get accepted in grad school. My grades in undergrad were nothing to write home about."

"I do have a school in mind for you. But it's not graduate school."

"What then?"

"The school of hard knocks," she said with a queer little smile.

"Excuse me?"

"It's my fault. After your mother died, I promised myself you'd want for nothing. That policy seemed to work just fine...until recently."

"What are you getting at?" The sweat on my palms was now spreading to my entire body.

"It's been eight months since your life took that nasty turn and—"

"Six!"

"And your pity party shows no signs of ending. Your father and I talked it over, and we decided you'll no longer receive your monthly allowance. And if you want to continue to live in that fancy condo of yours, you'll have to pay the going rental rate of three thousand dollars a month. Also all your credit cards have been canceled."

It took me a few seconds to process what she was saying. When it hit me, I grabbed the arms of my wing chair for support.

"You're...you're cutting me off?"

It was the last thing I'd expected. Cornelia could be a sourpuss but she'd always been generous with her pocketbook. In addition to free rent and payment of all my credit cards, she gave me a monthly check for five thousand dollars.

"What will I do for money? How will I live?"

She waved a hand bejeweled with ruby rings, her birthstone. "You'll get a job, of course. Like ordinary people. You do know what a job is, don't you?"

I winced. Her plan, I'm sure, was for me to begin a long term of indentured servitude at her company. I'd have to immerse myself in the world of beans and other fat-back laden foods. I imagined myself wearing a hairnet, stirring a huge vat of beans while my aunt barked into a megaphone: "Faster, faster."

"It's a mistake to make me work at the plant. I'd never be able to perform to your exacting standards."

"You're right about that. I choose the best people in the business. And that definitely does not include you."

"Where will I work then?"

"How should I know? I want you to find a job on your own. Develop some independence. You'd be surprised how much satisfaction you'll feel."

"But I have no skills."

Unless being good at the drinking game Flip, Sip, or Strip counted. And to be frank, I usually lost at that as well.

"Don't be a ninny. You have a college degree. Thank God I insisted you get that."

"In general studies."

"That's a perfectly respectable degree."

"No. It isn't." I shot up from my chair and paced the length of the study. "Do you know what the job market's like? I've heard of people with accounting and engineering degrees who can't get jobs. I'll starve."

"Quit being so dramatic. True, you'll have to downsize your lifestyle some but—"

"Downsize? Much worse than that. I'll be standing in line at soup kitchens or eating cat food. And not the Fancy Feast stuff either."

She wiped away imaginary tears. "Oh my. Where's a traveling violin player when you need him?"

"Please don't do this to me. I'll do better, I swear. No more goof-ups or trips to jail."

Cornelia shook her head. "Too late for that. Your father says he's tried to talk to you but you've shut him out. Time for harsh measures."

The walls of her study seemed to be closing in on me. "I need air," I said. Not to mention a drink.

My aunt stood. "Hold on. I'm not finished with you yet."

I ignored her and headed for the exit.

"Toni Lee. Stop this very instant."

I flung myself down the hall and out the heavy front door, slamming it behind me. The sky was choked with whorls of gray clouds; a hot wind roused the leathery leaves of an enormous black-barked magnolia tree.

Once inside my car, I slammed my foot on the accelerator and roared down the oak-lined road, watching Tranquility Hall disappear in my rearview mirror. Part of me wanted to keep on driving until I was a hundred miles away from Rose Hill. Unfortunately I'd only traveled a few more yards when my motor coughed several times and died. I tried to restart the car. It let out a petulant whine and refused to turn over. I glanced warily at the gas gauge.

Empty. It was the third time I'd run out of gas in the last six months.

I locked up and plodded down the residential street. Thunder muttered in the distance; the air was charged and damp.

I was cutting across the Rose Hill College campus when the first raindrop plopped on my forehead. Within seconds, the skies opened, releasing torrents of water, sharp with bits of hail. I dashed across the slick grounds. By the time I arrived home, my lungs burned, my skin stung, and my t-shirt clung to me like a wetsuit.

Inside, I checked my phone. No texts, but my father had left a message saying, "Sorry, Toni Lee. You spooked me so bad I felt like I had to call Corny. I know you're mad, but this is for your own good. You don't want to be totally dependent on your aunt for the rest of your life. Believe me—"

Delete.

"Chicken."

No doubt my father had requested an overseas sales trip so he wouldn't have to be around for the fallout. And no matter how hard he tried, he couldn't put a positive spin on my new lowly circumstances. Unlike him, I had no experience being poor. And yes, I know it made me seem like a spoiled brat, but I wasn't used to pinching pennies. I'd never saved a Bed, Bath and Beyond coupon, never bought a pair of used blue jeans at a thrift store, and never saved oil in used Crisco jars. To completely cut me off financially was like tossing a pampered Persian cat out into a back alley.

And my father was one to talk to me about being dependent. His sister-in-law was his employer and the source of all his money. The only reason he owned a grand house like Tranquility Hall was because Aunt Cornelia had given it to my mother and him as a wedding present. Nowadays she also paid for the upkeep. Supposedly one of the last things my mother had said to her sister before she died was, "Please look after Porter. Lord knows he can't take care of himself."

For the most part he was a token employee of Cornelia's Southern Foods, getting away with as little work as possible. Before he'd married my mom he'd sold firewood and cut down trees for a living. Without my aunt's money he'd be reduced to shaking down sofas for loose change.

Aunt Cornelia had also left me a message. "You're acting like an out-of-control toddler. Life goes on. It's been eight months."

"Six months," I whispered, deleting her message.

Although it seemed like yesterday when my life changed. Back in February, I was about to embark on my first year on the pro tennis circuit. I'd played the game since I was nine, and when I was twelve, I went away to Weil Tennis Academy in Ojai, California for the rest of my schooling. Afterward, I won a scholarship to Georgia Southern and played on their tennis team.

One brisk winter morning, I was playing a practice game with my hitting partner when I fell on the court and broke my wrist. The injury wasn't so bad, but the treatment nearly did me in.

Hours after receiving an anti-inflammatory shot, I got a staph infection that ballooned my wrist to three times its normal size. The infection was so bad my doctor feared I'd lose part of my arm. After being dosed with a round of antibiotics powerful enough to fell an elephant, the infection eventually receded, but my wrist was permanently weakened, and I could no longer play tennis.

After my accident, I didn't know who I was anymore. My

whole life had been about tennis. For several weeks afterward I didn't leave the house. I didn't bathe, I quit eating, and I slept eighteen hours a day. My life seemed hollow and purposeless.

At my family's insistence I went on anti-depressants and eventually the worst of my torpor lifted. I started spending my days roaming Rose Hill's shops or when I got bored with the local stores, I'd drive to Atlanta to browse in Phipps Plaza and or head to Charleston to hit the King Street shops. Nights were spent out at clubs and fancy restaurants, flirting with cute guys. Most evenings I didn't get home until after midnight, and some nights I didn't make it home at all.

Shopping, partying, and day-tripping didn't replace tennis but they helped to dull the pain. Now I wouldn't even have those niceties. I also wouldn't be able to help Joelle anymore. My friend's student loan payment for nursing school was enormous. Every month I sent her a check for $500. I knew she'd grown to depend on it.

It was almost impossible to imagine an existence without my hefty allowance. Money solved problems, smoothed feathers, and, in recent months, gave me a reason to emerge from my cozy cocoon of Egyptian cotton linens every morning and muddle through the day. The only thing it couldn't do was give me back my tennis career.

Six months later, I still dreamed of playing every night. I could feel the phantom grip of a racquet in my hand, hear the bounce of the ball against the clay court, and see it, fuzzy and fluorescent, eclipsing everything else as it soared toward me.

Three

The next morning I returned home after retrieving my stalled car. I stepped into my foyer and sensed an intruder. My muscles got as tense as piano wires, and I wondered if I should flee. Moments later I heard footsteps. Not a stealth creeping movement but a determined clacking of heels on hardware floors, followed by the scent of Red Door.

Aunt Cornelia was peering into my pantry. She was wearing a green dress the color of a poisonous African tree frog. Her assistant, a sleek-haired female who wore a hands-free phone and horn-rimmed eyeglasses, sat at the kitchen table. Her fingernails were bitten down to skimpy crescents, and she kept shuffling and re-shuffling a stack of papers in front of her.

"You know, most people keep food in their pantries," Cornelia said when she saw me. "All I see is an expired box of baking soda and a package of Trojan ultra-ribbed Ecstasy condoms."

My cheeks burned. "Why are you here? Am I not even entitled to my privacy anymore?"

"You didn't return my phone call. What could I do but make a personal visit?"

"I told you. There's nothing more for us to say."

"How wrong you are."

What did she want from me? My first-born? A kidney? My platelets? Speaking of which, I wondered what platelets were going for these days. Or eggs? Maybe I could sell a dozen of mine since I didn't plan on using them anytime soon.

"You remind me so much of Nina. Stubborn even when it didn't serve her."

Enough already. It always upset me when anyone compared me to my mother. I headed down the hall, intending to hole up in my bedroom until she left.

"Have it your way," she said. "I was planning to give you until the end of the month to leave this lovely condo but if you're going to be pigheaded I expect you to vacate these premises within twenty-four hours."

I whirled around to face her. "You can't do that. You're required to give longer notice to evict someone."

"Not for squatters. As I recall, you've never paid a penny of rent here."

"Squatter? I'm not a squatter. I can't believe...How could you...?"

"Quit your sputtering, and sit by me."

I obeyed, but inside of me a category-four hurricane was howling.

"When my sister died, I had no idea what to do with a four-year-old child," my aunt said. "Raising a youngster was not in my life plan. Not with an entire company on my shoulders."

"Raising" wasn't the right word; outsourcing was more like it. After my mother died, my father went on a Jack Daniels bender that ended in a nervous breakdown, a broken collarbone, and a ninety-day stay in rehab. While my father was drying out, Cornelia hired a nanny and tutor to see to my needs.

She stayed in Atlanta and managed my life from a hundred and fifty miles away. Mostly we communicated through phone, fax, memo and later on, email and Skype.

"You'll be relieved to know I'm not abandoning you completely," she said.

"You're not?" I felt a small surge of hope. Was it possible she'd just been trying to give me a good scare? If so, her plan worked. I was so spooked I'd gnawed my bottom lip into shreds.

"Of course not. You're my only niece, after all, and we don't want everyone to think you're completely on the skids. Thus, I've decided I will continue to tithe to St. Andrews in your name. Five hundred dollars a month."

Whoopee, I thought.

"There is one other thing."

"What?"

"If you get a job, keep it for one year and stay out of trouble, you'll receive...Hand me that contract, Kellie." Her assistant swiftly surrendered the papers, and my aunt held them at an arm's length; she was too vain to wear reading glasses.

"You'll receive..." she said again, and paused for dramatic effect.

"Tell me."

"Five million dollars."

There was a long, stomach-churning silence. Surely I'd misheard.

"Run that by me again?" Maybe she'd said five mink collars or five male scholars. Surely she hadn't said—

"I will continue to tithe in your name—"

"No. The other thing."

Cornelia clapped her hands together. "It's about time you started listening to me. Five million dollars. Quite the attention-getter, eh?"

Damn straight. Even the assistant looked taken aback. "You're serious?" I said.

She suppressed a yawn. "Of course. As you know, beans have been extraordinarily good to this family. Five million is the amount I'd planned to leave you in my will and the rest will go to charity. Now you won't have to wait until I die to get your inheritance, which is a happy occurrence, because I plan to outlast everyone."

My aunt had a habit of controlling people with her money. Although my daddy had never said as much, I was certain he never remarried because he feared my Aunt Cornelia might quit paying him an overinflated salary in exchange for hardly any work.

Several years ago, as an incentive to get me to finish college, she'd dangled a Porsche Boxster and the services of a private tennis coach as carrots. This was the very same thing, just a much bigger carrot.

"What's the catch?"

"You're so suspicious. There's no catch." She handed me a black Montblanc pen. "My lawyer hammered out the terms. Look them over carefully and sign when ready."

"What about my father? Does he know about this?"

"Yes, and he's all for it."

She pushed the contract closer to me.

I paged through it. Listed were dozens of offenses that would cause me to forfeit the money. She had covered every sin under the sun: loan sharking, vagrancy, joy-riding, tax evasion, firearm violation, drug use, moral turpitude, and bastardy. Another clause said I wasn't allowed to sell my Porsche during the year for extra money, and I couldn't accept cash from my father. Not that he ever had much extra; he was always covered up in his gambling losses. If I quit my job or was fired within the year, I'd forfeit the money.

I continued to read. "Excessive alcohol consumption?"

Knowing Cornelia, nibbling on a piece of rum cake might constitute excessive consumption. She never touched the stuff, except during the occasional communion.

"Boozers are losers, I always say. But an occasional sip of cooking sherry won't cost you your inheritance. An arrest for public drunkenness, on the other hand, will."

I pointed to a clause with the pen. "And I have to get a job within a month and you have to approve it."

"Correct."

"Is this your sneaky way of pushing me into nunnery?"

She laughed. "As if they'd take you....I want you to choose something challenging. I don't think you'd get much from selling jeans at the Gap or waiting tables at Hotties."

She meant Hooters. Which I'm sure was plenty challenging, what with having to fight off hordes of men while wearing sprayed-on orange shorts.

"To make sure you follow the contract, I'm setting up a satellite office in Tranquility Hall to keep an eye on you. I'll go back to Atlanta now and then, but for the most part, I'll telecommute."

Her statement shocked me. If she intended to hang around Rose Hill for a year—a place she claimed was stuck in the Eisenhower era—it meant she was serious about monitoring my behavior. My every move would be on display like a firefly trapped in a jar. Still, for five million dollars, I suppose I could endure a chorus line of meddling aunts.

"I didn't mean to seem ungrateful earlier. I appreciate you giving me this wonderful opportunity."

She lifted her chin, and I could see the faint line of her creamy foundation. "What's the point of having money if you can't share it with your family?"

I seized the pen, eager to sign.

"There is *one* more thing you should know," she said.

I knew it! A catch.

"I've added a final clause to the contract. If you fail, you'll lose any chance of getting your inheritance. And if your father lives longer than me, I'll set up a trust that will make it impossible for him to pass his money onto you."

It was a harsh stipulation, but I wasn't worried. I had no intentions of failing.

"Keep in mind your task might not be the cakewalk you think. Change is tricky for most people."

Not for me. Not for that kind of money. For five million dollars I would work three jobs, take celibacy vows, and recite the entirety of Revelation everyday while kneeling on a pile of cornmeal. Cornelia could have made the stakes much higher.

"Who knows?" she said. "Maybe during the year you'll even find another passion, one to replace tennis."

"Maybe," I said, even though I doubted that would ever happen. Tennis was my passion, and I couldn't imagine replacing it with anything else. It'd be like telling Stephen King he should forget about writing horror novels and start crocheting tea cozies.

Four

I knew finding a job was going to be a bear, but I didn't think it was going to be impossible. After a week of nonstop searching I hadn't gotten the tiniest of nibbles. I'd heard the economy was in bad shape but it'd never affected me before. Now it was up close and personal, like a guy with bad breath on a crowded elevator.

One morning, ten days into my search, I attended a Professional Career Fair and spent ninety minutes lucklessly wandering around a convention center. Most of the jobs offered I'd never even heard of: systems analyst, histology manager, fiber optic installer. Weren't there any normal jobs in the world? Ones that required only a warm body, an easy smile, and a flair for Pinterest?

I continued fighting the crowds, ignoring my growling belly and aching feet, until I reached one of the last tables with a wall banner hanging above it that said, "Calling All College Graduates: The Teacher Corps Want You."

Didn't people need a license and special degree to be a teacher? Still, the sign did say *all* college graduates welcome, and I fit that category, although just barely. Days after I'd received my diploma I kept checking it to make sure Georgia Southern hadn't printed it with invisible ink.

A woman manning the table explained to me the mission of Teacher Corps, saying it was an accelerated teacher training program for anyone with a degree, even general studies. The classes were held at Rose Hill College in the evenings, and it was possible to secure a job in the school system while completing the program.

Teaching seemed like an easy gig, but would Aunt Cornelia approve? No telling. Maybe she wouldn't think it was challenging enough, what with having summers free, vacation days galore, and going home at three o'clock to watch talk shows.

The woman told me there were openings in math and special education.

Math wasn't my strong suit. I'd never balanced a checkbook before. My bank account was attached to my father's, and Aunt Cornelia covered any overdrafts.

"Tell me about the special education job."

"You'd be dealing with young people who have some mild learning and behavior disabilities. They need extra attention and your classes would be small. The position is at Harriet Hall High School." She paused for a moment, waiting for my reaction.

The name of the school meant nothing to me. I'd gone to a private school until I was twelve and then I attended the tennis academy. I wasn't familiar with Rose Hill's various high schools. None were located in my neighborhood.

I was pleased to hear the opening would be at a high school. It'd be fun to go to proms, pep rallies, and football games. The students were close to my age, and we probably liked the same music and movies; it'd almost be like hanging out with my friends. I could be the easygoing teacher who sits on the edge of her desk and is beloved by all her charges.

"I'm interested," I said quickly.

"You are?"

She sounded a little surprised.

"I'm sure you have hordes of other candidates but—"

"You'll have to interview with Dr. Lipton, the principal. Are you familiar with him?"

"No."

"Dr. Lipton's something of a celebrity in the school system and a gifted leader. People say he'll be chosen as the new superintendent once Dr. Scott retires. I'll set up an appointment with him at the Board of Education this afternoon."

*   *   *

I arrived at the Board of Ed, a nondescript brick building with a scorched-coffee smell and phones that continually rang. During a brief moment of quiet, I stated my business to the harried receptionist.

Shortly afterward, the front door opened, and a tall, black man strode in wearing a yellow silk tie and a well-cut suit. The suit was made from such fine hand-finished wool it practically shimmered. His longish hair was combed back from his head in gentle, wet waves. When he reached the center of the room, the overhead lights appeared to burn brighter, and the sickly green color of the walls looked more robust. It was as if he was traveling with his own secret power source.

The receptionist ignored the ringing phones to greet him, and alert him to my presence.

He turned his attention to me; his gaze was intense.

"You're here for the teaching job?"

I extended my hand. "Yes, sir. My name is—"

"Sorry," he said, ignoring my hand. "Position's been filled." He turned away from me and walked out the door.

I trailed behind him. "Wait! There's been a misunderstanding. The lady who interviewed me—"

"Must be smoking crack." He pushed open the door.

What was his problem? I followed him outside and lengthened my stride to keep up with his. "Please give me a chance. I'm enthusiastic with plenty of energy and—"

Dr. Lipton whirled around and looked me in the eye.

"Young lady, I told you the position is filled. Now please, quit tailing me."

"I might be young, but that doesn't mean—"

"Young? You're an embryo. I have vegetables in my crisper that are older than you."

He continued on his way, and I stood in the parking lot, the heat bearing down on my scalp like a hot iron skillet. My spirits sunk to new lows as I watched my sole chance of getting a decent job walk away from me in a pair of black wingtip shoes. I was about to return to my car, when I decided I wasn't going to give up that easily. I needed this teaching job. My deadline was breathing down my neck.

I caught up with the principal, took a deep breath for courage, and talked to his departing back. "Listen. I'm not just some young greenhorn off the street. Last year I was about to start a career as a pro tennis player. Do you have any idea what kind of dedication that takes? Every day I practiced until my arm was on fire. I'd make myself play a match even if I felt like I had to scrape my body off the floor. I was the most driven player on the circuit. I'd be playing right now if I hadn't hurt my wrist."

When I was finished, I surprised myself. What I'd said was true, but the girl I'd been talking about was a stranger to me now.

Dr. Lipton faced me. Again, he studied me so intently I almost expected him to ask me to open my mouth so he could check my teeth. Go ahead, I thought. I'd let him inspect every molar if it got me the job.

Finally he spoke: "Under normal circumstances I'd never hire someone so young and obviously inexperienced, but I'm having a heck of time trying to fill this slot. In fact, you're the only pony in this race."

Yes!

"Tomorrow is the first planning day for teachers, and by law I have to fill that special ed position. I need someone who can control a classroom of teenagers. I took one look at you, and saw this very skinny, obviously privileged young lady..." His eyes cut to my Kate Spade bag. "And I said to myself, 'She won't last five seconds.'"

"With all due respect, Dr. Lipton, you're underestimating me."

Truth was, I saw my youth as an advantage. I could deal with the kids on their level.

"Your little speech made me think twice. I was on my college's varsity basketball team and I, too, intended to go pro until I busted my knee. I know exactly what it takes to compete as a top-notch athlete. Made me think you're not quite as lightweight as you look."

"Thank you." I was tempted to throw my arms around him in gratitude but resisted the urge.

"Understand this, Ms. Wells. I don't care how many tennis matches you've won or how badly I need a new teacher. If you don't give me a hundred and ten percent, I'll show you the door."

"Does this mean you're considering me?"

"More than that. Go back inside. Ask for a Ms. Wrigley. Tell her you're the new special ed teacher at Harriet Hall High School, and she'll take care of your paperwork. See you tomorrow. Eight a.m. sharp."

Five

The first day on the job I popped out my front door carrying a steaming coffee mug and a new briefcase. Nature was staging a beauty pageant. Whipped cream clouds raced overhead, crimson cardinals darted across a dew-kissed lawn, magnolia trees flaunted leaves of jade.

Normally on a day like today I'd be marinating in Hawaiian Tropic and lying by the club pool with a mojito in one hand and a Mary Kay Andrews novel in the other. Made me feel a stab of longing for my former life of leisure.

"Keep your eye on the prize," I said softly.

As soon as I got inside my car, Joelle called. A few days earlier I'd told her about my family cutting me off, but I didn't discuss the deal I'd made with my aunt.

Afterward there'd been a brief silence; she was probably thinking about the loss of her monthly check but didn't bring it up. The second I got my inheritance, I planned to pay off the mortgage on her overpriced cottage.

"I'm shocked you answered the phone," Joelle said. "You're never up this early. I expected to leave a message."

"I've been up for hours."

"Liar. Admit it. You haven't gone to bed yet. I can smell the alcohol fumes rolling out of the receiver. The reason I'm calling is I read in the paper that the main library is having a free resume workshop at ten a.m. You should get over there. Soon as I'm finished working these long shifts, I'll be able to help you more with your job hunt."

"I don't need a resume," I said, pulling out of the drive.

She laughed. "Naiveté, thy name is Toni Lee. You can't get a job without a resume. It'll need more padding than a preteen's bra but—"

"I don't need a resume because I already have a job." Proudly I told her about my new gig, and how I was heading out that very moment for the first of five planning days before students arrived.

"They hired you just like that? With no teaching degree? No license?"

"It's a program called Teacher Corps. What they do is—"

"I know what they *do*. You hear about them in the news all the time. They place people in undesirable teaching positions. Where is it you're teaching?"

"Harriet Hall High School."

Silence.

"Joelle. Did I lose you?"

"Did you say Harriet Hall?"

"Yes. What about it?"

"Good God almighty." Her voice was so loud she sounded like she was on speakerphone. "You didn't sign a contract, did you?"

"I guess. To be honest they were shoving so many papers in my direction that I—"

"Doesn't matter. I doubt the school system sues too many people for breaking their contracts."

"Why would I want to break my contract? It's the perfect job for me."

Even Aunt Cornelia had been impressed. Last night when I told her, not only did she approve of my new job, she wondered if maybe it was a bit too challenging. Little did she know how small my classes were going to be.

"Gotta go. I'm being called over the P.A.," Joelle said. "We'll talk about this mess you've gotten yourself into later."

Why was she acting so funny? Did Joelle question my ability to look after a class full of students? Not that I could blame her. A couple of months ago she'd gone to a medical conference and asked me to care for her African violets. By week's end I'd murdered most of them. Before she returned, I replaced the ones I'd killed, thinking she'd never know the difference. *Wrong.* She knew those flowers better than some people knew their children. Thank God teenagers were more resilient than African violets.

After Joelle hung up, I turned right on Parkway Avenue, a street lined with the city's most majestic homes—stately colonials, Greek revivals, and candy-colored Victorians. All the homes were separated far from the traffic by sprawling green grounds. The crepe myrtles were in full bloom, and their ungainly flowered branches bobbed in the breeze. Rose Hill's nickname was the City of Flowers because something was always springing into bloom, strewing the air with colorful petals.

I traveled a few miles, obeying the pleasant yet bossy voice of the GPS, and clattered over railroad tracks. I passed a tired strip mall boasting a Title Pawn Auto, EZ Loans, Bulldog Bonding, and Suds Laundromat. A portable sign outside one store advertised chicken wings and human hair. No thanks, I thought.

A final pass over more railroad tracks landed me in a creepy area with boarded-up buildings, weedy vacant lots, and low-slung, cinderblock public housing. A grim industrial plant belched smelly plumes of blue smoke.

The further I went from home, the more my surroundings seemed like a Chinese nesting box, revealing one inner layer after another of ugliness. No wonder Joelle had acted so wary when I told her where I'd be working. Unbeknownst to me, I'd accepted a teaching job in Rose Hill's underbelly.

As I continued to drive, I half expected the GPS lady to say, "Get out while you're still breathing." Instead she prompted me to make a left turn. I arrived at my destination: Harriet Hall High School.

I'd expected the worst—a crumbling, graffiti-defaced eyesore cornered off with crime tape—but compared to its surroundings, the school looked perfectly decent. A white columned portico and triangular gable softened the building's institutional appearance. The grounds were well-kept and looked like a public park with decorative street lamps, stone benches, and tidy squares of green space.

My panic lessened. True, I'd accepted a job on the wrong side of town, but at least the school looked safe and welcoming. Maybe I wouldn't be ambushed by muggers as soon as I opened my car door.

Still, my red Porsche was going to stick out like a fire truck. I circled the school, looking for parking, and discovered a fenced area with a locking gate. A sign said, "Faculty and Staff Only." The lot was nearly full, and my car was easily the flashiest. I parked and quickly abandoned the vehicle. First impressions were important, and I didn't want to be known as the teacher who drives a Porsche. From now on I'd take my motorcycle to school.

Harriet Hall's foyer smelled of floor wax and fresh paint. A glass case, glinting with gold and silver trophies, stood in the corner, and a mural of an orange jaguar—obviously the school mascot—splashed an entryway wall. There wasn't a bullet hole or dead body in sight. Not that I expected such things, but I had no idea what I'd been in for.

I entered the office, and a willowy black woman with high cheekbones smiled warmly. She looked like she should be strutting down a catwalk in a Helmut Lang frock instead of stuffing envelopes in a high school office.

"Welcome to Harriet Hall," she said. "My name is Ms. Ware. How may I help you?"

"I'm Toni Lee Wells, the new special education teacher. Is the principal in?"

The smile wilted; her chin hardened. Her distaste was so obvious I looked over my shoulder to see if maybe an IRS agent was standing behind me.

"Teachers are supposed to report to the chorus room for a meeting," she said tersely. She wheeled on her heels and returned to her task.

"Where is the chorus room?"

She either didn't hear me or was ignoring me. Undeterred, I asked again.

"Next to the vocational building," she snapped. Then she clipped across the floor into an inner office and shut the door, making it clear she was done answering my pesky questions.

Had I done something to insult her? It was a little early in the game to be making enemies. Reluctantly I left the office, having no idea where to go. Glancing about, I saw two women traveling down the main hallway with purposeful strides. I followed them across a breezeway to a large room filled with student desks on risers.

Dozens of teachers milled about. I was easily the youngest faculty member. I caught a few people sneaking peeks at me, the new fish, but no one greeted me. Made me feel like I was crashing a private party.

I hadn't been there for more than thirty seconds when I heard a voice shout, "Are you ready to change a child's life?"

The faculty, obviously trained for such questions, responded in unison, "We are!" Dr. Lipton trotted up to the podium, instantly energizing the room, and shouted, "Are you ready to touch the future?"

Again the faculty said, "We are!"

"You sound like a bunch of meek mumble mouths," Dr. Lipton said. "Let's hear it again."

"We are!" the faculty responded. They shouted so loud my ears rang.

"That's better," Dr. Lipton said. "There's only one reason we're here today. Not to socialize and definitely not to drink the school's God-awful coffee. We're here today and every weekday for one reason only, to educate our students."

He immediately launched into a story about a student named Rodney who grew up two blocks away in a project with a meth-addicted mother but beat the odds to get his college degree and eventually became a state senator.

"And do you know who he thanked first in his acceptance speech?"

Dr. Lipton slowly scanned his audience. "Not his campaign manager, not his wife, not the voters. No, ladies and gentlemen, he thanked his history teacher who retired from Hall only three years ago."

When Dr. Lipton was done with his speech, the room swelled with the song "Ain't No Mountain High Enough."

"Sing it with me, team members," Dr. Lipton shouted as he slung his arms around two nearby teachers and swayed to the music.

The faculty sang along, and many of the teachers were gazing at Dr. Lipton with awe as if he were a teen heartthrob instead of a middle-aged principal with a bit of a beer belly. I had to admit he was inspiring.

When the song was over, Dr. Lipton said, "Before we adjourn, I'd like to welcome our new staff members to the Hall team. First, our math teacher."

A brawny black man stood. His biceps were so big they ballooned out of his short sleeve shirt.

"Mr. Gerald used to be a staff sergeant in the Army and a bodyguard for James Brown," Dr. Lipton said. "How do you feel today, Mr. Gerald?"

"I feel good!" Mr. Gerald briskly saluted the faculty.

"And I knew that you would," Dr. Lipton said. He slapped palms with the teacher.

Next Dr. Lipton introduced a new English teacher, a broad-shouldered woman who was close to seven feet tall and had a face so mean it could turn milk. She was a retired police officer with a black belt in karate.

"Last but not least, we have a new special ed instructor," he continued. "Ms. Toni Lee Wells."

I stood, feeling like the punchline of a bad joke. They were likely expecting someone who'd wrestled alligators in the Amazon or pinned Hulk Hogan in a wrestling match.

Instead they got a skinny, wild-haired blonde wearing a sunny yellow suit and daisy earrings. No wonder a couple of people snickered.

After the introductions Dr. Lipton dismissed us. I didn't know where I was supposed to go. I was about to approach the principal and ask but several faculty members already thronged him.

"Are you the person who was crazy enough to drive a Porsche to this school?"

I turned to see who'd made the remark. It was a black woman in her early thirties with a cap of brassy gold hair. She wore a single-breasted navy suit that, despite its severe tailoring, couldn't disguise her curvy figure.

"Yes, but my other car's a Ford Fiesta."

"I drive a Ford Fiesta," she said, giving off strong whiffs of annoyance.

"I'm sorry. I didn't mean to—"

"I'm Deena Sprague, department head of Special Education. I'll also be your buddy teacher."

Her brown eyes were hard, like dull pennies, and deep frown grooves marred her nearly flawless olive skin. Frankly, she seemed more like a fuddy-duddy than a buddy.

"Nice to meet you. I'm delighted to be here and I—"

"Follow me. I'll show you to your room. You taught before?"

"No, ma'am. I'm a recruit in the Teacher Corps program." It sounded so militaristic I almost felt like saluting or clicking my heels together.

"God save us all," Ms. Sprague muttered. Then she strode out the door and down the locker-lined hallway, making great time in her peep-toe pumps. I had to practically run to keep up with her. When she reached the end of the hall, she pushed open the school's back door, chains rattling against its pitted metal surface. In the distance I spotted a huddle of battered trailers.

"Where are we going?"

"To the portables. Hall's overcrowded so we have some temporary buildings out near the field house. You should consider wearing sensible shoes to work. This grass gets muddy when it rains."

After walking several yards across the hot and seemingly airless field, we reached the cluster of portables. Ms. Sprague paused by the oldest and most beat-up of the bunch. It looked like a FEMA trailer on its last leg, or a hideout for a serial killer.

"This used to be the in-house suspension portable. You're very lucky to get it."

Lucky? Cursed was the better word. We climbed the rickety wooden steps leading to the classroom, and when Ms. Sprague opened the door, a wall of heat slammed into us. She flipped a switch, and the lights stuttered for several seconds. Eventually they settled down to a garish glow, revealing walls covered with obscene graffiti. Something gray, possibly a big rat or an undersized possum, darted across the floor. I bit my lip to stop from screaming.

"You may want to put out some traps," she said.

The walls bulged with mysterious tumors, and the classroom was empty of furniture. A door leading to a small closet was splintered, as if someone had punched it. I gazed around helplessly. Was she hazing me? What next? Eggs in my hair? Minnows down my underwear?

"I'll leave so you can get settled in." She gave me a key and headed to the door, hips twitching.

"Excuse me?"

Ms. Sprague stopped. "Yes?"

"I hate to complain on my first day, but are you sure this is my room?"

She planted a hand on her tiny waist. "I realize it's not the chi-chi environment you're probably accustomed to but—"

"I'm not worried about me. I'm more concerned about my students. I don't see how anyone could learn anything in this..." I swallowed the words "House of Vermin."

"This portable's been in use for years. And the students who've come here for classes have learned just fine. You're fortunate to get a room at all. Most new teachers float."

"Excuse me?" I imagined a group of faculty members bobbing in the water like buoys.

"Floaters have to travel from classroom to classroom whenever someone has a planning period. You've escaped that unpleasant fate. This room will look better once you get some desks. Hopefully by the first day."

"Will someone at least be painting?"

Ms. Sprague pointed to some graffiti that said, "Isaac Rogers, Class of '92."

"Not likely," she said.

"I've just never seen anything like this before," I said.

"Welcome to the inner city, Ms. Wells. Most of the kids who attend school here come from families on public assistance. They're the forgotten children. Angelina Jolie isn't going to be adopting any of them, and no relief workers are going to come to their aid. In other words, the community couldn't give a fig about them or this school. We're always fighting for our fair share of resources."

"But the outside's so nice. And the main building looks newly renovated."

"Thanks to Dr. Lipton. He has a very special interest in this school; it was his alma mater, you know. He fought for the renovations, and he's fighting to get an addition built so one day portables won't be necessary. But until then, remember this: Harriet Hall, our founder, taught her first class in horse stables; we've come very far since then."

Not that far. Frankly even Seabiscuit would turn up his nose at my bleak accommodations.

"Incidentally," Ms. Sprague said, "you'll need to put up a bulletin board. Dr. Lipton requires it."

As if that would help. It'd be like spritzing cologne on raw sewage. It was hard for me to believe that Dr. Lipton cared about such superficial matters.

After Ms. Sprague left, I brushed my hands together purposefully, wondering where to start. *Firebombing? Dynamite? Wrecking ball?*

"Now, Toni Lee," I whispered. "Be positive."

First, I needed to fling open the front door to let fresh air in and allow for a quick getaway in case of close encounters with creatures of the disease-riddled kind. Once that was done, I made a brief inspection of the room and found a baseball-sized hole in one of the walls. No wonder the place had attracted unwelcome guests.

I spied a thermostat in a corner of the room and turned the temperature all the way down. *Nothing.* No cough, no hum, no reassuring whoosh of air. The portable was on the edge of a treeless field and probably had as much insulation as a Campbell's Soup can. I'd been inside for five minutes, and sweat was already rolling off the tip of my nose and plopping onto the tops of my shoes.

I wondered how I was going to spend eight hours a day in a pest-infested hot box. And it was isolated. If I screamed nobody would hear me. As if on cue, I heard the approach of heavy footsteps.

"I've got something for you," said a voice behind me. The voice was baritone and slightly menacing.

I abruptly turned. A muscular black man loomed in my doorway. A small diamond glinted from his earlobe and a two-inch scar grazed his cheek. He looked both sexy and dangerous. I didn't know if I should flirt or flee.

"Your supplies." He handed me a package so small it could have come from Tiffany's. "They were accidentally delivered to my room."

He introduced himself as Carl Rutherford, teacher of psychology and sociology.

"It's so hot in here you could steam cabbage," he said.

I fanned my face with my hand. "I've only been here a few minutes and I can barely stand it. I need to call someone, I guess. I don't suppose the school has a concierge."

"There's no concierge, and even if there was it wouldn't help.

The board won't turn on the air until the first day of school. Budget cuts. And don't expect any repairs either. The portables are so old they don't want to put money into them. In fact, I thought they'd retired this one because of the asbestos."

"Seriously?"

He smiled. "Just a joke, and not a very funny one. First year teaching?"

"Yes. I'm doing Teacher Corps."

"Ouch." His wince revealed a dimple on his right cheek.

"I got the same reaction from my buddy teacher. What's wrong with Teacher Corps?"

He scratched his temple. "Let's just say most of the people in the program can't teach their way out of a paper bag, and they usually quit the first day if not the first hour. How long was your training? A few weeks?"

"I haven't had any training yet. I start Monday."

"So basically you have no idea what you're doing."

"Last night I streamed *Dangerous Minds.*" I didn't mention I fell asleep before it was over.

He snorted.

I also decided not to mention that I also used to play school when I was little. Of course, real-life kids were apt to be trickier to manage than a classroom full of Care Bears.

"Sorry. I shouldn't be so discouraging. If you need any advice, just ask. I'll be glad to help."

It was great to finally meet someone who was nice, not to mention nice-looking.

After Carl left, a teacher's desk was delivered to my room, but it was so banged-up it looked like it'd been thrown from a three-story building. Several drawers wouldn't open. Not that I had much of anything to store in them. I'd gone through my tiny supply box. The only items inside were a box of fat crayons intended for young children, thumbtacks, a tape dispenser but no tape, and a package of rubber bands.

I visited the office and asked Ms. Ware, the secretary, if she could order me some additional supplies. Her attitude was just as curt as the last time I saw her. Told me I should have ordered them at the end of the year. When I very patiently reminded her I hadn't been at Harriet Hall last year she said, "That's not my problem then, is it?"

Sexually frustrated, I decided. I, too, got crabby when I didn't get any nookie.

Later, Mr. Rutherford appeared in my room again, carrying a stack of three large boxes. As soon as he got a few feet inside, he took a couple of steps back. "Feels like walking into a dragon's mouth. How can you stand it?"

"I try not to move around very much." I'd found an oscillating fan in one of the closets and set it out but it was only stirring the dust and hot air around.

Carl dropped the boxes on the floor.

"What's all this?"

"Supplies. I was in the office and overheard your conversation with Ms. Ware."

He opened the box on top. It brimmed with things I could use: a stapler, scissors, file folders, even a globe.

"Where did you get all this swag?" I picked up the globe and examined it. A strip of masking tape was attached to the base. A message in black marker said, "Property of Ms. Ferris. DO NOT TAKE!"

He snapped his fingers. "Meant to remove that before I gave it to you."

I nearly dropped the globe. "You stole this?"

Holy cow, I thought. If the teachers at Harriet Hall were thieves what would the students be like?

"Of course not." His eyes were wide with mock indignation. "I just redistributed it. Teachers are notorious hoarders. I took the stapler from someone who has five. They're buffing the floors in the main building so these things were lying around in the hall, just begging for a new home."

"You're an outlaw."

He smiled. "Not that much of an outlaw. Trust me, everyone does it. It's practically a sport around here."

I glanced hungrily at the boxes, shiny new supplies, some still in their original packaging. Who could have predicted I'd one day find myself drooling over a stapler? "Thank you. I was afraid I'd have to buy this stuff myself."

"At your service," he said, bowing at the waist. "Anything else you need?"

Plenty, I thought, admiring his lanky yet well-built form, but now wasn't the time or place.

"Where's the teachers' lounge? I was told I have a mailbox there."

"I'm headed in that direction. I'll take you."

Even though it was probably ninety degrees out, the outdoors felt cooler than the inside of my portable. I followed Carl to the main building, which was awash with students—mostly female—as well as numerous babies and toddlers, many shrieking and crying. A long-legged girl in a short skirt and towering heels approached. Her arms held an infant with frantic eyes.

"Mr. Rutherford! Mr. Rutherford!" she yelled.

"Slow down, Chantrelle," Carl said. "You're going to crack your skull and the baby's."

"This is Kwanna, Mr. Rutherford." The girl thrust the stunned child into Carl's arms. Kwanna wore a frilly pink dress; her scalp was dotted with dozens of multi-colored plastic barrettes. I expected Carl to act like he'd been handed a live lobster—he seemed too hip to appreciate anyone under the age of twelve—but to my surprise, he gently bounced the child. After a moment, he handed the baby back to the student. "Who's going to watch Kwanna while you go to school this year?"

"My auntie." Chantrelle held the kid sideways as if she were a battering ram. "Mr. Rutherford. I heard they changed the rules for the Miss Hall pageant this year."

"That's right," Carl said. "Student mothers can no longer participate."

"Mr. Rutherford!" Chantrelle said, stamping her shoe. "That ain't right. I wanted to compete."

"I'm sorry. That's what the committee decided. And would you please get a better grip on Kwanna? She's going to shoot right out of your arms."

We left Chantrelle and continued down the noisy corridor.

"Miss Hall pageant?" I said.

"Huge deal at Harriet Hall. Girls dress up in gowns their parents can't afford, and they curtsey and preen in front of Dr. Lipton, who's the judge. Some female students would rather be in the pageant than get their diplomas. I wish they'd discontinue it."

"And why are all these little kids here today?" I said, indicating the ruckus around us.

"Annual baby parade. Every year before school starts, students bring their kids to show them off to the staff."

"How does that happen? All these young girls having babies?"

He winked slyly. "If you don't know, I'm not the guy to tell you."

Heat surged up my neck and into my cheeks. "You know what I mean. I feel bad for these young girls being tied down with children. Their lives are over at sixteen."

"I'm more worried about the babies being raised by girls who are kids themselves."

"Why do so many get pregnant?"

"Many of our female students think that giving birth is a source of accomplishment and self-esteem. It's practically a rite of passage here, and the baby is their trophy."

He paused at a door marked Teachers' Lounge. "After you," he said.

"Wow. This is my very first visit to a teachers' lounge. Do I need a password?"

"No," he said, opening the door. "Just some very low expectations."

As soon as I stepped inside I saw what he was talking about. Hall's teachers' lounge had as much mystique as a bus terminal waiting room. The walls were painted a queasy green, and the furnishings included a big clumsy table, a butt-sprung couch, a wheezy refrigerator and a Coke machine covered with angry notes from people who'd lost their money. One said, "I'd have better odds in Vegas."

"Too bad," I said. "My mouth was set for a Coke."

Carl gave the machine a couple of nudges with his hip and two Cokes rattled down the chute. He tossed me one. "On me."

I caught the soda. "Nice move."

"I try."

We were grinning at each other like a couple of randy crocodiles when a stern voice interrupted us.

"Ms. Wells. Are you in there?" It was Ms. Sprague.

I glanced around, not sure where the disembodied voice was coming from. Carl pointed to an intercom box suspended on the ceiling. Then he waved goodbye to me before slipping out of the room.

"Yes, ma'am." I felt weird talking to a box.

"I've been looking everywhere for you. Your textbooks have been delivered, and I wanted to go over what you'll be teaching this year."

"Great. I was just—"

"Report to your room immediately."

I hustled over to my portable as fast as humanly possible, determined not to get on the wrong side of my supervisor. When I arrived, Ms. Sprague was standing in the middle of the room, mopping her brow and frowning. Strands of damp hair were plastered to her cheeks.

"About time. I thought I might die of heat exhaustion waiting for you."

"I'm sorry, I was just—"

"Wasting my time?" Ms. Sprague thrust her arm in the direction of a precarious stack of books. "Here are your textbooks. You're teaching Life Skills."

Sounded like a class I could stand to take.

"What kind of life skills?"

"Not the four Cs of diamond selection, if that's what you're thinking. I'm talking about real-folk life skills. Like what you have to do to impress the manager of the DQ so you can get a job as a cashier for eight dollars an hour. Not that you'd know anything about that."

I ignored her dig—partially my fault for driving a flashy car to school—and picked up the top textbook on the stack. Someone had taken a Sharpie to the cover and written a terrible word in big block letters. I tossed it into the metal trashcan where it landed with a loud thunk. Then I made a big show of wiping my hands of it.

"What did you do that for?" Ms. Sprague said. She'd raised one of her over-plucked eyebrows.

"There was a racial slur written on the front."

"I don't care if it was crawling with brown recluse spiders; you can't throw away books. There's a shortage as it is." She pointed at my boxes of supplies and said, "Where did you get those?"

"Someone on the staff lent them to me," I said quickly.

"Who?"

"Mr. Rutherford."

She continued to stare at the boxes, as if they were a Sudoku puzzle she couldn't quite solve. Seconds ticked by, and I felt sure that at any moment, she was going to take a closer look and see the masking tape on the globe that marked it as someone else's property. Then she'd call the police, they'd arrest me, and I'd be led out of the building in shackles.

After a long, uncomfortable moment she flared her nostrils and said, "How very generous of him."

Her gaze slowly ran the length of my body, as if I were one of many plucked chickens she was picking out for a stew. Abruptly she looked away from me and left the room.

Six

I survived pre-planning at Harriet Hall! I was so proud of myself I wanted to silkscreen my accomplishment on a t-shirt and parade down Main Street. *I know.* It wasn't like I'd cured cancer or invented Instagram, but, to me, it was still a big, honking deal. Since my injury there'd been days when the most challenging thing I'd done was to open the childproof cap of a Pepto-Bismol bottle. To get up on time, go to work, and stay there doing purposeful things for eight hours (mostly meetings and getting my classroom ready) was a huge and exhausting undertaking. Yet I'd weathered it. Already I could see the armored truck driving up to the bank to deposit five million bucks into my account.

When the weekend arrived, all I wanted to do was wander around in a bathrobe all day, occasionally flopping down on the sofa to take a nap. No time for that.

I had to clear out of my airy home with its coffered ceilings and marble fireplace and move into a very cheap condo painted the color of a Mary Kay Cadillac. The condos in my new neighborhood all looked exactly alike, and the landscaping was skimpy, a scraggly bush here, an anemic tree there. Standing outside was like standing on the moon.

Once I was settled in the new place, Joelle came over with a housewarming gift, a plastic ficus plant. Obviously she didn't trust me with the real item, which was just as well. My condo got about as much light as the inside of a shoebox.

"Who moved you?" she said.

Today Joelle was dressed like a python. A python that just swallowed a mouse. Her dress was a wee bit too tight.

"Place called Cheap Joe's Moving Company."

I was sure the two college-aged boys who did the work were curious about my reduced circumstances. I could practically see the thought bubbles over their head: *Bankruptcy? Foreclosure? Dumped by sugar daddy?*

I traded thirty-two hundred square feet for just over nine hundred; most of my furniture was now in storage. After paying the movers and all my deposits, I had two hundred bucks left in my bank account. I used to blow that much on a bottle of champagne.

"The carpet in this living room is an interesting color. What would you call it?" Joelle said.

"Mud?"

"Well, at least it won't show dirt. And you have to admit it's convenient to step out of your door and be only yards away from a dozen different restaurants."

"Yes. I can see the Cracker Barrel sign from my bedroom window."

"I'm sorry. I know this must be hard on you, especially getting a job at Harriet Hall."

"The school's not so bad."

"That's because the students haven't gotten there yet. I deal with Harriet Hall girls and their boyfriends every day at the hospital. I don't think you have any idea what you're in for."

"Aren't you always telling me how attached you get to your patients?" Joelle worked in labor and delivery.

"True, but if they give me any sass I can poke them with a needle. You don't have that option. Ten minutes into your first class, you'll probably want to run out the door screaming."

"Will not," I said, feeling a little stung.

From the beginning of our friendship, Joelle had always taken on a maternal role with me. She was two years older and naturally bossy. (Her brothers used to say she was so bossy she'd tell water which way to run.) She also considered herself to be far more worldly than me. To her, my years at the tennis academy and my participation in countless tournaments was sort of an airy-fairy Disney World existence that had little resemblance to real life. But once my teaching year was over Joelle would have to admit I was no longer a naive girl living in a gilded cage. Working at an inner-city school would give me a little street cred.

Monday morning arrived like an uppercut to the jaw. Sunday night my next-door neighbors kept me up all hours. I don't know what they were doing until three a.m., but it sounded like either bowling or demolition. Unfortunately I lingered too long over coffee and Cocoa Puffs and ended up pulling into the faculty parking lot five minutes late.

I signed in, fudging the time (thankfully the mean secretary wasn't skulking about) and sprinted across the field to my portable. When I opened the door, a blast of refrigerated air greeted me. I raised a victory fist over the working air conditioner, but my elation petered out when I ventured further into the room and found myself awash in a sea of desks. There were so many I could barely move without bumping into one. It was as if they'd been mating over the weekend.

Carl strode in. He looked professional in a crisp white shirt, diamond-patterned tie, and dark linen suit. His earring was absent; I guess he took it off to teach. I was about to toss off some flirty remark when I noticed a gold ring on the appropriate finger glinting the Morse code message, "Married. Hussies keep away."

I could have sworn he hadn't been wearing a wedding ring during our previous encounters. My disappointment must have shown on my face, because he said, "Problem?"

"Look at all these desks. I only need about ten or twelve, and there must be forty in here."

"No big deal. Throw out the extras. I'll get some help."

Three young men were hanging out near the entryway of the portable. Carl beckoned them over. They were all garbed in baggy denim jeans and tennis shoes big enough to stomp out a campfire. They also wore shifty expressions like they were plotting a Circle K robbery.

"Tavaras, Steve, Drequann. I need you to go in and take out nine desks apiece," Carl said to them.

I almost expected them to whip out switchblades and say, "Make me," but the boys didn't hesitate. They obediently headed inside to complete the chore.

I could see their toughness didn't hold up at a distance. Up close they were gangly-limbed and had the kind of baby-faced cheeks grandmas loved to pinch. Made me feel sheepish for stereotyping them.

"Wait," I said. "What if it rains?"

"Not your problem. And if you have too many desks that means someone else is short. They'll probably be gone in an hour. By the way, I brought you a little first-day-of-school present."

He handed me a brick-sized piece of stained wood. Carved into the surface was my name: T. L Wells. Too bad I had no idea what it was.

"Thank you so much for this lovely...uh...*objet d'art.*"

He laughed. "You have no clue, do you?"

I shook my head, embarrassed.

"It's a hall pass. I had Doc, the shop teacher, make it for you."

"Of course! Thank you. I shall cherish it always."

"Just a gift from one friend to another. Hope you have a good first day. I better get a move on."

It was freezing in the portable so I turned the thermostat up. The frigid air continued to blast from a large vent in the ceiling.

Shivering, I made a final inspection of my classroom. I'd covered up some of the filthiest graffiti with construction paper, and plugged up the hole with old towels. I also visited a teacher supply store, but all the prepared bulletin boards seemed babyish. I decided to put up a black-and-white poster of a wild-haired Janis Joplin. I'd always been a huge Joplin fan, and although my students probably didn't know who she was, maybe they'd be curious and we could have a lively discussion about her. Kind of a history lesson.

Just then the bell rang. Actually it was more like a buzzer and it sounded like the whine of dozens of gnats.

Show time!

I went to the portable's porch to greet students. The field teemed with loitering teenagers, shrieking with laughter, chasing each other in the dirt, and talking so loudly you'd think they were attending a school for the hard-of-hearing. The mood was festive, and no one seemed even mildly interested in going to class. Was that typical?

A skinny girl with an oversized head skipped up the stairs to the portable. I smiled. Maybe this was my very first victim? Oops. I meant student.

"Are you taking Miss Beecher's place?" the girl said. She stood too close, elbows jostling me, hot breath in my face.

"I'm not sure."

"Ms. Beecher was in this classroom last year." The girl smiled, revealing two prominent front teeth covered with a scrim of yellow plaque. I made a mental note to plan a lesson on oral hygiene ASAP.

"She had to leave because they took out one of her lungs. It was rotten."

"Are you sure?" I remembered Carl's joke about the asbestos.

The girl nodded. "I'm Janey. Who you?"

"I'm Toni Lee."

"Ms. Toni Lee?"

"Just plain Toni Lee. That's my first name and that's what you should call me." Letting students call me by my first name was in line with the loose management style I had in mind for my classroom.

"What kind of candy you brung?"

"Brought," I corrected, switching into teacher mode so smoothly it surprised me. "I didn't bring candy."

"Oooh. Mrs. Toni Lee. You done messed up. You supposed to bring candy."

"It's not Mrs. Toni Lee. It's Toni Lee. As for the candy—"

"Can I hold a dollar? I need it for lunch."

"Well, if it's for lunch." I rifled through the wallet in my purse and plucked out a bill. "I only have a five."

Janey seized the money. "I'll be back."

"Wait a sec. It's almost class time and—"

I was talking to empty air; Janey had already banged down the steps. The second bell rang but there was no sign of my students. I couldn't imagine what was going on. I knew my classes were supposed to be small but this was ridiculous.

I returned to the portable and sat at my desk, rubbing my goose-pimpled arms, wondering how long I should wait before I went to the front office to investigate the Case of the Missing Students. I was glancing at my class roster when the door opened and six teenagers tramped inside, two females and four males.

Like members of a synchronized theater troupe, they each picked up a desk and placed it in the very back of the room against the bulletin board. One boy with a long face and hooded eyes slumped backwards in his desk. Surliness rose from the group like smoke from a cigar. On their heels came Janey, holding an oversized Butterfinger candy bar and a can of Mountain Dew, bought, no doubt, with my money.

"Why are you tardy?" I said to the new arrivals.

No response. Six sullen faces glared at me. Janey's mouth was too stuffed with Butterfinger to answer.

"Since it's only the first day I'll excuse you, but I do expect you to be on time from now on. Understood?"

The students in the back of the room merely glowered and slouched in their desks.

"They're scared," Janey said. She was licking chocolate off her fingers. "They don't want anyone seeing them going into the special ed room. People make fun of them."

I smiled, pleased to have a chance to show them how caring and easygoing I could be. "You know, it's not a shame to need extra help. All through high school and college, I was a jock, and I had tutors to get me through. Even though I was a little embarrassed at first, in the end, I was grateful for the assistance."

Their expressions didn't change; my words were like bullets bouncing off a Kevlar vest.

I cleared my throat, wondering why I wasn't getting through to them. "In fact, some of your classmates may be jealous you're getting so much help and attention. Bet you didn't think of that."

One of the girls shot up and marched to the exit. She was pretty with long, dark bangs fringing her wide-spaced eyes.

"Where's the fire?" I said pleasantly.

"Goan. Ursh," the girl mumbled.

"You've lost your purse?" I said.

"Monica's going to the nurse," Janey shouted.

"Are you sick?"

"Of you," the girl said haughtily. The class laughed, and Monica continued toward the door. Was she making a joke? If so, I didn't find it particularly funny.

"Slow down there, Speedy Gonzales." I followed her with the pass Carl had given me. "You need a hall pass."

"Leave me alone, cracka," she said. "I got a migraine."

She left the portable and slammed the door behind her. A chunk of ceiling tile fell to the ground. Snickers flew around the room.

Perhaps Monica's migraine was making her a little testy. In fact all the students seemed edgy. Maybe their defenses were up because they were accustomed to heartless, hard-driving teachers. It might take them a while to figure out I hailed from a more mellow tribe.

"Monica called the teacher a cracka!" Janey ejected herself from her desk and frolicked over until she was inches away from my nose. "Want me to take the write-up to the office? Want me to, huh?"

"We will not get all worked up over Monica. We have more important things to do. Like learning!"

Now that most everyone was assembled, I decided to plunge

into the lesson for the day. Thankfully I'd been issued a teacher's edition of the textbook. It gave step-by-step instructions on how to present material. At least that part of my job would be a breeze.

I stood in front of the class with the book open on the podium and began to read:

"The purpose of this course is to learn about the world of work and how to live independently. You will become familiar with possible career options, and—"

A boy with heavily tattooed arms jolted out of his desk. "Who let out the turd cloud?"

"Whoever smelt it dealt it," Janey said.

"Holy crap," said a boy whose teeth gleamed with silver. "That's enough to knock you flat."

"Young man," I said.

"His name's Vernon," Janey said.

"Vernon. Profanity is not allowed in this classroom. And I don't know what you're talking about because I don't smell...Oh! You know, maybe I should open a window. It *is* a little stuffy in here."

The students abandoned their desks and scrambled for the door, shouting and screaming.

"It's not that bad."

Actually it was so strong it could peel the paint off the walls; the only person who seemed unconcerned was Janey, which led me to suspect she was the source of the stench.

It took several minutes to herd the students back into the portable. After that was accomplished, I began to read from the textbook again.

"We're not supposed to be doing work," Janey interrupted.

"Why not?" I said.

"Everyone knows the first day is a free day," Janey said. "No teachers make you work. Ms. Beecher never made us work on the first day."

Murmurs of agreement came from the back of the room. Were they right? Had I violated some kind of sacred classroom tradition?

"The first day is supposed to be fun." Janey flitted about the room chanting, "Let's get krunk. Let's get krunk." The other students joined in.

No, let's get *drunk*, I thought. I'd been at work for only a few minutes and already my classroom was in chaos.

Over the din, I heard a knock on my door. "Quiet, please," I said to the class but the shouting continued. I opened the door, and Carl came inside accompanied by a pouty Monica.

At the sight of Carl, the students quieted down. A couple shouted out, "Hey, Mr. Rutherford" like he was an old buddy. Certainly they were friendlier to him than they were to me. Carl returned the greetings and said, "Ms. Wells. Does Ms. Steele here belong in your class?"

"Yes."

He crooked his finger, indicating I should follow him to the porch. Away from prying ears he said, "It's never a good idea to give Monica Steele a pass. She's a notorious hall-walker."

"She said she had a migraine."

Carl laughed. "Monica lied. She doesn't get migraines; she gives them."

"Thanks for the tip. Incidentally, is there a rule about not doing any work on the first day of school?"

"Of course not. Students will tell all kinds of fibs, especially to new teachers. In fact, you should make a special effort to keep your kids occupied today. Beulah Jefferson is on campus."

"Beulah Jefferson? Who's that?"

"President of the Harriet Hall Alumni Association. Likes to pop in on teachers' classes and give them grief. She can be a pain in the behind, but you have to take her seriously. She's managed to get a few teachers fired in the past."

"What does this Beulah person look like?"

"Very old. Always wears pillbox hats and lace-up shoes. Walks with a cane. Unfortunately for you, she doesn't much care for white teachers. Doesn't think they should be teaching black children. "

I sighed. "Is it lunchtime yet?"

"Before you know it. Hope you eat fast."

"How long is lunch?"

"A half-hour for the kids. Fifteen minutes for staff. The other fifteen minutes you'll be on lunch duty. There's a list of assignments in the teachers' lounge."

Lunch did come, freakishly early at ten forty-five a.m. Turned out there were three lunch periods, and my class was assigned first lunch. I hadn't packed food because I assumed I'd have a nice restful repast at some nearby café. But when I tried to leave, the security guard told me teachers were prohibited from leaving the campus during the school day. Therefore it was the cafeteria or nothing.

Unfortunately the ambiance at *Chez* Harriet Hall was far from inviting. Noise level? Deafening. Lighting? Bright as an operating room. Décor? Cinderblock walls, and long, fold-up tables with plastic dots for seating. I'd have liked to skip lunch altogether but the morning's dramas had made me ravenous. Bring on the pink slime.

Ambiance aside, business was booming. A long line snaked around the room. How was I going to get through the line, scarf my food, and report to duty in fifteen minutes? I took my place at the end of the line.

Carl entered the lunchroom, and I waved him over.

"Line's so long you'd think they were giving away the food," I said over the racket.

"They *are* giving it away. Over ninety-eight percent of students qualify for free lunch. What are you doing in that line? You're a teacher. You can cut."

"Finally a VIP privilege."

"One of the few."

"Would you like to join me?"

"Can't. I have duty the first half of lunch."

"Where do teachers eat?"

Carl pointed to a closed door just off the cafeteria. "There's an anteroom with a few tables inside for faculty."

I proceeded to the head of the line. Two coaches were in front of me. A lunch lady in a hairnet and a green polyester uniform heaped generous portions of a pale noodle casserole on their trays as well as extra bread. When I slid my tray in front of her, she dished up a dainty dollop, not enough to satisfy the nutritional needs of a teacup poodle. I glanced up at her as if to say, "Has there been a mistake?" Her hard-eyed glare answered my question.

Holding my tray aloft, I muscled through a sea of jostling and shouting students to the anteroom. I opened the door, expecting a peaceful refuge, maybe even some classical music tinkling in the background. But the teachers were almost as loud as the students. A few people, including Ms. Sprague, my so-called buddy teacher, glanced at me when I came in, but nobody called me over.

I scanned the room, looking for an open seat or a friendly face. Mr. Gerald, one of the new teachers, was sitting alone at a table. I walked over to him. "May I join you?"

He nodded, chewing vigorously. His portion of noodles was as paltry as mine. Perhaps you had to develop some seniority before you were fed decent-sized rations.

"How's your first day going so far?"

Considering that he had biceps the size of my thighs, he'd probably already whipped his kids into shape. Mr. Gerald chewed some more, swallowed and took a dainty sip of water before answering. "I can't hold a conversation while I'm eating," he said, his soft, breathy voice out of sync with his burly appearance. "I have acid reflux. Talking aggravates it."

"Sorry."

I silently picked at my pasty, under-seasoned noodles with my plastic spork and eavesdropped on conversations at nearby tables.

"I had fifty students in my homeroom and twenty desks. It was the Middle Passage all over again."

"One of the windows in my room won't close; every bug in Kingdom Come is flying around in there."

"Who's in charge of bells this year? First period was eighty minutes long, and second period was twenty minutes."

The commotion churned and eddied around me, and even though I was in the eye of it, I didn't feel a part of it. I couldn't help but wonder if I'd ever fit into this strange new world. *One year, one year*, I kept telling myself. It felt like a prison sentence.

Seven

I sat on the side verandah at Tranquility Hall, eating grilled shrimp salad from the Publix deli with Aunt Cornelia. The air sweetly smelled of Confederate jasmine. No body odors or gas emissions. No roaches or mice, only cute, disease-free wildlife like hummingbirds buzzing the feeder and yellow butterflies flitting among the lantana plants. Best of all, it was blissfully quiet; no shouts, no backtalk, no lockers slamming. Just the soft creaking of the magnolia tree branches whenever a breeze blew in. How could I have taken all of this loveliness for granted?

My aunt jabbed at her salad with a fork. "I forgot how dull Rose Hill can be. They roll up the sidewalks at seven p.m."

For the last few minutes I'd been gathering up the courage to discuss a ticklish topic with my aunt. Now was as good a time as any to bring it up.

"Not all of Rose Hill is dull," I said, keeping my voice casual. "I know of one area where it's plenty lively. In fact, they have gunshots all night long."

Cornelia dabbed her lips with her napkin, leaving a hot-pink imprint. "Last Monday night I swore it was the Rapture and I'd been left behind. That's how quiet Main Street was."

I laughed at her joke and scooted my chair a few inches closer to her. Was it possible she hadn't heard what I'd just said?

"It's not just gunshots," I said, this time in a louder voice. "There are also the screams of women as they run from rapists, and the squeal of tires from drive-by shootings."

The sun slipped out from behind a bank of clouds, and Cornelia donned her initialed Dolce and Gabbana sunglasses. My aunt loved clothing and accessories that trumpeted how pricey they were.

"What in the world are you jabbering about?" she said.

"Did you know Harriet Hall High School is located in a very dangerous neighborhood?"

"No," she said, sounding a little bored.

"It's in a ghetto."

"I'm sure that must be challenging, but gratifying as well. You should be proud of yourself."

Praise was not what I was after.

"Maybe I'm not making myself clear. I'm talking *terrible* neighborhood. Drugs. Gangs. Prostitutes. Extremely misogynistic rap music."

"Have you experienced any of these things directly? Beyond the rap music, I mean?"

"Not yet. But it's probably only a matter of time. And the kids are definitely a product of their environment. Completely out of control."

She waved dismissively. "It takes a while to learn how to discipline young people. Give it time. Charleston wasn't built in a day, you know."

"It's not just *my* students. It's the whole school. There are fights every day. Girl-on-girl fights with fake nails and hair extensions flying, and a few days ago I witnessed two parents, both mothers, sparring in the library. They broke a bust of Socrates."

Her eyes widened; finally a reaction beyond the blasé.

"Are you expected to break up these fights?"

I wasn't. A security guard named Mule busted up the battles, but certainly if a teacher was in the wrong place at the wrong time, he or she could get swept up in the action. I decided it wouldn't hurt to tell a little fib.

"Yes. If I'm in the vicinity."

"That's difficult for me to believe." She took a sip from her

Arnold Palmer and swallowed. "Do you know how easy it would be for me to check that out? All I have to do is pick up the phone."

I glanced down at the last shrimp floating in a leftover pool of mayonnaise on my plate. "Well, maybe I don't actually have to break up fights but I could still get hurt working there." I flexed my weak wrist to illustrate my point. A blatant move, but I was desperate.

Her mouth puckered. "Well then...Maybe you should think about giving it up."

"Maybe," I said, trying not to appear too overeager. "Then I could go out and find a safer job."

"You could do that."

Was it really going to be that simple? If so, I should have talked to her days ago. Would have saved myself hours of misery.

She sighed. "Except it would be such a shame for you to lose your inheritance."

The last bit of salad I'd swallowed stuck in my throat.

"I'm sorry, but it sounds to me like this job is just what you need. After all, it's adversity that changes people the most."

"But I had no idea—"

"This was a job you chose, Toni Lee. Don't forget that. You need to take responsibility for your decision."

She was right, of course. I'd willingly waltzed into the belly of the beast, unarmed and with such annoying hubris. Now it looked as if there was no going back. I was stuck at Harriet Hall.

"One more thing. Do *not* come to me with any more tall tales about your job. It's only a year. You can make it. And once you're finished, you'll be handsomely rewarded."

I nodded quickly, but I wasn't certain anymore. I'd been such a fool; teaching was not what I'd expected.

Eight

"THAT'S ENOUGH! Stop talking right now. Do you hear me? You're stepping on my last nerve. What's wrong with you, you wicked, wicked children?"

That was me. The person who said she'd never be a yeller. The hip teacher who wanted a laid-back classroom. Instead I sounded like Ms. Capers, my third grade teacher, who wore an ill-fitting wig and was so disliked by her students they used to leave dead Palmetto bugs on her chair.

I even stole some of her most famous lines: "stepping on my last nerve," and "wicked children." Any day now I'd wear polyester pantsuits and come to school smelling like cat pee.

It wasn't as if I hadn't tried to be patient with my charges; after all, they *were* disadvantaged, and special education students to boot. What kind of heartless person would I be if I got cross with them? But, as time wore on, I found it almost impossible not to lose my temper in class.

Who could blame me? Whenever I tried to teach, they'd talk over me as if I wasn't in the room. If it was early morning, many of their heads would drop down on their desks with a loud *thunk,* followed by snores. When they weren't asleep they were squabbling with each other or giving me backtalk. The only student who seemed to tolerate me was Janey; she tailed me around the campus, chatting incessantly. Carl called her my shadow.

As for my bi-weekly Teacher Corps classes, they were useless. I kept hoping I'd be given tips on classroom control, but instead the instructor, a slight elderly man with creepy long fingernails and a monotone voice, spent hours talking about educational theory. How was Bloom's Taxonomy going to help me when my students were running amok?

I turned in several discipline forms daily but I might as well have been stuffing them into Coke bottles and tossing them into the ocean. Periodically the assistant principal called kids to the office but I never heard my students' names.

On Friday Ms. Sprague stopped me in the hall in between classes.

"I have a question about your lesson plans," she said, clearly peeved. Her tailored suit did nothing to disguise her figure. The woman could wear an iron lung and still look sexy.

"What's wrong?" I was practically shouting over the *bam, bam* of slamming lockers and yelling teenagers. The halls were a war zone; a person needed body armor and a canister of tear gas to walk through them.

"For homework you have students researching various careers."

"That's right."

"And how exactly do you think they'll conduct that research?"

Why she was asking me such a basic question? I flattened myself against the wall. A long line of girls were surging in my direction, their voices husky and querulous. I feared being trampled.

"How about Google?" I said.

"With what computer? Very few of our students have computers in their homes."

"Are you sure? You're always hearing about the expensive tennis shoes and phones welfare recipients own. Surely they have computers."

"Pull up those pants!" snapped Ms. Sprague.

Alarmed, I glanced down at my outfit; I was wearing a dress.

"Not you," Ms. Sprague said. "Him." She pointed at a young man whose jeans were practically puddling around his knees, revealing bright red underwear. "You heard me, Mr. Owens." The student reluctantly adjusted his trousers, and Ms. Sprague turned to address me again. "I've been to these children's homes and seen their circumstances up close. Fact is, some of our students are lucky to have electricity or hot water, much less an assortment of electronics. Nor are there any libraries within walking distance of where they live."

"What about the library here? It stays open a couple of hours after school. Will it kill them to hang around for a while?"

"And who'll pick them up when they're done?" Ms. Sprague said, arms folded over her chest. "Mom in her Lexus SUV?"

I felt my cheeks getting warm. "I'm sorry, I guess I wasn't thinking."

"You don't have a clue, do you?"

I didn't argue because I knew she was telling the truth. It was as if I'd traveled to a foreign land where none of the usual rules and customs applied. If I was ever going to survive the year, I needed to get the hang of things.

Friday afternoon arrived, and I was so jubilant I felt like pounding my chest and breaking dinner plates. For the first time I understood all the hoopla about TGIF and "working for the weekend."

I was in the office, itching to make my escape, when Carl sauntered in my direction, whistling an upbeat tune. He always seemed happy, even on Monday mornings. What was his secret?

"I see you've got a smile on your face," he said.

"Ready to relax," I said.

Relax was code for downing a drink as big as a goldfish bowl. During the week I tried to avoid alcohol. Teaching at Harriet Hall was harrowing enough, but teaching at Harriet Hall with a hangover was like chewing glass.

"Doc Brewster, the shop teacher, and I are going to The Steer for happy hour," Carl said. "Join us?"

"I don't want to intrude." I was still disappointed that the only attractive guy at school was married.

"No intrusion at all. We'd love to have you."

I agreed and as soon as I was done signing out, I headed over to The Steer. When I arrived, the dimly lit restaurant contained only a smattering of customers, mostly lone diners. I made my way to the bar area, peanut shells crunching underneath my shoes. "I've Got Friends in Low Places" played on the sound system, and the aroma of fried onions embroidered the air. Doc Brewster sat at a booth beneath the massive head of a glassy-eyed bull.

I greeted him, saying Carl had invited me, and he motioned for me to sit.

"Carl called. Said he was stopping by the bank first." He pushed a plastic basket lined with wax paper in my direction. "Steak nugget?"

I met the bull's accusatory gaze. "No, thanks."

"Gotta quit eating these. The wife will give me grief if I don't come home hungry for supper."

He was one of the few teachers who occasionally spoke to me in the halls. Doc was short and pudgy with a constellation of dark moles covering his cheeks. He was also notorious for his terrible taste in clothes. Today he wore red suspenders and a pair of very loud madras golf pants.

The bartender, a prim blonde with precisely cut bangs, stopped by the table asking for my order. A button pinned to her brown polyester uniform said, "Try a Texas Tumbleweed Today."

"What's good to drink here?"

"Debbie makes a mean gin and tonic," Doc said.

"I'll have two to start."

"House or premium gin?" Debbie said.

I was about to say "Bombay Sapphire" but then remembered my days of top shelf spirits were gone with the wind. Hello, rot gut.

The bartender was quick with mixing the drinks, and the first one loosened my tongue. Even though I barely knew Doc, I spilled to him what my life at Harriet Hall had been like so far.

When I was done, Doc said, "Looking for advice?"

"Definitely."

He swigged his beer and wiped the foam from his upper lip. "First, give up on the idea of a perfect classroom. Keeping order at all times is like putting socks on the arms of an octopus. Second, the most important rule of survival at Harriet Hall is CYA."

"English, please. I'm not up on all the educational acronyms yet." It seemed as if every time an educator opened his or her mouth, letters of the alphabet spilled out. My students, for instance, weren't simply slow, they were LD for learning disabled. A couple were also BD, which stood for behavior-disordered.

"You've never heard of CYA?"

"No."

He threw back his head and laughed. "You *are* a newbie. CYA isn't educational jargon; it's a way of life. It means cover your ass. Read the Teacher Handbook front to back, and do whatever it says. Turn in lesson plans on time. If you can keep your nose clean for two years, you'll get tenure and you're golden. Practically the only way they can get rid of you is to take you out with a sniper's rifle."

"So it doesn't matter what kind of teacher I am, as long as I cover my ass."

He banged his mug against my highball glass. "Now you're getting it."

"Isn't that kind of screwed up?"

"That's teaching. Legislators like to talk a good game but here's the reality: You've got some of the poorest and toughest students in the city in your classes, and it's your job to turn them into model citizens? Who are you, Gandhi? I'd love to see some of these policy makers darken the door of a real inner-city classroom. They'd probably pass a law that requires all teachers to carry Tasers." He devoured another steak nugget. "By the way, did you hear about Gerald?"

"The big guy?"

"Walked out on his class yesterday, blubbering like a baby. Couldn't handle these kids. You ought to pat yourself on the back for hanging in as long as you have. Most new teachers cut out after a week. The faculty doesn't bother cozying up to newcomers until they've been around for at least a year."

Aha. That explained why most of the teachers ignored me.

I also told him about my problems with Ms. Ware, and he explained that there were gatekeepers at every school—usually secretaries, lunchroom workers, or data clerks. As the least educated employees in the building, they often felt insecure, and as a result, sometimes got a little power-mad. He said I had to be courteous to Ms. Ware without turning into a doormat. According to him, doormats got no respect from gatekeepers.

"Gatekeepers also appreciate small bribes," he said over the roar of the blender behind the bar. "And Ms. Ware will practically roll over and beg for chocolate."

"Do you give her chocolate?"

"Don't have to." He patted his substantial belly. "It seems our Ms. Ware has an eye for a fine male physique."

"Lucky you."

He brayed, spraying droplets of beer on the table. "Just kidding. I bring the Countess of Cruel Dove bars at least once a week. The only teacher who doesn't have to bribe her is Carl."

I smiled over my drink. That I could understand. Carl could charm anyone, even a crab like Ms. Ware. Too bad he was already spoken for.

"Speaking of Carl, it wouldn't hurt to sit in on one of his classes. The man knows what he's doing."

"I might just do that."

"One more thing. Watch out for Beulah Jefferson. If she comes into your classroom, everything needs to be shipshape. She'd love to catch a white teacher screwing up."

"Carl mentioned her too. Does she drop in on all the teachers?" If Ms. Jefferson decided to pay me a surprise visit, I was doomed. My classroom was more chaotic than a runaway ant farm.

"Lucky for you, the old gal can't walk so well with that cane of hers. She'll probably never make it out to the portables."

Carl joined us, apologizing for being late, blaming a long line at the bank. He slid in the booth next to me. He'd been working all day but still smelled fresh, like fabric softener drifting from a dryer vent. I kept taking furtive whiffs of him.

Doc got a text from his wife, asking him to come home and attend to a leaking washing machine. When he left, I expected Carl to move to the other side of the booth, but he stayed put.

"There's always something leaking over at Doc's," Carl said. "It's his wife's sneaky way of getting him home."

"Clever. And how does your wife coax you home?"

"Coax? That's not her style. If she wanted me home, she'd burst in, upend a few tables, and drag me out by the nose hairs."

I nervously glanced around the restaurant. "You expecting her tonight?"

He rattled the ice cubes in his glass. "Actually, we're recently divorced."

Well, well, well. Suddenly the evening had gotten vastly more interesting.

"Sorry to hear that," I fibbed. "But you still wear your wedding ring."

"Checking out my fingers, huh?"

I shrugged. "I'm observant."

"I always wear my wedding ring to school. In the past I've had problems with flirty female students. The ring cuts down on that sort of thing."

Not to mention flirty colleagues. Inching closer, I peppered Carl with questions about himself. He told me he was twenty-seven, had been teaching five years, and was currently going to school at night to get his M.S. in Psychology.

"There's one thing I've been dying to ask you all night," I said. "What's that?"

I pointed to his cheek. "Where did you get your scar?"

He frowned. "You picked the one thing I don't like to talk about."

"Too painful?" I imagined a variety of disturbing scenarios: a drunken and brutal father, an ambush in an alley, or a gangland war. Carl looked fairly street-tough.

"Too embarrassing."

"Come on. I promise to keep it a secret."

He gritted his teeth. "Okay...It was a light saber accident."

"What?"

"When I was a kid, I was playing Star Wars with my younger brother Mitt. His light saber broke into a sharp edge, and it cut my face open."

I coughed to cover up a laugh.

"I told you it was embarrassing. It's like telling people you have a washable skull-and-crossbones tattoo."

Carl confessed that he grew up in a middle-class neighborhood with an Irish Setter and a swimming pool. He said he never lied to students about his upbringing but he didn't advertise it either. Didn't want to emphasize the differences between him and his kids.

"You certainly had me fooled." I nearly knocked over his bourbon on the rocks with my elbow. "Oops. My back."

Carl rumpled his brow. "Your back? What's wrong with it? You pull a muscle?"

"You haven't heard that expression? My students say it all the time."

He slapped his khaki-covered knee and laughed. "It's 'my bad,' not 'my back.' I can see I'm going to have to give someone slang lessons, shawty."

We'd gotten so close I was practically sitting in his lap and during the rest of our conversation I was constantly touching him on the arm or leg. In my part of town, a white girl getting friendly with a black man would probably have caught a few eyeballs, but here, on the scruffier Southside, no one was giving us any attention. He brushed the bangs away from my forehead, and said, "How about coffee at my house?" When he touched me, my body's pleasure receptors lit up like a pinball machine.

If I accepted his invitation, I guessed we'd do more than drink coffee. Was that a good idea? It could make things awkward at school next week. Who cares, I thought. Ever since I'd gotten the job at Harriet Hall I'd been a goody two-shoes, and I was already sick of it. Time for some racy recreation. Thankfully Aunt Cornelia's contract didn't prohibit me from participating in activities of the carnal kind.

I downed the rest of my G & T, and laid down a few bills for Debbie. "Let's go."

He pushed the money back in my direction. "My treat."

"Thanks, but I can pay for myself."

"Come on. You're a first-year teacher in the Corps program. I've got five years in. I can afford it much better than you."

We left The Steer, and I followed him to his apartment. I'd seen my share of guys' places, and sometimes they were so unhygienic, you were afraid to sit lest you catch scabies or fleas. Not true with Carl's home. His living room was well-kept and homey with a puffy oversized couch, crowded bookshelves, and a collection of glossy-leafed and thriving house plants.

"Have a seat and I'll get some coffee," he said, heading to the kitchen.

While he was gone, I glanced through a plastic bin that held dozens of DVDs, mostly action flicks but a couple of artsy films too. After a moment Carl returned with two chunky mugs on a tray, along with cocktail napkins, sugar, and cream. The guy was definitely well-trained.

"Do you realize you have absolutely no horror films?" I said.

"That's because real life is already plenty scary. Did you want to watch a movie?"

"Maybe not," I said, stirring sugar into my coffee.

"You have some other ideas?"

I smiled shyly. I wasn't normally so coy, especially after I'd had a drink or two, but something about Carl made me less bold than usual.

He immediately scooched closer to me and brushed his lips lightly against my ear. I shifted positions and when I did a high squeaky voice said, "I wanna go potty."

I pulled away. "What was that?"

Carl groaned. "Chatty Keisha." He pushed aside a couch cushion and withdrew a dark-skinned, naked doll. Its long, black braid had been chopped in half.

"And why, may I ask, do you have a naked doll in your couch?" At least it wasn't life-sized.

"She belongs to Katherine, my five-year-old." He tossed the doll aside and inched closer to me. "Sorry for the interruption."

"You didn't mention you had a daughter."

"Never came up."

He leaned toward me, his lips honing in on mine. I jumped up from the sofa. "Where's your restroom?"

"Down the hallway. First door on the left." He patted the couch cushion. "I'll keep your spot warm."

The bathroom contained more signs of Carl's daughter. A tub caddy held a rubber ducky, a plastic sailboat, and an economy-sized bottle of Mr. Bubble. I splashed cool water on my face and said to the mirror, "You've never slept with a father before. At least not knowingly."

I made a face at the prospect. Sleeping with some boy I'd met in a club and sleeping with a father were two different things. Fathers were responsible people who conducted committed adult relationships, and truthfully all I wanted was a little fun between the covers. Maybe this wasn't such a smart idea after all. I left the bathroom, and Carl motioned me to the couch.

"Come give me some company."

"I think I better go home."

"But you barely touched your coffee."

"Don't want to get all jittery on caffeine."

"It's decaf."

"It's late."

"What's your hurry all of a sudden?"

"I'm just tired."

As a consolation prize, I leaned down and briefly brushed my lips with his.

Nothing. It was like kissing a plaster wall. The sparks I'd felt earlier were gone.

"That's no kind of kiss."

Carl stood and his mouth sought out mine. At first I tensed, but the longer we kissed, the more my resistance rushed out of my body. He tasted of bourbon, and his skin emitted a burnt aroma, like roasted pecans.

A few minutes later I was kissing him as if I wanted to nibble him down to nothing. He was taller than me, and I climbed him like a tree trunk and wrapped my legs around his torso. Both of my shoes clunked to the carpet.

We wrestled our way to his bedroom and dropped to his mattress, clutching and scrabbling at each other's clothing, frenzied for the touch of bare skin. Buttons popped, cloth ripped, and zipper teeth were pried apart. I gasped at the heated sensation of his nude body against mine. His panting slowed, and his hand grazed my nipple. I could tell he was trying to rein in his urgency in the name of foreplay, but I couldn't wait.

"Now," I demanded.

"You sure?"

"Do I have to hire a skywriter?"

He hovered over me, and the bed jounced and shuddered. My conscious self dissolved into a pinprick as release roared through my body.

Nine

Carl was like human Cheez-Its; I couldn't get enough of the man. I ended up spending the entire weekend at his apartment, most of it in bed. Occasionally we left the bedroom for a half-hour to eat toast, sip coffee, or watch part of a movie but eventually we'd find our way back to the mother ship, i.e., his memory-foam mattress.

Sometimes the sex was leisurely, other times playful, but the end result was always the same: an orgasm so cataclysmic it blew off the top of my head. I'm not exaggerating. Carl was more practiced with the crevices and contours of the female body than any man I'd ever been with. I should know. After my injury, I'd shamelessly torn through quite a few.

The weekend was winding down and Carl had me on the edge of paradise—my fingertips mere millimeters from the fingertips of God—when his cell phone rang. It had rung several times before and he'd always ignored it; this ringtone was different from the others. It sounded like, "Thank Heaven for Little Girls."

He lifted his head. "I have to get it."

I seized his wrist. "No. Way." If I had a pistol handy I'd have been tempted to train it on his temple.

"Sorry." His lips skimmed my earlobe. "I'll make it up to you."

While I tried to beat back my ferocious sexual frustrations, Carl answered the phone and immediately his voice went from throaty lover to kindergarten teacher.

"Hi, sweet cakes. How's Daddy's girl?"

Pause.

"What happened with kitty?"

Pause.

"That's the way kitties roll. They don't like their tails pulled."

In the presence of such domestic sweetness, my nudity felt positively pornographic. No longer aroused, I eased off the bed, intending to put on my clothes.

Carl grabbed my elbow and pulled me back.

"Daddy loves you too, sweet cakes. I'll talk to you tomorrow." He tossed the cell phone onto the lamp table and straddled me. "Where were we?"

His hair was cut too short to yank, so I tugged on his ears. "We need to talk."

Carl jumped off of me. "Scariest four-word combination in the English language. Especially when it comes from a naked woman."

"Seriously."

"I'm listening."

I pulled the much-trafficked bedsheet up to my chin. Would have liked to pull it over my head for our upcoming conversation.

"Is this a one-night stand?"

"Since you've been here two nights I guess the answer is no." He ran his fingers through my curls, which were probably wilder than pampas grass.

"You know what I mean."

"Is that what you want?"

"Hell no," I said, maybe a little too quickly. I was hooked on the man. Wanted him in my bed every night. Wanted to have my way with him at least ten more times before I left. If I could sleep with Carl on a regular basis I might make it through the school year.

"I'd like to do this again too," he said. "But, to be honest, I want to keep it light."

I nuzzled his neck. "I agree. Sex isn't nearly as much fun in the dark."

He leaned back against a bank of pillows and rested his hands on his rock-hard stomach. "You know that's not what I mean. I definitely like being with you, but...I'm not ready to get serious with anyone. I'm recently divorced. I'm in graduate school. Now is not a good time to become emotionally involved. I probably shouldn't have seduced you in the first place—that's not really my style— but there's just something so sexy about you...I lost my head."

I agreed. The chemistry between us was crazy, and I supposed it was okay to keep our relationship on the physical level. It's not as if I had a lot of experience with deep relationships anyway. When I played tennis I'd been too driven to get emotionally involved with anyone, and after my injury, I was too reckless to even consider it.

"That's cool," I said, even though I felt a pinch of disappointment. I was really into the guy.

"What did you say?" Carl said. A jet was passing overhead, and it shook the apartment's thin walls. He lived less than a mile away from the airport.

"Let's have sex again," I said over the roar of the plane engines. "Hold the emotions."

"Are you sure? I don't want to create any false expectations. Don't want anyone to get hurt."

Honestly, after all the mental turmoil I'd been through in the last few months I didn't think I was capable of ever being hurt again.

"I'm sure." I whipped off the sheet. "Now that we've got that cleared up, could we possibly finish what we started?"

Ten

Every person has a breaking point and mine came Monday after lunch. I entered my portable and as soon as I sat down at my desk, I smelled something foul. I examined the heels of my shoes, but they were clean. I kept sniffing the room, tracing the stench to the closet.

I opened the door and nearly gagged. Inside was a sizable pile of poop along with a crudely scrawled note that said, "Toni Lee is a crappy techer." I didn't recognize the penmanship—my kids hadn't done enough work for me to be familiar with their handwriting.

For days, I'd been quietly putting up with rowdy students, roaches, mice, mud, and freezing air, but seeing that big, stinky pile of poop made me snap. I flew to the office.

The assistant principal in charge of discipline wasn't in. No surprise there. I was beginning to think he was a mythical creature like a unicorn or the Loch Ness Monster. Dr. Lipton wasn't around either. Who was running this loony bin? I returned to the outer office.

Ms. Ware was seated at her desk, spooning the last bit of blueberry yogurt out of a plastic container.

"I need to talk to you."

"As you can see I'm having lunch." She looked me up and down. "Why are you wearing earmuffs and a scarf? Hasn't anyone told you it's ninety degrees out?"

I whipped off my earmuffs; I'd forgotten I still had them on. My freezing room was the least of my problems.

"Someone went number two in my closet."

Ms. Ware gave me a withering look and said, "And why is that my problem?"

"Because you need to send a custodian to my portable immediately, and if someone isn't there in fifteen minutes, I'm going to come back here and haunt this place until it's cleaned up."

I didn't wait for her reply. I stomped out of the office, and slammed the door behind me.

I returned to my portable, and to my surprise, I only had to wait five minutes before a custodian appeared. Thank God Ms. Ware had taken me seriously. Maybe that's how it worked around Harriet Hall. Maybe you had to threaten people to get anything accomplished.

The rest of the day I was so traumatized I didn't even try to teach. I just let the students do whatever they pleased; no one seemed to notice except Janey, who asked me if I was feeling okay.

After the dismissal bell rang, Ms. Sprague stopped by my classroom. It was the first time my buddy teacher had dropped in on me since pre-planning days. Welcome to the jungle, I wanted to say.

"Why is it so cold in here?" She was shivering in a form-fitting sleeveless shift.

"Is it?" I opened my thermos and took a big swig of hot chocolate.

"Do you mind if I turn down the air?"

I laughed. "Good luck with that. It's busted."

"Have you contacted maintenance?"

"At least a dozen times."

"Never mind that. I have something more important to discuss with you." She loomed over my desk: I could smell her White Diamonds perfume, see the olive-toned face powder in her oversized pores. "Why didn't you tell me you were having classroom control problems? The assistant principal says you turn in a stack of disciplinary forms every day."

"That's correct." I tugged on the drawer that kept my copies of the forms but it wouldn't budge.

"Why?"

"Because my kids act like maniacs. Why else?"

She frowned. "It's not his job to control your students. Any teacher who turns in more than one form every few months is doing something wrong in the classroom."

I grunted, still pulling on the stubborn desk drawer. "Maybe I wouldn't be turning in so many forms if the assistant principal would get around to punishing some of my students. Does he use a lottery system or what? He hasn't called a single one of my kids into the office."

"That's because you teach special education students. By law, they can't be suspended except under very unusual circumstances. You're wasting your time turning in those forms."

The drawer came unstuck and fell to the floor with a metallic bang. I took a long, deep breath.

"So there's nothing I can do? The kids can poop in my closet, set the place on fire, build a nuclear bomb out of pencil lead, and suffer no repercussions?"

If I was the crying type, now would be the time to turn on the waterworks. I'd never been so frustrated in my life.

"It's your job to keep order in the classroom."

A roach skittered over my foot. I was so used to bugs by now I didn't even flinch. "So you're saying this is my fault?"

"Whose fault would it be? Incidentally, where's your bulletin board? I remember specifically telling you every teacher's required to have one."

Janis Joplin was still hanging on my mostly blank board but now she sported devil horns, a mustache and a little bubble coming out of her mouth saying, "Kill da white people."

"Someone's used my closet for a bathroom and you're worried about bulletin boards?"

"Dr. Lipton has several expectations for teachers. Putting up a bulletin board is one, dressing professionally as an example to the students is another." She took a glance at my thigh-high waders. I'd started wearing them every day to muck through all the mud in the field near my portable.

"Outside appearances," I said with a nod. "Like Ms. Ware who's sugary sweet to visitors but treats the staff like they're dog meat."

"If you give Ms. Ware the proper respect she'll return the favor."

"Not true. I'm always nice to her and she—"

"Several people overheard you threatening her if she didn't get a custodian to your room. That doesn't seem very nice to me. In fact, you owe her an apology."

"Fine. I just want to make sure I understand you correctly. You're telling me I can't expect *any* help from the administration."

"Of course I'm not saying that. If you're really having trouble with a young person, I'm certain the assistant principal will be glad to have a chat with him or her. But I'd wait a while before you ask. Right now you've cried wolf so many times you have zero credibility."

"Ms. Wells," said a tinny, disembodied voice. It came from the squawk box hanging from the ceiling.

"Yes?"

"This is Dr. Lipton. Please report to my office."

Ms. Sprague wagged a finger in front of my face. "Somebody's in trouble."

She was out of her tree. There was no earthly reason for Dr. Lipton to be mad at me. After all, I was the injured party in the situation. In fact, it was my guess Lipton had heard about my appalling incident and wanted to reassure me. At least that's what I would do if one of my employees was the victim of a poo-and-run.

Eleven

When I entered the main office, Ms. Ware was at her desk, using a pair of tweezers to pluck a hair from her chin. When she saw me, her eyes slanted into slits. "What do you want, crazy woman?"

"I'm not crazy. I was understandably upset. And I'm very sorry that I—"

"Ms. Wells," Dr. Lipton said from his inner office. "Come in, please."

"You better watch yourself," Ms. Ware said with a haughty toss of her heavily lacquered hair.

Dr. Lipton's office had a baronial feel with two matching burgundy leather wing chairs, drawn brocade draperies, and an oil portrait of an iron-haired Harriet Hall gazing sternly from an ornate frame. I doubted anyone had ever dared to poop in Harriet Hall's supply closet, but since she used to teach in a horse stable that would have been redundant.

"Take a load off," Dr. Lipton said. He hunkered behind a dark wood desk big as a barge; on each side were two wire baskets heaped high with paper.

I sunk into a wing chair; the legs were shorter than average, making me feel like I was sitting in a hole. He pushed a pen and a document across the shiny expanse of his desk. "Could I get your John Hancock?"

I leaned forward to pick up the paper. When I read it, my breath seized in my lungs. "I don't understand...This is a letter of resignation."

"The girl can read."

"Who says I want to resign? Yes, I was upset about what I found in my closet but that doesn't mean—"

"Do you know who was in the office while you were screaming threats at Ms. Ware? A member of the school board."

"I didn't know that, but I still think I had a right to be upset. Maybe you didn't hear the details of what happened."

Dr. Lipton let out an impatient sigh. "A student made a mess in your supply closet. I was informed."

"Not just any mess." I lowered my voice to a whisper. "It was poop. A huge pile. Looked like it came from a cow or some other very large mammal."

I clasped my hands on my lap, anticipating an appropriate show of outrage. Instead Dr. Lipton shrugged.

"That's teaching for you, Ms. Wells. Sometimes you have to put up with shit, but you can never lose yours. Besides, it was your fault; you failed to lock your classroom while you were gone. Where do you think you are? Mayberry?"

What's there to steal, I thought. Icicles? Rat droppings?

"May I have the key to your portable, please?"

I shoved the letter across the desk as if it were on fire. "Don't make me leave. I'll do anything. Apologize to the school board member. Pull extra lunch duty. Scrape gum from underneath the desks."

"Ms. Wells—"

"Anything."

Dr. Lipton's lips twitched; he toyed with his gold signet ring. After a lengthy silence he said, "I'm the top candidate for superintendent, and that means I'm like a bacterial culture under a high-powered microscope. And you're hanging out our dirty drawers for everyone to see."

"It'll never happen again. I swear. I'm very sorry."

He curled his fingers to inspect nails that shone with clear polish. "I've worked my backside off trying to get people to change their opinions about Harriet Hall. Do bad things sometimes happen here? Yes. But a whole lot of good goes on too. That's what we need to focus on.

He paused for a moment. The copier in the outer office whirred as it warmed up, and Ms. Ware's heels clacked across the concrete flooring. The silence between us was maddening.

"I'll probably regret this, but I've decided to give you one more chance."

I leaped up so quickly you would have thought a spring was attached to my backside. "Thank you so much. I promise I'll—"

"Down, girl," he said, with a hand motion.

I dutifully sat, but found it challenging not to fidget.

"There are conditions. Decorate your bulletin board, for God's sake. I'm told yours is almost bare."

"Done!"

"And you have to do something about your class attendance."

"Okay," I said with less enthusiasm. "By how much?"

"Ninety-five percent should do it."

"Ninety-five percent?"

That was impossible. How was I supposed to force students to come to school? Play Reveille on the bugle outside their windows? Drag them out of their beds by their feet?

"Also progress reports will be out in another week. I want to see As and Bs only."

"Are you joking?"

He was asking for a slice of the moon, as I'm sure he well knew. Most of my students were failing because they refused to do work. Bad grades did not seem to spook them in the least.

"Didn't you just say you'd do *anything to* keep your job?"

I'd meant anything within the realm of possibility. What would he ask for next? Milk from an electric eel? The still beating heart of a vampire?

"If you can shape up those three things, you can keep your job," he said. "I'll review your records in the next couple of weeks to gauge your progress. You're very lucky to be getting a second chance. Don't disappoint me."

I left his office and plodded down the nearly empty hallway with my head down, thinking I might as well have signed my letter of resignation, because what Dr. Lipton was asking me to accomplish was impossible. I wasn't paying attention to where I was going and nearly ran into Doc. His ensemble of a Hawaiian shirt and striped tie made my eyes ache.

"What's wrong, little lady? Students giving you crap?"

"You heard," I said in a barely audible voice.

"Heard what?"

I'd assumed everyone in the school knew. Briefly I told Doc about the "gift" I'd found in my supply closet and the unfortunate hissy fit I'd thrown in the front office.

"Aw. Don't feel bad. I'd have made a big stink too."

"Not funny. Lipton was really mad." I told Doc how he wanted me to improve my grades and attendance.

"No way can you do that. Lipton damn well knows that."

"So why did he ask then?"

Doc glanced in both directions and lowered his voice. "It's my guess he wants you to fudge your records."

"Seriously?"

"He's reluctant to tell you that outright; he's hoping you'll figure it out."

"But that's unethical!"

"Welcome to the real world, baby girl." He squeezed my shoulder. "Hey, don't look so upset. Lipton's just pushing you to see how much he can get away with. God knows you don't *have* to change your records. It's not like he's going to give you the boot if you don't."

Wrong, I thought. Lipton had made it very clear he'd fire me if my grades and attendance didn't improve, which meant, even though I knew it was unethical, I was definitely going to falsify my records in order to keep my job. But I wasn't going to tell Doc that. Didn't want him to know I was going to sell out.

Twelve

The poo incident taught me something very important about Harriet Hall: I was completely on my own and couldn't expect any help from the administration. Therefore, I promptly abandoned all my delusions about being some kind of cool, super teacher, and decided my goal was to merely make it through the year with my sanity intact.

With that in mind, I devised a plan I called Operation Survive Harriet Hall. As with all tricky maneuvers, there was a small glitch: My strategy required cash, and after receiving my first paycheck, I discovered I was making only a bit more than the average paper boy. I did, however, have one credit card in my name with a ten thousand dollar limit, one I'd been approved for in college because my father co-signed for it. Cornelia didn't even know I had it.

I took that card and made a trip to Best Buy, where I bought all types of electronics: iPods, iPads, three laptops loaded with video games, PlayStation, Wii and Xbox. I also charged some heavy-duty locks for my closet door. It killed me to max out my card – now I wouldn't be able to charge a stick of gum. Too bad. If I wanted to make it through the school year, it had to be done. After all, as Aunt Cornelia was fond of saying, sometimes you had to spend money to make money.

The next morning I spread the booty out on a card table in front of my class. A reverent hush fell over the room. I'd never seen so many big eyes; they could have doubled as manhole covers.

"Attention, please." I stood in front of the table to guard it from overeager students with their itchy fingers. "I'm about to tell you exactly how you can get your hands on this amazing merchandise."

Suddenly my audience was so transfixed you'd think I was a stripper gyrating in front of them in a gold lamé bikini. (Or a Chippendale dancer for the girls.) Slowly and deliberately, I detailed my plan: For the first thirty minutes of each class period they would be required to do their work and behave like civilized human beings, i.e., no backtalk, grumbles, or gas-passing contests. Then, for the rest of the period, they'd be allowed free time to play with the assortment of gadgets I'd bought.

After I'd finished laying down the rules, my gaze swept the classroom. "Do we have a deal?"

The room rang with whoops and whistles. The students thronged me, their new hero. If there'd been Gatorade handy I'm sure they would have gleefully dumped it on my head. It was thrilling to be popular for a change.

Here was the weird thing about the plan. Technically no one could give me grief for letting my students goof off for half the day. I was supposed to be teaching them Life Skills, and leisure activities were a component of the Life Skills curriculum. Still...it was definitely not a kosher thing to do, and I knew if classroom visitors continually saw my kids rocking out to hip-hop or plugged into a PlayStation, I might get into trouble. So, in order to give me advance warning of visitors, I tied a string of bells to the flimsy steps leading to my portable. It allowed just enough time for students to cut off the games, return to their desks, and direct their attention to the front of the room where I'd pretend to be in the middle of an informative lesson.

Over the next week, we staged several practice drills until we had it down. And yes, I knew I was encouraging my students to cheat the system, but I justified my actions by telling myself that my students were hardly dewy-eyed innocents. They'd earned their doctorate in street smarts long before I ever came along. Even Janey, the sweetest student in my class, was an ace at scamming money from people. (Me especially.) Sadly there wasn't an uncorrupted kid in the bunch.

No surprise the new program was a wild success. After a week, my discipline issues didn't completely disappear, but they were far less frequent. While my students were happily occupied with their gadgets, I caught up on my celebrity news and munched candy corn—my latest addiction to replace the sugars I used to get from alcohol.

On the odd day when I came to school feeling less than perky, I skipped the lesson portion of the class period and allowed my students to immediately dive into their diversions. Ironically both attendance and grades improved as a result of the new "curriculum," but I also helped the numbers along, reporting a ninety-five percent attendance rate and awarding only As and Bs.

My guilt over short-changing my students continued to nag me, but I periodically reminded myself that when bedlam reigned, my kids hadn't been learning anything either. Now, at least, a tiny stream of knowledge was trickling into their brains. Wasn't that worth something?

It was the best I could do. Before Poo-gate, I'd taken Doc's advice and observed Carl teaching a psychology class. I felt like a four-year-old Suzuki violin student listening to Itzhak Perlman play a Mendelssohn Concerto. His command of the classroom was a wondrous thing to witness. It also made me realize that teaching was an art, and I didn't have a prayer of mastering it. Unfortunately the only thing I'd ever been halfway proficient at was playing tennis.

After conquering most of my classroom discipline problems, I decided to tackle my issues with Ms. Ware. One afternoon I ran out of attendance forms and stopped by the office to pick up a stack. The secretary sat at her desk, examining her pores with a magnifying mirror. When I asked for the forms, I got the expected dark look and put-upon sigh. "Come back another time," she said. "I'm busy."

This time I came prepared. On the counter I plunked down a gold foil box tied with a silk bow. Ever so casually Ms. Ware glanced in my direction. "What's that?"

"Chocolate."

Ms. Ware swiveled in her chair to face me. "I've never seen that kind before."

"I ordered them from a place called Chocolate Fetish. Best in the world. One pound box, each chocolate lovingly handmade. Alicia Keys' treat of choice. She eats them in bed on her Egyptian cotton sheets. Doesn't care about stains because she buys a new set of sheets every day."

I'd embellished the last bit, having once overheard Ms. Ware say that Alicia Keys was her favorite recording artist.

The secretary licked her lips, rose from her desk and approached me, her gaze transfixed on the golden box. Slowly I tugged away the satin ribbon and opened the lid, revealing several rows of truffles tucked into fluted paper. Milk chocolates—some spangled with nuts—intermingled with darker, velvety varieties.

"Twelve little pieces of heaven," I crooned. "Yours for the taking."

Her pupils dilated as she reached for a dark brown beauty.

Swiftly, I jerked the box away. "Attendance forms first, please. Then chocolate. Two for each piece. And throw in some whiteboard markers while you're at it."

I'd never seen her move so quickly. Ms. Ware handed me a huge stack of forms that would last me through ten school years and three packages of board markers. Then she grabbed the box and plucked out a milk chocolate truffle, squiggled on top with caramel, and popped it into her mouth.

She closed her eyes and let out a rapturous sigh.

The transformation was astounding. From vicious tigress to purring kitten in under five seconds. Mission accomplished.

Thirteen

It was a sultry September evening. Carl and I stopped at a convenience store to pick up refreshments. Afterward we planned to head to his place for an hour or two of mattress gymnastics. Carl wore aviator sunglasses and a tight T-shirt with a skull appliqué that showed off his muscular torso. He stood in front of the cooler, looking like a sexy gangsta, so different than the way he dressed when he was teaching.

"What kind of beer do you want?" he asked.

"Doesn't matter to me." My warm breath steamed up the glass case.

He withdrew a six-pack of Natural Light from the shelf.

I frowned.

"What?" he said.

"Light beer? Don't you find it somewhat unfulfilling? Wouldn't you like something more substantial?"

I was talking in code, too afraid to say what was really on my mind. Over the last couple of days I'd been thinking I wanted more from Carl than just amazing orgasms. Since my injury, it was the first time I'd ever felt that way about a guy. Unfortunately he'd already made it very clear he wasn't ready for a serious relationship.

Carl gave me an odd look, put back the Natural Light, and grabbed a six-pack of Colt 45. I reached for a Nutty Buddy on an upper shelf, and he took the opportunity to playfully pinch me on my butt.

"You there," said a male voice. "What do you think you're doing?"

Carl leaped away from me, and I looked over my shoulder. My father stood behind me, holding a six-pack of Heineken in his hands. I hadn't seen him in over a month, and I certainly hadn't expected him to make an appearance in a convenience store on the South side.

"Daddy," I said, giving him a hug. "What are you doing here?"

He had a Band-Aid on his cheek from some mishap or another and a section of gauze taped to his arm.

"Just left the airport. Your aunt's in the car. She picked me up, and we stopped to top off the gas tank and grab some beer for me. I was going to call you as soon as I got home." He glared at Carl. "Move along or I'll alert the manager."

"It's not like that. He's—"

Aunt Cornelia entered the store, the smell of Red Door announcing her arrival.

"Porter, fetch me a Fiji Water if they have it." She stopped short. "Toni Lee?" Her sharp gaze swung to Carl, who was still clutching the Colt 45. "What's going on here?"

"This stranger was fondling Toni Lee," my father said.

"He's not a stranger. This is my friend, Carl."

"Friend?" My father looked Carl up and down.

"Yes."

His face reddened. "I'm sorry, young man. When I saw you pinching my daughter's behind I assumed—"

"Well, if he's pinching Toni Lee's bottom he must be more than a friend," Aunt Cornelia said.

I shot Carl a helpless look. Where was a trap door when you needed one?

"Toni Lee?" Aunt Cornelia said. "Manners?"

"I'm sorry." I quickly made introductions. Then I said, "We don't want to keep you. Daddy, I'm sure you're anxious to get home after being out of the country for almost two months."

"I ordered a Key lime pie to celebrate Porter's homecoming,"

Aunt Cornelia said. "You and Carl are invited to come and join us for dessert. I'm certain you're anxious to catch up with your father, Toni Lee."

"Tomorrow evening would be better. Carl and I were just—"

"I'm not taking no for an answer," Aunt Cornelia said. She met my eyes with her own, and I immediately understood I wouldn't be able to get out of the invitation. "It'll give us a chance to get to know your friend here."

I glanced at Carl. "Is that okay with you?"

"Actually, I—"

"Of course it is," Cornelia said. "Carl. I'm sure you don't intend to drink all that malt liquor on an empty stomach."

"No, ma'am," Carl said deferentially.

"Good. I'll expect you then."

I watched them go, and on the way out Daddy nearly tripped and fell into a Pepsi display.

"Be careful," I called out. Then I turned to Carl and said, "I'm afraid my aunt is extremely pushy. You don't have to go if you don't want to."

Carl returned the six-pack of Colt 45 to the cooler. "I don't know, Toni Lee."

His expression was solemn under the fluorescent lights of the store. I couldn't blame him if he turned me down. Meeting the family was only a few steps below exchanging internet passwords or getting matching tattoos. Not to mention my cover would be blown. He'd find out who the real Toni Lee Wells was. Not that I'd been hiding things from him. It was just that the particulars of my background had never come up in our conversations.

He rubbed the nape of his neck, an uncertain look on his face, and I was sure he was going to beg off. He surprised me by entwining his fingers with mine and saying, "I got a bossy aunt too. Might as well go ahead and get it over with."

"Thank you," I said, feeling relieved.

"I feel like I'm starring in a movie called *Guess Who's Coming for Key Lime Pie?*"

"Don't be silly."

My aunt, to her credit, considered herself socially enlightened, and would never say anything negative about me dating Carl. As for my father, he was more traditional in his views, but it wasn't in his nature to make waves.

I was more worried about how Carl would react when he saw Tranquility Hall for the first time. An eighteen thousand square-foot family estate hardly jibed with my persona as a penniless schoolteacher. Should I prepare him before he saw the house or just spring it on him?

"Take a right on Highland Street," I said. We were in his car, and we'd just reached the West side of town.

"Nice neighborhood." He shot me a sideways glance. "Your father lives there?"

"Nearby. Turn down Magnolia Way. "

He put his blinker on his Honda Civic and made the turn. When we were about a hundred yards away I made a decision.

"Stop!"

Carl put on the brakes. "What's wrong?"

"I've been giving you the impression I don't have a lot of money, and that's true. I can barely afford a package of Lance Crackers, but my family, on the other hand, has a few more coins in their piggy banks."

"So you're saying—"

"My aunt is a multi-millionaire."

"Seriously?"

I nodded.

"Yes. Well, a recent multi-millionaire, to be honest. My aunt's money is so new, the ink's not dry. She's CEO and primary stockholder in Cornelia's Southern Foods. It was started in my grandma's kitchen in Pinch Gut."

"The bean people?"

"Toot. Toot. That's us."

Carl still had on his sunglasses so I couldn't easily read his expression. "I don't get it," he said. "You drive a motorcycle to school, you live in an inexpensive development. Doesn't your family help you out?"

"It's complicated."

"Why didn't you tell me before?"

"Never came up. Does it bother you?"

"No, but it's a big surprise."

"We'd better get inside. Drive on. It's the first place on the left."

He accelerated until Tranquility Hall came into view. It seemed even more sprawling than usual in the orange light of the setting sun. The engine idled as Carl rubbernecked the estate. A vein in his cheek pulsed. What was going on in that handsome head of his?

"I've never seen a place like this before," he said. "It looks like a school or a plantation." He tugged on the edge of his skull t-shirt. "I wish I was wearing something more respectable. They're probably hiding the Monets as we speak."

"More like the Thomas Kinkades. And of course they're not hiding anything."

We parked the car in the circular drive and strolled toward the house, dodging the spray of a chattering sprinkler system.

"Where's your mother?" Carl said before we went inside. "Are your parents divorced?"

"My mother died when I was four," I said, hoping he wouldn't ask me any more questions about her. My mother was off-limits as a topic of discussion.

"You never told me that." He gazed up at the house, which cast such a large shadow it swallowed Carl and me along with most of the grounds. "There's a whole lot you haven't told me."

I couldn't tell by his tone if he thought that was a good thing or a bad thing.

The front door had a note stuck to it saying, "We're in the library," which was a timesaver since Tranquility Hall had at least a half-dozen places to entertain. When I was growing up, I was constantly hollering in the halls looking for my father or my nanny.

Carl and I headed to the library, which contained hundreds of leather-bound books bought by the yard. My father wasn't much of a reader, but there was an entire wall of built-in shelves to be filled. Many of the volumes were repeats. I'd once counted eight copies of Charles Dickens' *Great Expectations*.

I sat on a chintz sofa. Carl joined me. Beau, sitting at my father's feet, growled. Carl immediately scooted away from me. Daddy apologized again for his mistake in the convenience store and shooed Beau from the room. Aunt Cornelia said, "So glad you two could make it."

As if she hadn't held a dagger to our throats, I thought.

The Key lime pie was already dished up in Wedgewood plates. Just as we started to eat, Carl said, "Are you a tennis player, Mr. Wells?"

His question startled me. I followed his line of sight to a shelf lined with my old trophies. I swore sometimes they were multiplying behind my back.

"Those are Toni Lee's trophies," Aunt Cornelia said. "How long have you been seeing my niece?"

Carl shot me an uneasy glance. "About two weeks."

"And she hasn't yet told you she aspired to be a professional tennis player?"

"No. She hasn't."

"You two must not talk very much," Aunt Cornelia said, lifting her sharp chin. "How *do* you spend your time together?"

"More coffee, Carl?" I said.

"Toni Lee used to play tennis from sunset to sundown until she hurt her wrist," Aunt Cornelia said.

"That must have been disappointing," Carl said. He had a strange expression on his face, as if seeing me for the first time.

"She was inconsolable for months afterwards," Aunt Cornelia said. "Drinking like there was no tomorrow. Wilder than an acre of snakes. Can't believe she hasn't told you all that."

"Aunt Cornelia."

A wry smile tugged at her bright pink lips. "Maybe I should

change the subject. My niece is turning three shades of red. Would you like a tour of the house, young man?"

Carl agreed, just as I said, "We should be going."

Guess who won?

"Follow me," Cornelia said. "It's so large even I get turned around sometimes. Porter, send out a search party if we're not back in an hour."

I didn't want to surrender Carl to my aunt's clutches. God knows what else she might spill. She might even mention my arrests. I could imagine her saying, "We keep a bail bondsman on speed dial for Toni Lee just in case."

After they left, Daddy retrieved a silver flask he'd secreted in a potted peace lily. He added a little Irish to both of our coffee cups.

"Carl seems like a nice enough fellow. Two of you serious?"

"Not really."

"That's a relief. I mean...You're too young for that sort of thing right now."

"What if I were to get serious with him?"

My father cleared his throat. "That's fine too, I suppose, except I can't help but wonder..."

"Yes?"

"Is this your way of punishing me for cutting out of the country and leaving you in Corny's clutches?"

"Why would you say that?"

He rested the coffee cup on the swell of his belly. "Don't make me spell it out. Maybe it wouldn't be unusual for you to date someone like Carl in New York City or even Atlanta but it never happens in Rose Hill."

"Not true. I've seen interracial couples on the South side."

He grunted. "The South side hardly counts. There's a military base over there, for god's sake. That side of town might as well be in an entirely different country."

"Let's change the subject."

When it came to Carl I was completely colorblind. Far as I was concerned he could be paisley. I'd spent all of my teenage years at a tennis academy. There'd been kids of every ethnic origin in attendance, and the passion we felt for the sport took up so much of our gray matter, there was no room for judging someone based on their culture or the color of his or her skin.

"About this job of yours. Where's the school?"

"Aunt Cornelia didn't tell you? It's where I met Carl."

"She couldn't recall the name. Said it was Huckleberry Hound. Something like that."

"I'm teaching at Harriet Hall."

He choked on his coffee. "The project school? Are you out of your mind? You could get knifed or shot there. Why in the Sam Hill did you take a dangerous job like that?"

"It was the only one I could get, and the school isn't nearly as bad as people think. There's a new principal who's changed the school around."

I was stretching the truth, of course. I'd learned that the charismatic Dr. Lipton was all theatrics and little substance. No sense in getting my father all worked up.

He refreshed his coffee with the flask.

"This is my fault. Shouldn't have told Corny about your arrests. If I hadn't, you'd still be getting an allowance, living in your old house. You definitely wouldn't be working at some project school."

"But I also wouldn't be getting my inheritance early either," I said in a low voice.

"If you survive to collect. Lots of rumors about that place. Assaults on teachers and so forth."

Daddy was being overly dramatic. My students could be disobedient at times, but I couldn't imagine any of them harming me. At least I didn't think they would.

"Just be careful." He reached into his back pocket. "I had some luck gambling in Monaco so I got a little extra walking around money. Let me at least slip you a few bills so you won't have to struggle so much."

"I can't take your money."

"Why not?"

"You know why. I need to be completely independent. That's what Aunt Cornelia—"

Carl and Aunt Cornelia entered the room, arms linked like old school chums. I couldn't help but wonder what they'd talked about.

A few minutes later, we made our escape from Tranquility Hall. Carl was quiet on the drive back to his apartment. Had Cornelia spilled more of my secrets? Or maybe it was just the shock of meeting my family and finding out we had far more in common with the Trumps than the Joads.

When we arrived at Carl's place, I decided to act as if nothing happened and made an immediate beeline to the bedroom.

"Wait," he said.

I stopped and gave him a questioning look.

"We should have a talk."

I sat on the puffy sofa. My anxiety was cranked up several notches when he didn't join me on the couch. Instead he sunk down in the easy chair across from me.

"I was sorry to hear about your injury," Carl said. "That must have been devastating."

I nodded. In fact, it still was, and I hoped he wouldn't quiz me too much about it.

"I'm curious. What made you take a job at Harriet Hall of all places?"

"I need the money. And I also like teaching."

The second statement was an out-and-out lie, but teaching just for money sounded so callous. Especially to someone as dedicated as Carl. Recently I'd learned he gave out his home phone number to everyone in his class, and frequently helped the truant officer with home visits, even on weekends and holidays.

"Are you being honest with me?" Carl said.

My insides cringed. Had Aunt Cornelia told him about our five-million-dollar deal? I knew she had loose lips but I didn't think she'd go that far.

"Why do you ask?"

"I overheard your father offering you money and you turned him down," Carl said.

I swallowed hard, not knowing how to reply.

"Why not just be honest? It's my guess you're at Harriet Hall for the same reason I am. You love teaching, and you want to help the kind of kids who really can benefit from someone who cares about them. It's okay to come out and say it, even if it does sound a little corny."

To me it sounded sweet and sincere, and I couldn't help but feel flattered by his image of me. Too bad it was about as close to the real Toni Lee Wells as Velveeta was to aged cheddar. In fact, I was so taken with his rosy vision of me I couldn't imagine setting him straight.

And what would I say? That I was a lousy teacher and that the only reason I was working at Harriet Hall was to get an early inheritance? Talk about a turn-off. It made my heart clench just thinking about what a lowlife I was.

Carl left his chair and cuddled up to me on the sofa. "Teaching means a lot to me too. In fact, my passion for it pretty much cost me my marriage."

I didn't respond, hoping he'd say more. Carl never talked about his ex, and I was definitely curious about the woman who'd stolen his heart before I came along.

"My ex-wife didn't think it was enough that I was a teacher and was always nagging me to get an administration degree and become a principal," he said in a halting voice. "She has a supervision degree herself, but hasn't gotten an administration job yet. She assumed I would have a better chance. She was also very jealous of my brother Mitt's lifestyle. He lives in Charlotte and works as a personal injury attorney. You may have heard his slogan, 'If you've been hit, call Mitt.'"

"I have heard of him! Those ads are everywhere."

Carl nodded. "My ex was always throwing Mitt's wealth in my face. She acted like money was more important to her than I was. And she got mad at me when I wouldn't let Mitt pay for my graduate school. I told her I prefer to make my own way in life. Just like you, I guess."

Not like me at all, I thought.

"I'm glad you didn't decide to be a principal. You're way too talented of a teacher. I wish I'd been lucky enough to have a teacher like you when I was in school." In fact Carl's fervor for teaching reminded me a little bit of my love for tennis.

He picked up my hand and gently pressed it to his lips. "You know what? I think your aunt's right."

What else had that blabbermouth spilled?

"We don't do enough talking. Maybe we should remedy that."

"What are you saying?"

"We should go a little deeper with this relationship. Get out of the kiddie pool and go for an adult swim."

My heart started doing a crazy little samba. It was exactly what I'd hoped would happen between us, but hadn't dared to expect.

"What changed your mind?"

He pushed a stray curl behind my ear. "Sometimes if two people feel right together, you just have to go for it. Even it comes at an inconvenient time. Are you game?"

I was so tickled I covered his face with kisses to let him know my answer.

After we sealed the deal in the bedroom, I felt even more bothered that Carl had the wrong idea about my reasons for taking a teaching job. Deception was hardly the ideal way to kick off a serious relationship. Yet I couldn't imagine telling Carl about the contract with my aunt. Hopefully he would never have to find out.

Fourteen

Many people looked slack-jawed and rubbery-faced when they were in dreamland, but not Carl. He was an extremely appealing sleeper, eyelids fluttering, lips curved into a half smile. Was it any wonder I was thrilled he wanted to take our relationship to the next level?

It was Saturday morning, and I carefully slipped out of Carl's bed so as not to wake him, shrugged on a robe, and tiptoed out of the room. I went into his galley kitchen to draw a glass of water. As I stood on the cool tiles, drinking and gazing out at a flat gray sky, the front door opened with a creak.

I swallowed a gasp. Who could it be? Occasionally I'd spotted some shady characters in the apartment parking lot. Did Carl lock the door last night?

I slowly slid open a kitchen drawer and extracted a steak knife. Then I tiptoed to the entrance of the living room. I didn't spot anyone, but rustling sounds were coming from the hall closet. I couldn't see who'd come inside; the open door blocked my view of the intruder. Trembling, I considered my next move. Should I scream, dash for the exit, or sneak back into the bedroom to call the police?

While I debated, I heard a toilet flush. Carl was up. Thank God. The rummaging in the closet stopped. I took a step into the living room, holding the steak knife aloft.

"What are you doing here?" said a female voice.

I blinked rapidly, my mind denying who I was seeing: It was

Ms. Sprague, wearing a t-shirt, flip-flops, and a pair of tight tomato-red shorts that left little to the imagination. She stared at me with a horrified expression.

Carl strode into the living room wearing only tighty-whiteys. He surveyed the scene, and uttered an expletive. He must have been startled because the man never swore.

His wife, on the other hand, was much more practiced in the art of profanity. "What the fudge is going on here?" (To be honest, she used a much stronger word than fudge.)

"That's none of your business, Deena," Carl said. "What are you doing here?"

"I'm here because *your* daughter wants to ride her bike today, and you forgot to bring the helmet back last time." She spit out the words like they were bitter tobacco juice. "I let myself in."

"Where's Katherine?" Carl said.

"Coloring in the car, thank you, Jesus," Ms. Sprague said. Her glance volleyed between Carl and me. "Or she'd have seen you with this...this...*whore* of yours."

I felt like scuttling back into the bedroom and hiding under the covers.

"That comment's out of line." Carl managed to look authoritative even in his underwear. "And Katherine shouldn't be in the car by herself."

Ms. Sprague fixed her burning gaze on me. "I thought I'd seen it all, but you've definitely lowered the bar with this one. I haven't liked her since I laid eyes on her."

"Don't talk to my girlfriend like that," Carl said. "Especially in my home."

"Oh. She's your girlfriend now, is she? I guess that's why you forgot your daughter's helmet. Too busy screwing this—"

Carl's lips flattened into angry slash. He pointed to the exit. "Deena. Out. Now."

"Slut," Ms. Sprague said just before she left. The word stained the air long after she'd uttered it.

Carl rushed to my side. "You okay?"

I stiffened in his arms. "Ms. Sprague is your ex-wife? Why didn't you tell me?"

"I assumed you knew. Everyone on the faculty knows. It's not a secret."

"I barely talk to anyone on the faculty. And you and Ms. Sprague don't have the same last name."

"Deena kept her maiden name when we got married. I've been meaning to get my key back from her. She's always busting in here like she owns the place."

My mind was still careening from the drama of it all; it was like an episode of *Real Housewives,* only in 3-D.

"Did you fight a lot when you were married?" I said. My guess was Ms. Sprague wielded a mean iron skillet. I could also imagine passionate sessions in the bedroom afterward, images I immediately shooed from my brain.

"Unfortunately, yes. We even had some blowouts when we dated," Carl continued. "But then she got pregnant and marrying her seemed like the right thing to do. Anyway, the divorce was for the best. I'm not one for drama, and Deena seems to thrive on it."

I was glad to hear Carl was not a fan of fireworks. Most of my life I tried to keep my emotions in check. If I let them loose, I worried they'd spew out uncontrollably, like the contents of a can of Silly String.

"I wonder what she's going to do to me at school," I said warily. No telling what kind of tortures Ms. Sprague could dream up.

"No worries about that. Deena can be a witch-on-wheels in her personal life. But when she's at work, she's a consummate professional. She'll never mention it."

Recently I'd seen a movie on the Lifetime channel called *A Woman Scorned: The Betty Broderick Story.* It had started out with Betty calling her ex-husband's girlfriend an "oversexed syphilitic piece of white trash" and ended with gunshots from a Smith and Wesson.

While I doubted Ms. Sprague would riddle me with bullet

holes, after seeing her today, I was certain she'd figure out some way to make me pay for sleeping with her ex. She'd barely tolerated me before. Now she had a legitimate reason to despise me.

Monday morning arrived, and I kept waiting for Ms. Sprague to burst into my classroom, hurling insults. Every time the door opened, my heart hitched, but it was always a false alarm. When the final dismissal bell rang with no ambush from Ms. Sprague, I wondered if maybe Carl had been right about his ex. After all, he knew her much better than I did.

After my last class I left my portable and stopped by the teacher's lounge. The air inside was thick with the buttery aroma of popcorn. Three female teachers were congregated around the table, talking loudly and munching popcorn kernels. As soon as they spotted me, they clammed up.

"Good afternoon," I said.

Usually I got a hello or a nod but this time, *nada*. Three faces hardened into judgment, eyes sharp as flint. I didn't have to guess why. Deena was chummy with many of the female members of the faculty. No doubt she'd given them an earful about me and Carl.

I continued to my mailbox. The women's gazes penetrated my backside so hard they might as well have been branding me like a prize cow. Inside I found the lesson plans I'd turned into Ms. Sprague the week before. Across the top of the page in red block letters she'd written, "REDO!" Below that it said, "Include measurable behavior objectives."

Lesson plans were a county requirement but many teachers dashed them off with less thought than a grocery list. I stuffed the plans into my briefcase, and slunk past the star chamber who'd yet to speak a word but said volumes with their stony silence.

By the end of the week it was obvious that my relationship with Carl was a juicy topic at Harriet Hall. Whenever I encountered faculty members, conversations halted, giggles were stifled, eyeballs tracked me as I passed by. I heard a coach whisper "jungle fever" and wink. Just like high school, I thought, until I remembered it was high school. One afternoon I was in a stall in the ladies' room when I overheard a conversation between two teachers.

"Where does that skinny blonde get off sleeping with Rutherford? Can't she find one of her own kind?" a voice said over the sound of running water.

The other replied, "Don't know what he sees in her. She has the rear end of a twelve-year-old boy."

They had more to say but the hand-dryer drowned out their stinging words. When they left, I came out of my stall and stole a glance at my butt in the mirror. It was a bit on the slight side, but Carl didn't seem to miss the extra padding.

When I got home I googled "jungle fever" and discovered it was slang for an interracial relationship. In addition I learned that a white woman dating a black man was sometimes called a chocolate dipper or a charcoal burner.

There were plenty of stereotypes about such women, none flattering. Overweight white women supposedly sought out black guys because not only did the men not mind muffin top or thunder thighs, they celebrated the fluffier female form. Female druggies were said to go for black men, hoping they could hook them up with illegal inebriants. Perhaps the most degrading stereotype assumed white women dated black men solely for the superior size of their packages. Far as I was concerned it was all a bunch of nonsense.

During my week of torment, I barely saw Carl. He'd been holed up in the public library laboring over a term paper for one of his graduate classes. I kept quiet about the flack I was getting; he already had enough to worry about. Any interference from him would only make things worse.

The next week I redid my lesson plans four times; each time

they came back from Ms. Sprague faster than a boomerang. On the fourth go-around, she attached a note saying if I couldn't get them right, the next time she'd place a disciplinary letter in my file.

Meanwhile, her friends on the staff continued to give me grief. The guidance secretary, a whip-thin woman, purposely jostled me in the hall, saying, "You need to watch what you're doing, homewrecker."

You can't torch a house that's already in ashes, I wanted to say, but decided to keep my mouth shut.

One morning I tried to make copies, only to discover I'd reached my allotment for the year, which was impossible. I'd only used about a hundred copies so far.

Ms. Ware was in charge of the copy machine, and when I visited the main office to ask her about my allotment, she said, "Machines don't lie," and turned her back on me.

"I'll bring extra chocolate tomorrow."

"Chocolate makes me break out," she said. "Maybe Mr. Rutherford will loan you some of his copies since y'all are getting so cozy."

So Ms. Ware was a member of Team Deena as well. No big shock. Nearly everyone on the faculty seemed to be siding with Carl's wife. It looked as if I was going to have to make all my copies at Kinko's from now on.

On Friday morning I overslept and didn't have time to make copies beforehand. When I arrived at school and checked my mailbox, I found the last lesson plans I'd handed into Ms. Sprague, plans I'd worked on for hours. She marked them "Unacceptable" and said she'd placed a letter of reprimand in my file.

I grabbed the plans and headed to the main office. At that moment, I was more worried about my copies, wondering how I was going to wheedle Ms. Ware into giving me a paltry few. A package of state-required paperwork needed to be reproduced and turned in that day. If it was late I'd be in big trouble. The pencil-pushers up in Atlanta did not play.

The second bell had already rung, and I was the only one in

the office. The secretary was seated at her desk feeding documents to a shredder.

"Ms. Ware. I need more copies. We both know I haven't used them all. What will it take to get more?"

She ignored me.

I opened my purse and looked in my wallet. "How about five bucks?" I laid the bill on the counter.

I brightened when she took the cash, thinking I'd gotten off cheap. Then I watched with horror as she fed it into the shredder.

"Ten?"

This time I wisely left the money in my wallet.

"Forty," she said without looking up. "And you can't tell a soul."

"I don't know if I have that much." I scrabbled through my wallet for stray bills. It was money I could ill afford to spend. "Wait a minute. Maybe I can scrape it together." I counted out thirty-nine dollars and set out another dollar in quarters, laying it out on the counter. "It's all there."

She stood to retrieve the money and was scooping coins into her palm, when a voice said, "What's going on here, ladies?"

Dr. Lipton stood in the doorway that led to his office; I had no idea how long he'd been there or how much he'd heard.

Ms. Ware batted her lashes, long as black widow legs, and said sweetly, "Ms. Wells was paying me back some money she owed me." Not unexpectedly the secretary was an exceedingly smooth and quick liar.

"Ms. Wells," Dr. Lipton said. "Why don't you mosey on into my office?"

I nodded and followed him; the secretary watched me, pupils shooting death-rays in my direction. I knew if I ratted her out to Dr. Lipton, the only thing I'd ever get from Ms. Ware again was a view of her backside.

Dr. Lipton didn't take a seat behind his palatial desk. Instead he sat in a matching chair across from me, toying with one of his slick curls.

"Mind telling me what that was all about?"

I thought it best to stick with Ms. Ware's tale, because I couldn't imagine Lipton siding with me over his sexy secretary. For all I knew they might be sleeping together. The principal had an eye for the ladies. I'd witnessed him inappropriately checking out the booties of some of our more comely female students. Some seemed to return the fascination even though Lipton was far too old for them. It was his crazy magnetism. At times it could be as thick as the smell of his hair tonic.

"Like she said. I owed her money."

He grunted. "Tell me another joke. I know Ms. Ware. She wouldn't lend you the time of day, much less forty dollars. Be straight with me."

I glanced at the closed door. Ms. Ware likely lurked behind it, drinking glass pressed to the wood, eavesdropping.

"I don't want to get anyone in trouble."

"Too late. I overheard the conversation. Now I want to hear it from you."

Reluctantly I reiterated our exchange, leaving out the reason why the secretary was withholding copies from me. When I was finished, he was silent, banging the end of his pencil against his thigh.

"You're getting it all around, aren't you? I had a reprimand from Ms. Sprague about you in my box this morning. Says you write poor lesson plans and don't respond to redirection. True?"

I handed him the lesson plans I'd just retrieved. "See for yourself."

He examined them for a moment. "These belong in the lesson plan hall of fame. How many times did you redo them?"

"Five times so far."

Before speaking, Dr. Lipton tightened his gold cufflinks on both sleeves. The man was the king of pregnant pauses.

"Don't bother turning your plans into Ms. Sprague anymore," he said. "Just keep them on file and go back to doing them the way you used to before she started picking on you."

"Thank you." I stood to leave. I was hardly his biggest fan but I was grateful he was siding with me instead of Ms. Sprague.

"By the way, I'm mighty pleased with your attendance numbers and your students' grades."

"Glad you're happy," I said, even though fudging records was hardly a stellar accomplishment. Anyone with a complete lack of scruples could do it.

"Need your help with something else," Dr. Lipton said. "I want you to be in charge of mid-year testing for some of the students who are in danger of failing. I feel confident that with you as their proctor, the scores will be much better this year than last."

My stomach twisted into a tight knot. I was no longer naïve. This time I knew exactly what he was asking; Dr. Lipton wanted me to help the students cheat. It was one thing to pad grades and attendance, but another to falsely skew state testing results. All kinds of weighty decisions were made based on those scores.

I measured my words. "I'm not sure if the scores would improve just because I'm the proctor."

"Sure they will. In fact, your job depends on it."

"That's not fair. I've done everything else you've asked."

He laughed. "Who told you life was fair? Is it fair that the Board of Education thinks I should magically improve test scores even though I'm dealing with the most disadvantaged student population in Luckett County? I didn't create this social problem, yet the board thinks I can change things with a snap of my fingers. Where's the fairness in that?"

God. I was so bored with the board. Far as I was concerned they existed to give teachers grief. "I understand your position but I still don't—"

"If the public and the school board are asking for the impossible, they shouldn't be surprised when I do what it takes to achieve my results...So I'm asking you, can I count on your help or not?"

In a crazy kind of way his argument made sense. Since I'd been working as a teacher, I'd been paying more attention to education articles in the *Rose Hill Chronicle*, and it was true that everyone seemed to expect the school system to perform miracles. As far as I was concerned, No Child Left Behind was a lot of unrealistic mumbo jumbo. It was like requiring doctors to save every patient. Even someone with my limited experience knew that some kids were going to fail no matter what a teacher did.

"Ms. Wells. My hair's turning gray waiting for your answer," Dr. Lipton said.

I thought about going to Cornelia and saying, "In order to keep my job I will have to cheat on state testing. I'm sure that's not what you had in mind when you made this deal." Unfortunately, because I'd already lied to her once, she wouldn't believe a word of it. I scarcely believed it myself.

"Fine," I said, because I didn't have a choice. "I'll help you."

"Don't think I'm not grateful. You'll be rewarded. I always take care of my own. Remember that."

"That all?" I cringed at the idea of being one of Lipton's "own." It was like being in cahoots with a cobra.

"One more thing. There's a rumor going around the school that you're fraternizing with a fellow faculty member. Any truth to that?"

I squared my shoulders, prepared for a fight. "I read the teacher's handbook from cover to cover, and there aren't any policies against dating other teachers."

"No need to get your back up. I don't have a problem with you dating a colleague so long as you don't take out a billboard. I just hope that going out with Mr. Rutherford won't interfere with your job performance. Nice fellow, but I've never considered him to be a team player."

Translation: Unlike me, Carl wouldn't cheat and lie for Dr. Lipton.

"It won't be a problem," I said curtly.

I left Lipton's office and nearly knocked skulls with Ms. Ware who, as predicted, was hovering outside.

"What did you tell him?" she whispered viciously.

"Ms. Ware," Dr. Lipton said from inside his office. "May I have the pleasure of your company?"

Her pupils widened, and she looked genuinely scared. I almost felt sorry for her.

"You better not have told him." She poked a lethal red fingernail dangerously close to my eyeball.

Then again, maybe she deserved whatever was coming to her.

The next morning I entered the front office, leery that Ms. Ware might be lying in wait with a stapler gun. When I peeked around the corner I saw, not a secretary bent on revenge, but a young, creamy-skinned blonde woman in a plaid jumper and white blouse standing behind the desk.

"Hello," she said merrily. "Welcome to Harriet Hall. Care for a kiss?"

"Excuse me?" I definitely wasn't used to that type of greeting.

She thrust a glass bowl heaped with silver-foiled Hershey Kisses in my direction.

I ignored the candies and nervously glanced about the office. In a near whisper I said, "Where's Ms. Ware?"

"Ms. Ware is no longer working at Harriet Hall," said the woman. The braid down her back was as thick as a hank of rope. "I'm Jackie Blem, and I'm her replacement."

"She's not coming back?"

Seemed like it should have been harder to get rid of Ms. Ware. Kinda like Jason in *Friday the 13th*. I expected her to pop out of a closet wielding a nail file.

"I'm afraid not," Jackie said, still holding the bowl of Kisses.

Relieved, I grabbed a handful and introduced myself.

"Nice to meet you, Ms. Wells," Jackie said with a dimpled smile. "Dr. Lipton asked me to give you a message. He's moving you up to the third floor today. Some maintenance people from the board will help you transport your things."

"The third floor? Are you sure?"

"That's what he told me."

The third floor, known affectionately as "the penthouse," had been recently remodeled and every classroom was equipped with a bank of computers, an overhead projector, a DVD player, and a SMART board. A smaller but more tastefully decorated lounge was also located on the floor.

"Wait a minute. Who's moving out?"

Jackie glanced down at a paper in front of her and scanned it with a plump finger. "The name is Sprague. She's been transferred to the alternative school."

Another shocker. Not only had Dr. Lipton gotten rid of Ms. Sprague, he'd exiled her to the county's version of Guantanamo Bay. The alternative school was home to students who'd been kicked out of their neighborhood schools for serious infractions like teacher assault, drug dealing, and gang membership. Rumor had it the floors were painted red to disguise frequent bloodshed, and the building contained certain shadowy corners no staff member dared to enter alone. I couldn't help but feel a bit badly for my ex-buddy teacher even though she'd brought it on herself.

After all my things had been moved, I sat in my comfy ergonomic chair, admiring my new environs and munching on candy corn. Sunlight streamed through clean windows that overlooked a row of Bradford pear trees. The walls smelled of fresh paint, and the overhead acoustical tiles soaked up any noise louder than a whisper. It was as different from my portable as a lean-to shack was to the Taj Mahal.

Dr. Lipton had kept his word; he took care of the people who were loyal to him. On the flip side, he was not a man you wanted to tangle with. Ms. Sprague and Ms. Ware had certainly discovered that.

Once my students arrived in the new classroom, I spent the better part of the day policing their actions, insisting they wash and spray their hands before touching the new equipment. I shooed them away from the SMART board, and threatened Indian burns to anyone who dared deface the desks.

After the final dismissal bell rang, Ms. Evans, third-floor chair, visited my room. "Welcome to our neighborhood." She handed me a wicker basket heaped with goodies: a coffee mug, a box of Andes thin mints, Sharpies, Post-its and a gleaming, cherry-red Swingline stapler, the so-called Cadillac of staplers.

I picked up the stapler and stroked its sleek finish.

"That's from me," said Ms. Evans. She wore her honey-colored hair in a glossy bun; red apple earrings dangled from her earlobes. "I had an extra one, almost brand-new. Very low mileage."

"Thank you."

"Have you given any thought to your flag?"

"Excuse me?"

"All third-floor residents hang decorative flags outside their doors. I teach geometry so I have a flag with a parallelogram. You can choose whatever design you want. Ms. Klasky in room 301 hand-stitches the flags. We also have a door decorating contest at Christmas. It's completely optional, of course, but we've had one hundred percent participation for three years running."

"Count me in. For the door and the flag."

I had no idea what image should appear on my flag. A couch potato? A wormy apple?

"I almost forgot." She handed me a keychain with two newly minted keys. "Your keys to the lounge and the faculty restroom. Welcome to the third floor family."

That evening Carl was in his kitchen pulverizing a chicken breast with a meat mallet, his biceps bulging with every hit.

"I wish you would have told me about Deena," he said.

Smack.

"I'd have set that woman straight."

Smack.

I was perched on a stool, ducking bits of raw chicken and

wishing for a pair of safety glasses. Carl liked to cook but he was lousy at it. He burned most of his dishes and over-seasoned others.

"That's why I didn't tell you until now. I didn't want it to be this big to-do. I had no idea Dr. Lipton would go so far as to transfer her."

"I'm not blaming you. Your lesson plans are written proof she was unfair to you. She's lucky she wasn't fired."

"I still feel bad about it," I said, mainly because what happened to Ms. Sprague affected Carl. He told me she was making some noises about moving to Atlanta with Katherine.

"You shouldn't think like that." Carl held the mallet aloft as he prepared to give the meat another wallop. "Deena deserved everything she got."

"Isn't that chicken tenderized yet?"

He laid the mallet on the cutting board. "There's something else you should know. Deena had the colossal nerve to accuse you of being a terrible teacher."

"She did?" I willed my facial muscles not to twitch.

"Crazy, huh?"

"What did she say exactly?"

Carl wiped his hands with a paper towel. "There are two types of teachers at Harriet Hall. The first have a true passion for teaching. Some people make fun of them, calling them apple-heads, but the bottom line is they take pride in what they do. The second kind are just marking time, counting the days until summer vacation. Deena says you're the second kind."

I didn't respond. Mostly because I knew exactly how many school days there were until summer vacation. In fact, I went as far as to X out the passing dates on the calendar.

Carl grabbed my flute and took a sip. "Do you know what I told her?"

"What?" Not that I wanted to know the answer. I was ninety-five percent certain it was going to make me want to throw darts at my photograph or, at the very least, slap myself around a little.

"I told her she was suffering from a nasty case of sour grapes and that you were one of the most devoted teachers I'd ever known."

I simply could not smile and pretend I was Teacher of the Year. It was like begging to be lightning bolt bait.

"Carl," I said. "It's very sweet of you to defend me, but the truth is, you've never seen me teach before."

Nor did I ever want him to. I was probably the worst teacher at Harriet Hall. Yet I was passing myself off to him as a good teacher.

"Don't sell yourself short, babe." He kissed my cheek. "I've seen the way your students wait outside your door before class. It's like they can't wait to get in. Not even the kids in my classes do that. You've got a gift, admit it."

I felt sick to my stomach, listening to him heap undeserved praise on me. Hopefully he would never find out the truth.

Fifteen

That week I learned I wasn't the only person with a new beau or, as my students said, "boo." Joelle was also keeping company with a brand-new guy. She'd been seeing him for over a month, and that was the reason I hadn't heard more than a couple of peeps from her.

Her new man was Trey Winston, a member of Rose Hill's old guard and owner of Winston Insurance and Realty. He'd asked Joelle out to dinner at the Club a few weeks ago, and they'd been canoodling ever since. Now she was ready to go public with the romance and had planned a dinner party. Naturally yours truly was on the guest list.

I eagerly accepted her invitation. It was a good night for me; Carl had his daughter Katherine for the weekend. He and I never saw each other whenever he had daddy duties. Plus I really missed my old friend, and was curious about her new squeeze.

On the night of her dinner party, Joelle answered the door, and I barely recognized her. She looked as if she'd lost at least ten pounds and was garbed in skinny slacks and a waist-skimming cashmere top. Her bright red hair was dyed a more sedate burgundy, and she'd wrangled it into a towering bun. New diamond earrings winked from her earlobes. Joelle didn't have extra money for splurges. Trey must be giving her the rush.

"Sorry," I said. "Wrong house."

She grabbed my arm and pulled me inside. "Get in here."

"You look amazing," I said.

"Thank you." She twirled in front of me. "Twelve pounds down and counting. Master Cleanse."

I imitated her twirl. "Five pounds up and counting. Almond chicken."

When Carl's cooking experiments backfired we ordered Chinese take-out.

"And where are your animal prints? There's not a spot or stripe in sight."

"You haven't seen my underwear. Trey says that's where animal prints belong. He's a little bit on the conservative side."

I sniffed the air. "What are you cooking? Your famous shrimp and grits, I hope."

"Nah. Trey's not a fan of Southern cooking. We're having grilled salmon. I should warn you," she said, lowering her voice. "Baby Bowen's here."

I shrunk away from Joelle. "What is she doing here? Y'all aren't friends."

"I didn't know she was coming," Joelle whispered as she looked over her shoulder. "She's the date of this guy named Donnie who works under Trey."

"Is she being civil?"

"Sucking up more than a Hoover upright. I'm loving it."

"I should leave."

Joelle dragged me further inside. "She knows you were on your way. It'll be fine."

I entered the sparsely furnished living room (Joelle could only afford to buy a piece here and there) and as soon as Baby saw me she acted perfectly nice, saying, "Well, hello there, Toni Lee. Long time no see." Her blue eyes, however, looked cold and suspicious. I could hardly blame her.

Along with Baby, there was also a spare male, a colleague of Trey's. His name was Kirk, and he was obviously there for my amusement. I'd yet to tell Joelle about my relationship with Carl, mainly because it had only recently gotten serious. I wanted to have a long, leisurely visit with her and tell her all the details of my new love affair. But between her crazy hospital hours and my job and Teacher Corp classes, we hadn't been able to get together in weeks.

Joelle introduced me to Trey. He was over six feet tall and towered over Joelle. Beyond that he had thinning, colorless hair, a weak chin, and a mushy midsection. When Joelle stood beside him she glowed like a nightlight, and that's all that mattered.

Dinner at Joelle's house was usually a riotous affair. Relatives, from great aunts to second cousins twice removed, would come rattling out of the woodwork. The sideboard splintered under the weight of at least a dozen steaming Southern dishes: collards, pole beans, and sweet potato casserole. Earthenware dishes were passed around family style and heaped on colorful, mismatched plates. Everything was washed down with a river of sweetened iced tea.

Tonight was a much more formal affair, with stiff linen napkins, tapered candles, peonies, composed plates, and chilled bottles of Chardonnay. Everything was so white I felt like I might get snow blindness.

At dinner we discussed the stock market, golf, and the opening of a new branch office of Trey's company in Atlanta. Baby's boyfriend Donnie told a couple of jokes so raunchy I wanted to spray the room with air freshener afterwards.

I nursed one glass of wine to show Baby I was perfectly capable of getting through an evening without getting wasted. Joelle, who was usually such a chatterbox, barely said a word.

During a disappointing dessert of lime sorbet and angel food cake—I'd been hoping for Joelle's famous blackberry cobbler—Baby leaned forward, big breasts straining against her sweater. "Toni Lee, I haven't see you around in a while. Where have you been hiding yourself?"

"Toni Lee's a teacher now," Joelle said.

"Teaching?" Baby said. "Teaching what?

"Life Skills," I said. "I'm a special ed teacher at Harriet Hall."

Baby tittered politely. "Now, Toni Lee. What are you *really* doing?"

"Seriously," I said.

"I don't understand." Baby twisted a strand of her strawberry blonde hair around her finger. "Is this to fulfill some kind of community service requirement?"

"No. It's my job."

"That's the project school, isn't it?" Trey was cutting his cake into small, precise pieces. Although he was in his early thirties, poor fellow was already developing jowls. "I bet you see a lot of kids wearing two-hundred dollar tennis shoes."

"I saw this woman in the Kroger the other day," Baby said. "She was talking on an iPhone but she paid for her groceries with food stamps. What's wrong with that picture?"

Donnie nodded in agreement. He had a receding hairline, watery gray eyes, and skin coarse as cement, probably from a bad case of adolescent acne. "People on public assistance know how to work the system. It's shocking."

I glanced at Joelle. As a delivery room nurse, she saw indigent people nearly every day, and was always sympathetic to their plights. Normally she'd be hammering these people's hides to the wall. I knew she was trying to impress Trey, but I assumed she'd still make some gentle objections. But no, she was staring dreamily into her sorbet, clearly unconcerned by the elitist comments flying around her ears.

"That's not the way it is," I said.

"That so?" Trey gave me a patronizing smile.

"People on public assistance are hardly a bunch of fat cats," I said. "At least the ones I know. Some of my students have pretty bad teeth and come to school dirty because they don't have hot water or a place to wash their clothes. I haven't seen a lot of pricey tennis shoes or fancy cars either. If they're working the system, it doesn't seem like they're doing a good job."

I glanced at Joelle for support. "Right, Joelle?

She looked up from her sorbet, startled. "Sorry. I wasn't really listening. More coffee anyone?"

"I'll have more coffee," Baby said. She glanced at me. "And maybe we could talk about something a little less depressing?"

Kirk, who'd barely said a word all evening, smiled at me and said, "I admire your courage working at a school like that. Can't be an easy job."

"Thank you," I said softly. In the candlelight he looked like a younger Hugh Grant with brown hair that continually flopped over his forehead.

After dinner Trey, Donnie, and Kirk went out on Joelle's deck to smoke cigars. Baby excused herself to go to the powder room, and I stacked the china plates and took them into the kitchen.

"So why didn't you say anything when I was talking about my students?" I said to Joelle over the grinding of her garbage disposal.

"Guess I zoned out. Did you think the salmon was too dry?"

"It was fine," I said, even though it tasted like fishy sawdust. Joelle was obviously not used to preparing bland preppy cuisine. Most of the stuff she usually made was deep-fried or cooked with ham hocks. "Were you afraid you'd offend Trey?"

"Of course not," Joelle said, a shade too quickly. She was scraping food leavings into the trash. "And the reason I didn't defend you is because I hoped the topic would die a natural death. I hate to agree with Baby, but she's right; it's depressing. To be honest I'm getting a little burned out working with patients who have one baby after another. I'm thinking about trying a different field."

"But you love the baby floor."

"And I've been grinding away at it since I graduated nursing school. Just wait. If you have to keep this job for any length of time you'll get tired of it too."

Before I could respond Baby returned from the bathroom, and asked Joelle if she wanted to come to a Spinsters' Club meeting with her. Spinsters' was an exclusive club that young wealthy Rose Hill women joined to kill time between the cotillion and the Junior League.

I was hoping Joelle would say, "I'd rather eat a live chipmunk," but no, her eyes got shiny and she said, "Why, I would just love to be a part of that. Thank you, Baby."

After that, Joelle was lost to me, thoroughly sucked into Baby's vortex. A couple of times she made some wimpy efforts to draw me into the conversation, but they never took. I was so bored I poured myself another glass of wine. A second one led to a third. That was more alcohol than I'd drunk in a good while. After about an hour, I decided it was time to call it a night. I hastily said my goodbye.

"You okay to drive?" Joelle said.

"I only had one glass of wine with dinner," I said defensively. I refused to admit to the other two I'd poured down my throat; not that Baby or Joelle noticed.

The moon was so yellow and luminescent it looked like it was impersonating the sun. I decided to walk home. It wasn't that far, and I didn't want to risk a DUI. I wasn't the least bit nervous about walking alone. Harry Potter had his cloak of invisibility, and I had my cloak of inebriation. I felt as if nothing could touch me when I was buzzed.

I was whistling "Don't Worry, Be Happy" when a Jeep pulled up beside me.

"Need a ride?" said a male voice.

"I'm good," I said, even though I was already getting a blister on my heel from my shoes. Not that it hurt much.

"Come on, Toni Lee. It's dangerous for you to be walking out here alone."

I squinted at the driver. It was Kirk. "Sorry. Didn't know it was you. Why'd you leave Joelle's?"

"It wasn't any fun without you there."

I hopped into his BMW and told him where I lived. He slowed

the car as he approached the Club. "Want to go in for a drink?"

Twice a month on Saturdays after nine, the Club hosted evenings aimed at the under-thirty set. I hadn't been inside since my father canceled my membership. In recent days I'd been missing some of the perks of my former privileged life.

"Maybe for one drink." I couldn't afford to get too tipsy, especially at a place where everybody knew me and could report any unladylike antics to Aunt Cornelia.

The Rose Hill Country Club's main building was tucked behind a canopy of oak trees and looked like an Old South plantation, with six looming white columns out front and wraparound porches on all three levels. You could almost imagine Scarlett flouncing across the lush lawn, hoops skirt billowing behind her. One might wonder if the club founders were nostalgic for the antebellum days. All the employees, except Henry and a couple of others, were black, and there were no black members.

Inside the main dining room, I nearly collided with Henry. It was the first time I'd seen her since she'd told me my membership had been canceled.

"Don't get any ideas about kicking me out, Henry," I said. "I'm his guest." I jerked my thumb in Kirk's direction.

"Nice to see you again, Ms. Wells." She was holding aloft a tray of martini glasses. "The place isn't nearly as lively without you around."

"Are you the sort of girl who gets tossed out of clubs?" Kirk said.

"Only the most exclusive ones."

At the table he ordered a bottle of Pinot Noir, and he asked me why I left the dinner party so early. The wine loosened me up and I foolishly confessed that I thought Trey was far too vanilla for Joelle, but begged him not to tell a soul. I also told Kirk far more than he probably cared to know about the history of my friendship with Joelle.

I'd been in kindergarten when we met, and Joelle was in second grade. Initially it was Joelle's mom who'd gotten us together. She had carpool duty and had seen me go through three nannies in one year. At some point she said "enough," and informally adopted me, inviting me to gatherings in the family's modest stucco bungalow, always strewn with her son's footballs, basketballs, skateboards, and oversized sneakers.

The first few years we were acquainted, Joelle occasionally called me a baby and battered me with her My Little Pony. By the time I was in third grade, we were best friends and had been that way ever since. I spent countless nights in Joelle's childhood bedroom, a tiny pocket of femininity in a house musky with testosterone. The walls were painted hot pink, and Joelle had the entire collection of *Sweet Valley High* books on a rickety metal shelf, books she bought herself doing odd jobs in the neighborhood, starting at the age of eight. There was never any extra money in the Posey house.

"I'm more like a sister than a friend to Joelle," I slurred to Kirk. "And I'd hate to see her hook up with some guy who's all wrong for her just because she wants financial security."

I'd said too much. Essentially I was suggesting to Trey's friend that Joelle might be a gold-digger. Not the smartest move in the world. If she knew, Joelle would do much worse than pummel me with a My Little Pony.

"Let's dance," I said, hoping to distract Kirk from my last statement. A fast song gave way to the drowsy tune "Three Times a Lady." As usual, the club band's playlist was from the Jurassic era.

"Love to." Kirk led my stumbling self up to the cramped dance floor, where three other couples were already shuffling about.

He had mountainous shoulders and smelled pleasantly earthy. I liked the way he swayed his body to the music and the weight of his strong guiding hand on the small of my back.

"Sorry," I said to him. "I didn't mean to chew your ear off."

"My pleasure," he said. "You're the sexiest ear chewer I've met in a long time."

He leaned in for a kiss, and instead of pushing him away, I let him press his lips against mine.

Looking back at my actions, I realized I was simply operating on automatic pilot. Kissing Kirk seemed perfectly natural, what with the sultry music, the dim lights, and my red wine high. The second I came to my senses, I immediately pulled away. A couple of months ago my bra and undies would have definitely ended up in a heap on his bedroom floor, but those days were gone. Carl was all I needed.

"What's wrong?" Kirk said. He ran a finger down my cheekbone.

I knotted my fingers together. "You should take me home."

"Why?

"I'm in a relationship. I'm sorry. I shouldn't have come here with you."

I thought of Carl and was instantly lonely for him, wishing I could drive over and give him a big, grateful kiss for being so amazing.

Sixteen

I woke up the next morning thinking *who sandpapered my tongue?* Also I heard an insistent ringing sound that made me wonder if I was suffering from tinnitus. *Oh.* The phone.

"Hello," I said. Only it came out *Rhe-ro.* I sounded like the Cookie Monster with bronchitis.

Carl said, "I think I have the wrong number."

"It's me, Toni Lee. I was just...uh...clearing my throat. What's up?" I said. He didn't usually call me when he had Katherine.

"Deena's just announced she might move to Atlanta; she's got an interview for a teaching job there."

I sat up in bed, scrubbing the sleep out of my eyes. "I'm so sorry. This is my fault."

"It is not. Deena has been threatening a move since our divorce, and she can do it too, so long as she doesn't move more than two hundred miles away. That's what the custody agreement says. But that's not why I'm calling. I have a huge favor to ask."

Turned out Carl had an exam Monday and desperately needed to visit the library to study. Deena was supposed to pick up Katherine in the morning, but she woke up with a stomach flu and asked Carl if he could keep her for the day. He called his mother and a few other people, but nobody was home.

"Hate to ask you this, but I've run out of options," he said. "Could you please, please help me out?"

My foot had fallen asleep, and I gave it a shake. "You want me to babysit?"

"Just for a couple of hours. I know it's an enormous thing to ask."

My head lolled on my neck, heavy as a medicine ball. I was in no condition to be responsible for a kid.

"I might be getting a cold myself." I sniffed a couple of times to add authenticity to my claim. "I felt a tickle in my throat this morning."

He didn't respond, but his disappointment surged through the phone tower, rose out of my iPhone, and stared at me with big, sad puppy eyes.

"Okay. I'll do it," I said quickly.

"Thanks. Saved my life, babe. See ya soon." He hung up.

How was I going to handle a five-year-old? I was at home with little children as a pacifist is with an Uzi. It'd been ages since I'd been around a child that age. Unlike Joelle, I'd never been one to babysit. What if Katherine stuck her finger in an electric plug or ate dishwashing soap? Carl would never forgive me, and I would never forgive myself.

I almost called him back to say I didn't have enough experience, and that I needed to read a bunch of back issues of *Parent* magazine before I could be entrusted with his child. But I couldn't let him down. If Carl and I were going to get any more serious, I needed to learn to get along with his daughter.

"Thank you, thank you, thank you," Carl said when I appeared at his door. He already had his briefcase in his hand and was so distracted he didn't even notice that I looked like death warmed over. Worse. I was death left out in the desert for the buzzards to pick apart. I'd spackled a thin layer of makeup over my Lily Munster pallor but it hadn't helped.

I peered over the top of my sunglasses. "Are children toilet-trained at five?" I was only half-joking. In these permissive times who knew when young kids said "so long" to their Pampers?

Carl ignored my question and herded me inside. On the sofa

sat a big-eyed girl with sooty eyelashes and a pouty expression. Hastily, he implored Katherine to be a good girl, tossed a few instructions my way, and blew out the door, leaving me in complete charge. After he left, Katherine didn't say a word. She remained on the couch, holding a Barbie doll by her long black hair and gaping at me.

"Your daddy says you're five. Does that mean you're in kindergarten?"

No reply. She continued to gawk. Her hair was pulled into pigtails, making her resemble an oversized mouse. She wore a poofy pink dress and matching shoes with an oversized purple bow.

"What's the name of your doll? She's pretty."

The child's gaze didn't waver from my face; she almost looked stoned. Was she on medication? Or maybe she was staring deep into my soul and finding it lacking.

"Want to watch TV?"

More silence. More staring. And then she said, "Are you a princess?"

"Uh...not officially. Why do you ask?"

"Because you have fairy princess hair. Can I play with it?" She dropped to her knees like a little beggar. "Peeese? Peeese? Peeese?"

I raked my fingers through my long curls and said, "Fine by me."

For the next thirty minutes Katherine's busy little hands were in my hair, braiding, combing, and tangling. I noticed a piece of paper on the coffee table, in Ms. Sprague's handwriting. It was a list of rules for Carl to follow:

1. Limit TV watching to one hour a day; educational programming only.
2. No sugary sweets, including gum.
3. No fast food *ever*.
4. Bedtime promptly at eight.
5. Never, ever let her be around that skank.

As if there was any doubt as to who "that skank" was.

When Katherine was done rooting around in my hair, she

wanted to play Barbies. She had a whole slew of them; all were dark-skinned but still had the requisite long, swingy Barbie hair, except for Tonya Barbie who sported a crew cut courtesy of Katherine.

We played dolls for at least a half-hour. Katherine was a bossy companion, telling me how to dress my Barbie and fix her hair. A few times I warned her not to put any of the tiny shoes in her mouth lest she swallow one. Finally she said, "Only babies put toys in their mouths, silly lady."

Once we'd exhausted Barbies, she said she was so starving she could eat a goat. Just before he left, Carl had told me that Katherine's lunch was in the fridge. I retrieved a brown bag decorated with a SpongeBob sticker; inside was an egg salad sandwich, an apple, carrot sticks, and a juice box. Very healthy stuff, if not boring. Poor little imp. What fun was childhood if you couldn't stuff your face with things that were bad for you? At restaurants I used to open sugar packets and pour them in my mouth and Daddy never said boo.

Katherine folded her arms over her tiny chest. "I want a cheeseburger."

"We don't have a cheeseburger." A shame, because I wouldn't mind gnawing on some greasy red meat myself. I dangled the lunch in front of her. "Just this scrumptious sandwich. Made with prime goat meat."

My goat tease backfired; she batted the bag away, and said, "Ewww. I don't want it. Let's go to the park."

I glanced out at a sky that was growing increasingly grayer. "It's going to rain."

"That's okay. We can go to the indoor park."

"Where?"

"Mickey D's," she said, breathlessly. She jumped around the room like she had fire ants in her underwear. "They have bouncy balls, the crawly tube—"

"Your mom says you can't have fast food."

"She took me last week."

"She did?"

Katherine bobbed her head. "She takes me every Saturday. We always meet my friend Lizzie and her mom."

"Is that so?" I said softly. I wouldn't be surprised if Deena held Carl to a higher standard than herself, and frankly the idea of thwarting her strict agenda was appealing.

"All right. We're off to get a cheeseburger."

McDonald's was lit up like a football stadium on game night and crowded with shrieking children and howling babies. I couldn't think of a worse place to nurse a hangover, except for maybe the tarmac at Hartsfield International Airport.

I ordered Katherine a Happy Meal. For myself I requested a super-sized order of French fries and a double cheeseburger, hoping to soak up the alcohol tainting my bloodstream. Katherine was more interested in the meal's toy, a plastic gewgaw designed to promote a kid movie featuring a pink and purple dragon. Like a responsible babysitter, I insisted she eat all her nuggets. When she was done, she screamed, "There's Lizzie in the balls! Can I go?"

"I don't know." What if some kid jumped on her head and gave her brain damage? What if some pedophile spirited her away across the country in a van with dark tinted windows?

"Peese!" she screeched in my ear. "Peese. Peese. Peese!"

My jangled brain was no match for those high-pitched "peeses."

"You can go. But don't talk to strangers, and don't let anyone jump on your head or any of your vital organs."

She gave me a weird look and pranced off to the indoor playground. I continued to feed my face with fries, savoring each salty, grease-soaked bite.

"Toni Lee Wells."

A tall, familiar woman stood beside my table. It was Henry from the Club. I was so used to seeing her in her uniform I almost didn't recognize her. Today she wore a pink warm-up suit and her brown wavy hair hung loose on her shoulders. She held a plastic orange tray with a chicken sandwich wrapped in waxy yellow paper, a skimpy side salad that looked as if it was suffocating in its plastic globe, and an apple pie.

I gestured for her to join me, and she slid onto the bench across from me.

"You live on this side of town?" I said.

"A few blocks away. I come here every Saturday. My grandchild is generally here with her mother and I visit with them a bit." She glanced about. "I don't see them today. Maybe there was a last minute change of plans."

"Grandchild? How old?" I said.

"Just started kindergarten. And what are you doing on this side of town?"

"I'm babysitting."

"That so? Where's the child? You haven't misplaced the poor little dear, I hope," she said in a teasing voice.

"Nah. I've been trying to shake the scamp but she keeps finding me."

Just then I spotted Katherine skipping toward the table. "Look, here comes my charge now."

Henry squinted. "The child in the pink dress?"

"Hideous, right? The dress, not the kid. No accounting for mommy's taste."

Katherine arrived at the table, brain and organs seemingly intact. She took one look at Henry and said, "Hi, Grandma!"

"How cute!" I pointed at Henry. "She thinks you're her grandmother. Not that you look old enough to be a granny, of course."

"Can I have a bite of your apple pie?" Katherine said.

"Katherine. This is my friend Henry, and I'll get you your own apple pie. It's not polite to ask strangers for food."

"I am not a stranger," Henry said. "And what are you doing with my granddaughter?"

I gaped at Henry. "What? No! You're kidding, right?"

"I'm not. In fact, I'm the one who bought her that hideous dress."

"But you're not...I mean, you're—"

"White? That's correct, and Carl's late Daddy, God bless his soul, was black. That's who he favors, obviously...Katherine. Go back and play a while. I need to talk to Toni Lee for a minute."

The little girl rocked back and forth in her matching pink Mary Janes. "If I do, can I have my own fried pie?"

"Yes, ma'am." Henry swatted her on her butt. "Go on now."

Once she'd left, Henry shook her head. "Don't tell me you're dating my son."

"Guilty."

She didn't look pleased. "You, of all people, do not need to be toying with my Carl."

"I'm not toying with him. I really, really like him."

"That so?" She pointed her drinking straw at me. "Have you forgotten what happened last night?"

"What?" I was momentarily puzzled. Then last night's caper bubbled up in my mind.

Me and Kirk.

At the Country Club.

His tongue down my throat, tickling my tonsils.

I'd been so buzzed I'd forgotten I'd seen Henry at the Club last night.

"Please don't tell Carl," I whispered. I was tempted to pull a Katherine and say, "Peese, peese, peese."

"And why shouldn't I?"

My throat was so dry I took a quick sip of my Coke. "Because nothing happened. I didn't want to kiss that guy. He kissed me."

"Looked to me like the kissing was mutual. Then the two of you left to do God only knows what."

"I didn't go home with him, I swear. Please. I'm begging you not to tell. I don't want to lose Carl."

"Of course you don't. Carl's ten times more a man than anyone you'd ever meet at that club."

"I know that. Why do you think I'm going out with him?"

She blinked a couple of times, and I saw a flash of Carl in the almond shape of her eyes and thoughtful way she held her head.

"Here's the bigger question. Why is he with you? I don't mean to be unkind, Toni Lee, but it's no secret that since you stopped playing tennis you've been completely out of control. Carl's a family man with responsibilities. He doesn't need your kind of drama in his life."

"I've calmed down. I'm not like that anymore." The prospect of inheriting five million dollars was one heck of a wild-hair remover.

Her expression remained stern. "I'm sorry, but this is my son you're talking about. He needs to know what he's gotten himself into. I don't know what lies you've been telling him, but you're not his type of woman. At all."

When Katherine and I returned to Carl's apartment, I violated another one of Deena's sacred rules and let Katherine gorge on the Disney Channel. I was too distracted and upset to play with her anymore. When she fell asleep on the couch, I cut off the TV. Not long after, I heard Carl's key in the lock. The door opened, and he entered the apartment, wearing a scowl. His mother certainly hadn't wasted any time.

"Where's Katherine?" he asked brusquely.

I put a finger to my lips and pointed to the couch.

"Good," he said in a low voice. "Follow me. There's something we need to discuss. "

He strode to the bedroom, and I shuffled behind him.

"Listen, Carl—"

"Deena's on her way over to pick up Katherine. Did you two go to McDonald's?"

"Yes. I'm sorry, but Katherine said—"

"It's okay. Lizzie's mom saw her and called Deena. Now Deena's on the warpath because I let you babysit her. Do you mind hiding out in here until she leaves?"

"Maybe I should go." Obviously Henry hadn't yet reached her son, but it was only a matter of time.

"Please stay," he said, kissing my cheek. "Won't take long."

Just then the doorbell rang and continued to ring as if Deena was leaning on the button. If Carl didn't hurry up and answer, the next sound we'd probably hear was the sound of an axe splintering wood. Carl sighed. "I hope this doesn't take long."

He left, and I remained in the bedroom with the door closed, anxiously fingering the nubs on his blanket. I couldn't hear much. Deena was whispering, obviously for Katherine's benefit, but I could tell by the intensity of her voice that she was ticked off. She hardly sounded like a woman weakened from stomach flu.

A few minutes later, the door slammed so hard the thin apartment walls shook.

"Coast is clear," Carl said. "Come out, come out wherever you are."

I entered the hallway on watery knees. "Sounded heated. Sorry I got you in trouble with Deena."

"She'll get over it. Thanks so much for helping me out this morning. I got a lot of work done at the library."

"You're welcome. Listen, I need to tell you—"

"I almost forgot," Carl said. "I have an important question for you." He dug into his jeans pocket and withdrew a small black velvet box.

I eyed the small box, which seemed to pulsate in his hand like a living, breathing organism. It was true we'd gotten closer in recent weeks, but I hadn't expected *the* velvet box.

"Are you okay?" he said.

"Fine."

I was over the moon for Carl, but marrying him would mean that, not only would I become his wife, I'd also be Katherine's mother. My brief encounter with the five-year-old had been less harrowing than I'd expected, but to become a permanent fixture in her life...How could I make him understand I didn't yet have the maturity to be a mom, even to a child as cute as Katherine?

Carl opened the box so slowly I felt like I was watching the scene of a movie on a DVD that's gotten stuck. When the contents were revealed, I saw not the expected diamond engagement ring, but a simple pair of pearl earrings. I was relieved but also oddly disappointed. It was like unearthing a treasure chest and finding only a cache of tarnished pennies.

"These are for my mother's sixtieth birthday. What do you think?"

I felt like I'd just run a hundred-yard dash over hot coals. It took a few seconds for my pulse to slow to manageable levels. "They're gorgeous."

"You sure? Because you're acting kind of—"

"I'm still recovering from Deena's visit. When is..." I almost said "Henry" but managed to choke back her name at the last second. "Your mom's birthday?"

"I'm going over there tonight to give them to her."

That explained things. Henry hadn't yet called her son because she knew he was coming over, and she wanted to tell him about my exploits with Kirk in person. More satisfying that way.

"Carl. There's something I should tell you."

"Yes?" He was looking at me with such a trusting and earnest gaze, I could not bring myself to confess my late-night antics with Kirk, not just then. I knew it would hurt him too much, and to be honest, I was a coward. Let his mother be the one to tell him. I couldn't bear to see the betrayed look in his dark brown eyes.

"I let Katherine watch Disney Channel. I'm very sorry."

He reached out to muss my already tangled hair. "I'm just glad my two favorite girls got along so well. Not that I ever doubted it. I'm a lucky guy."

Wait until tonight, I thought. Maybe you won't feel quite so lucky anymore.

Seventeen

The next day at school Carl was AWOL. No accidental encounters in the teacher's lounge, no hallway sightings or stolen kisses in the supply closet. When a faculty meeting was called in the library after school, Carl was also absent and obviously avoiding me with a capital A.

I was so worried I wasn't paying attention to the guidance counselor who was giving a presentation during the faculty meeting. I wasn't the only one zoning out. The teacher across from me was happily making a rash of angry red marks on her students' math quizzes. Another was looking at funny kitty pictures on her iPhone. A third was sleeping, his lips buzzing softly with each exhale. It wasn't until Dr. Lipton took over the floor with his usual theatrical flair that everyone, including me, snapped to attention.

"I don't always nominate a candidate for a promising rookie teacher, but this year, I have a sure-fire winner. Please join me in congratulating Toni Lee Wells for being chosen as a finalist for the Luckett County Rookie Teacher Award."

It took a minute for Dr. Lipton's words to catch up with me, and when they did, I shyly smiled and said, "Thank you very much. I'm honored to be nominated." Secretly though, I was mortified. A spider monkey would make a better teacher than me. Obviously this was just another way Dr. Lipton was showing me how he took care of "his people."

"A winner will be chosen at the end of the year," Dr. Lipton said. "Finalists will also be required to write a personal statement on their teaching philosophy. I have no doubts Ms. Wells will bring home the award come June. Isn't that right, Toni Lee?"

"You can count on it." I gave him a thumbs-up like a dutiful team player.

"If you need any help winning that award, you let us know," Dr. Lipton said. Then he led the faculty in an impromptu rendition of "I'll Be There."

After the meeting was adjourned, several teachers offered lukewarm congratulations. Later, while I was checking my mailbox in the lounge, the door to the ladies' room swung open, and two teachers emerged. One, an older woman with whorls of tight curls covering her scalp, said, "Ms. Walker says she peeks into her room every day, and her kids are always playing games. I have no idea why Dr. Lipton chose—"

She quit speaking as soon as she spied me by the boxes. I pretended to be deeply engrossed in a flier urging teachers to nominate young ladies for Harriet Hall pageant. The two women left the lounge without speaking to me.

I returned to my classroom to finish up some paperwork. The door flew open with a bang and in hobbled an elderly black woman with a cane, her spine curved like a cashew, her face webbed with wrinkles. She wore a Chanel-like navy blue suit with matching pillbox hat, oversized gold button earrings, and old-fashioned black lace-up shoes. Everything about her seemed frail and ancient, except for her eyes. They were sharp and dark as a bottomless well.

"Are you Toni Lee Wells?"

I'd been warned about this woman, first by Carl, then Doc. There was no mistaking her identity: It was the infamous Beulah Jefferson.

"That's me."

I hastily grabbed a chair for her, fearing she might topple over as she leaned on her cane. She waved it away with a white-gloved hand.

"Did you know my granddaughter Janey is in your class?" It sounded more like an accusation than a question.

I couldn't have been more terrified if Freddie Krueger or Leatherface were in my room.

"She talks about you constantly," Ms. Jefferson said.

Of course she did. Janey was one of the bigger chatterboxes I'd ever encountered; she probably babbled in her sleep. The big question was, what had she said to Grandmother? I thought of all the hair-raising possibilities. Had she told her how much time we wasted each day? Or how carefully I'd trained my class to fool outsiders?

"Students have a tendency to exaggerate. I'm sure that—"

"Let me say my piece," Ms. Jefferson said. She sounded like a fire-and-brimstone preacher preparing to embark on a damning sermon. "Janey tells me you're the best teacher she's ever had, but I was skeptical. So I sat that child down and said, 'What makes Ms. Wells such a fine teacher? What does she do that's so special in her classes?' Frankly her response shook me to my very core."

It was all over. I imagined my check for five million dollars sprouting wings and flying away. Not only was I going to be fired, but I was probably in for a cane-whipping as well.

"Do you have any inkling why I was so shook up?" Ms. Jefferson said.

"No," I whispered. Although I could definitely make some educated guesses.

"Janey told me you purchased all the latest gadgets to make learning more fun for your students. With your very own money. In all my years of dealing with the teachers here at Harriet Hall I've never heard of such an unselfish gesture."

I was so traumatized it took me a minute to decipher the meaning of her words. I couldn't believe it. The much-feared Beulah Jefferson wasn't censuring me; she was praising me. How had that happened?

"I've already told Dr. Lipton how pleased I am," Ms. Jefferson continued. "But I'd also like to give you a small token of my gratitude."

She rustled in her coat pocket, withdrew a small, clumsily

wrapped package covered with lint, and handed it to me. I tore away the tissue paper. Inside was a photo of Janey in a plastic heart-shaped frame. Her usual bushy hairstyle had been subdued with several colorful barrettes, and she wore a round-collared blouse that made her seem very young and vulnerable. I could hardly stand to look at it.

"This is lovely. Thank you."

Ms. Jefferson's dark eyes got moist. "Her mama died of a drug overdose when Janey was six. I've had to raise that girl myself, but I'm not going to be around forever. One day she's going to have to stand on her own two feet. I can't tell you how grateful I am to you for teaching her the things she needs to make it in this troubled world. Thank you kindly."

"You're very welcome," I said, even though I hardly deserved her thanks.

"God bless you and all the other teachers who genuinely care about these babies." She reached into her oversized shiny black pocketbook with a tarnished gold clasp, withdrew a lace handkerchief, and daintily blew into it. "Some folks are only too happy to throw them away and forget them like they're yesterday's potato peelings. I sure do wish God had made more like you, Ms. Wells."

After she left, I sat at my desk, turning Janey's photo over in my hands. The earlier relief I'd felt had been replaced with a stomach-twisting shame; I didn't deserve a word of her praise, and had, in fact, been shortchanging Janey as well as the rest of my students with scarcely a second thought. Ms. Jefferson's visit to my classroom had shone a spotlight on my failings. These were young people's lives I was tinkering with. Didn't they deserve my best efforts?

I tucked Janey's photo into the very back of my desk drawer—I couldn't bear to look at her trusting eyes a second longer—and laid my head down on my desk. I didn't know what I was going to do in my classroom, but I knew I could no longer continue along the same path.

*   *   *

An hour later I heard a knock on the front door of my condo. I peered through the peephole of the front door, but all I could see was a huge bouquet of deep pink roses, at least two dozen. They blocked the face of whoever was delivering them.

I opened the door. On the feet of the walking bouquet was a pair of familiar sneakers.

"Carl?"

His face peeked out from behind the roses.

"Surprise," he said.

What an understatement. I hadn't expected to see Carl on my front stoop anytime soon—not after his mother had given him an earful about my two-timing ways—and I definitely didn't expect him to appear bearing pricey foliage.

"What are these for?" I said. I felt so guilty I was tempted to prick my fingers on the thorns.

"Let me inside, and I'll tell you."

"Of course." I relieved him of the roses and headed to my galley kitchen. Carl followed me and told me he'd missed school that day because Katherine had the sniffles, and Deena had a doctor's appointment and couldn't stay home with her. After Deena had retrieved Katherine, Doc called and told him about my nomination.

"That's what the roses are for. Not that I need an excuse to bring you flowers."

I arranged them in a vase. "They're stunning."

Although poison ivy or hemlock would have been more appropriate. Why wasn't he saying anything about Kirk? Was he trying to torture me?

Carl came up from behind me, circled his arms around my waist, and kissed me on the part of my hair. "I'm so proud of you."

Unable to endure the suspense any longer, I whirled around to face him. "We both know I don't deserve them."

"Don't be modest. I can't remember the last time Dr. Lipton thought enough of a new teacher to make a nomination for the Rookie honor. I don't always approve of his decisions, but sometimes he makes a good one."

"Come on, Carl. I'm not talking about my teaching. I'm talking about Saturday night. Your mother must have told you she saw me out. Why aren't you saying anything about it?"

I braced myself for his reply, which didn't come immediately. A bird chirped outside my window. The icemaker in the fridge rumbled. Carl scratched a bit of peppery stubble on his usually clean-shaven chin. "Do you want to discuss Saturday night?"

"Desperately. Don't you?"

He didn't look at me, but instead made some minor adjustment to the rose arrangements. Then he said, "I didn't feel like I had the right to comment. We've never said anything about being exclusive."

But it was implied, and we both knew it.

"Kirk doesn't mean a thing to me. Let me explain what happened. It was—"

"And it's not like I could ever take you to that country club. According to my mother, they don't admit any black members."

"Good Lord. I could care less about that stupid club. Sit for a minute. There are a couple of things about myself I haven't told you about yet."

He perched on a stool at my breakfast bar, and waited expectantly for me to speak.

"Remember when we went to Tranquility Hall?" I said tentatively. "And my aunt mentioned to you that I went a little crazy after my injury?"

He nodded.

"Well, you have no idea how wild I was."

Telling him about my out-of-control behavior after the accident made me feel exposed, but I held nothing back: The boozing, the pot smoking, the slutty one-night stands, even the arrests for public intoxication.

I kept waiting for him to curl his upper lip in disgust, but he was just listening intently.

I ended my soliloquy of unsavory sins with the kicker: I confessed to him what I'd done to Baby Bowen at Lois Atkin's funeral.

"Lois was my tennis coach. And I always thought of her as a surrogate mom. After my wrist got infected she came to visit me in the hospital once, and then I never heard from her again. I'd call her, and she'd never get back to me."

"That's harsh," Carl said softly.

"I was heartbroken over it. Then, not too long afterwards, she had a heart attack on the tennis court and died before she made it to the hospital. On the day of her funeral I chugged a few shots of Wild Turkey and smoked a fat joint. When I got to the church, I was sitting beside this girl named Baby Bowen, who'd also taken some lessons from Lois. She was wailing and keening like she wanted to throw herself on a funeral pyre. As for me, I couldn't shed a tear."

"Because Lois treated you unkindly?"

"No. I'm not a big crier. I haven't shed a tear since I was a little kid." I paused, suspended in an embarrassed silence over what I was about to reveal.

"Go on," Carl said gently.

"So I'm watching Baby Bowen bawl her eyes out, and I want to cry so badly, but I can't. My body was begging for some kind of release, and since I couldn't cry, I did something else. Something revolting. It's almost too disgusting for words."

I pushed a snarl of bangs over my eyes as if to hide behind them.

"I'm still listening," Carl said.

It took me a second before I could continue. "My stomach was queasy, and I knew I was going to lose my lunch at any second. I was frantically looking around for something to catch the vomit. I'd brought a little clutch purse, so I couldn't use that. Lord knows, I didn't want to sentence myself to eternal damnation and vomit into a hymnal. Then I looked at Baby, who was wearing a straw hat."

I could tell Carl was struggling not to smile. "You didn't."

"I did. I snatched her hat off her head and threw up into it. But that was just the beginning. I threw up on her dress, in her hair, on her face. It was horrible projectile vomiting, like a geyser, and it reeked of Wild Turkey. Baby was covered in it. She screamed and made a huge scene, ruining the funeral. Not that I blame her."

"I'm sorry. That must have been an ordeal."

"It was. I tried to make light of it because I didn't want people to know how badly I was hurting. It was one of my lowest moments...But the main reason I'm telling you this story is because I had a bit of a relapse into the old Toni Lee last night. I got upset with Joelle and drank too much. The guy I was with kissed me, which took me by surprise, but that's as far as it went. I forgot myself for a second."

He sighed. "I can't tell you how glad I am to hear that."

"Your mother wasn't jumping up and down when she discovered I was dating you. I understand if you don't want to continue to see someone she doesn't like."

"To be honest, my mother and I aren't all that close."

That surprised me. "Why?"

"She's a lot like Deena. She also thinks teaching's beneath me and wants me to find a more lucrative career. She wishes I was a big-time breadwinner like my brother Mitt. He got her a Lexus for her birthday. Made my faux pearl earrings look pretty pitiful."

"I'm so sorry."

"It's okay." He brushed his lips against mine. "I'll take you as a consolation prize any day...One more thing."

"Yes?" I said, relieved we'd worked things out.

"Why don't you ever cry?"

I had good reason for never shedding any tears, and it had to do with my own mother, but I wasn't yet ready to tell him about that. I'd given up more than enough secrets for one day.

"I can't say really. Maybe my tear ducts are just jammed up."

He gave me a skeptical look but didn't press me any further.

*   *   *

That night, I put Norah Jones on my iPod and lit a collection of vanilla-scented votive candles, transforming my tiny bedroom into a flickering, golden haven. The ceiling fan whispered above, and we slowly unpeeled each other's clothes. We entwined, a tangle of dark and light limbs.

Neither of us had yet used the "L" word, but lovemaking was what we were doing. Like a pair of alchemists, we'd spun lust into something much deeper and more fulfilling. Afterwards, as we lay next to each other, our skin glazed with a fine mist of sweat, Carl said, "Let's not have any more secrets, okay?"

"Okay," I whispered.

I hated to sully the moment with a lie. But how could I tell Carl about my deal with Cornelia or my unholy alliance with Dr. Lipton? If I did, he'd surely leave me, and I loved him far too much to fathom a world without him in it.

But if you love him, how can you deceive him, I thought.

I shook away the question. I knew I was being selfish. Carl would never sacrifice his integrity, not even for five million dollars. Furthermore, I had no excuse for my slacker approach to teaching. No one was paying me to be a slouch. I was doing that for free. Carl had been led to believe I was the female version of John Keating in *Dead Poets Society*, and if I loved him, that's the kind of teacher I should try to be.

The next morning I downloaded an assortment of education books on my e-reader: *Setting Limits in the Class, Assertive Discipline* and my personal favorite, *Teach Like Your Hair's On Fire*. For a week, whenever I had a free moment, I devoured the books, taking notes on techniques that might work in my classroom.

The texts made it seem so simple, like a recipe for frozen margaritas. Do this, dump in a little of that, and *voila*...well-behaved students.

For several days I immersed myself in the teaching books until I felt ready to try out some of the tricks I'd learned. I listed rules on a big piece of cardboard—only five—the teaching books said that too many rules were confusing. I also wrote the rules in positive terms, i.e., "Do keep quiet when the teacher is talking" instead of "hush up or I'll skin you alive." I'd also planned a seating chart, a rewards program, including intangible incentives such as teacher praise, and individual behavior plans for each student.

I was surprised to discover my new knowledge made me feel virtuous and exceedingly organized, like a real-life teacher instead of playing one on TV.

Monday morning I was half-tempted to hang a sign on the door: "Under New Management." I stood outside my classroom, anxiously nibbling a hangnail as I watched teenagers stream by in squealing packs.

When the bell rang, I calmly greeted students as they filed in with their usual shouts, hoots, and hilarity. After the tardy bell sounded, they sat in their desks, waiting for their daily worksheet so they could scribble down a few facts and move on to the electronic portion of the day.

I felt a flutter of excitement in my throat. "People. I'd like to talk to you about some exciting new changes in our classroom starting today."

I launched into my spiel, hoping to ease them into the new plan without too much drama or bloodshed. First, I explained the rules, and then I went over the seating chart; the kids had begun to fidget but were still listening, which made me feel hopeful. Then I reached the most ticklish part of my lecture: the explanation of rewards.

"Free time every day is officially over. If you meet all your academic goals for the week and follow the rules, you'll be allowed a half period of free time on Fridays."

I braced myself for howls of protest and flying tomatoes.

Instead silence reigned, which made me wonder if I'd been worrying for nothing. Maybe change would be as easy as the books promised.

"Questions?"

Vernon raised his hand. "I got one."

"Yes, Vernon?"

He flashed the metal in his mouth. "Are you tripping? Do you really think we're going to bust our tails for one half-hour of free time every week?"

"Well—"

Other students immediately chimed in with their own prickly protests. Within moments everyone in the room was shouting so loud, I was tempted to yell, "ZIP YOUR YAPS" like in the olden days, but every book I'd read said teachers needed to remain calm no matter what kind of crap storm was going on in their classrooms.

Stupid books.

"I hate you," Monica said several times, and the rest of the class joined in and chanted it over and over. They were so loud I thought they might bring the ceiling down. I grabbed the PlayStation, rushed to the open window, and held the game system aloft. "Everyone needs to pipe down or the PlayStation gets it."

Silence fell over the room. The PlayStation was the most popular gadget. While I had their attention, I said, "Today we'll go back to our old ways. But, I warn you, tomorrow there's going to be a new sheriff in town."

I heard a few "yeah, rights" and "we'll see about that," letting me know that they weren't going to give up their free time without a bitter battle.

For the rest of week, I continually tried to institute the new world order but it went over like an astronomer addressing the Flat Earth Society. I'd begin a lesson, such as the correct way to fill out a bank deposit slip, and moments into it, someone would shout, "Boring!"

and the rabble would chime in until I relented and let them do as they pleased.

Over the next few days I received several complaints from my neighbors. Ms. Evans served me with a violation of the third-floor noise ordinance, which I didn't even know existed. Almost made me nostalgic for my battered portable where I could set off plastic explosives and no one could hear it.

Unfortunately I couldn't ask Carl or any of my peers for advice. Since my Rookie teacher nomination they'd been led to believe that I was Super Educator, able to quell unruly students with a single raised eyebrow. Nor would my Teacher Corps instructor be of any use. During his classes, people whispered, texted, and played Candy Crush.

Occasionally I tried to reason with my students. "How are you going to earn any money without an education? What will you do if you flunk out?"

Blank looks. Shrugs. Eyerolls. Carl had once told me that the graduation rate at Harriet Hall was below sixty percent. And what happened to the forty percent who dropped out before they got their diplomas? Let's just say they weren't sipping champagne at the Grammys or going one-on-one with a New York Knicks player, as many of them fantasized. In general the dropouts would be choosing between two gloomy fates: poverty or prison.

Eighteen

Discretion is advised. Some might find the following incident disturbing. Think of *Silence of the Lambs* when Buffalo Bill says to the girl trapped in the pit, "It rubs the lotion on its skin or else it gets the hose again." Or just about any scene in *Human Centipede II*.

Yes, that disturbing.

The kids showed me their most repellent sides over the next week. One afternoon Vernon shouted, "Go to hell" several times in my face, his spittle spraying my cheeks. Another day I opened a desk drawer and found a naked plastic doll bristling with straight pins. Someone had written my initials across the doll's chest.

But that was kid stuff compared to what happened next.

Since I'd been teaching I learned that teenagers were masters at discovering a person's weaknesses, and my students were no exception. During our battle of wills, they'd lob various insults at me, trying to make me crack:

"You so dumb you got stabbed in a shootout."

"You so ugly you shave your pits with a lawn mower."

"Your teeth are so yellow you spit butter."

The worst came from Monica, which wasn't surprising. Besides Vernon, she was the one student who seemed to hate me the most. One day she interrupted my lesson and rapped a song called "Can You Control Your Hoe?" I ignored her and she got into my face, so close I could see the down on her cheeks and the gold flecks in her brown eyes. She said, "I'll bet even your mother couldn't stand you. I bet when you were born she took one look at you and said, 'Put that thing back in; she's broken.'"

I flinched as if she'd slapped me. Immediately I experienced a deep burning heat in my belly. I'd heard people say "I saw red" before and until that second I always thought it was an expression, but I was wrong.

I definitely saw red, and the red I saw was blood.

Monica's blood.

I wanted to scratch her face with my nails until I broke the skin. I had to squeeze my hands into fists to stop myself. She must have sensed my rage because she immediately darted away from me. I took several quick breaths, trying to calm myself, but it was too late. She'd found my Achilles' heel.

"Your mother hates you, hates you, hates you," she gleefully shrieked but this time from across the room, out of scratching range.

Stop it, I wanted to scream but I knew it would make things worse. I had the urge to lock myself in the closet or hide underneath my desk. Never had I been closer to fleeing Harriet Hall.

Luckily the bell rang. Before Monica left, she threw one last taunt over her shoulder. "Your mother hates you!"

After the students were gone, I closed the door and leaned against it for support. *Who was that out-of-control freak?* I wasn't thinking of Monica; I was thinking of me.

I'd been angry plenty of times in my life, but those instances were like small trashcan fires compared to the inferno I'd just experienced. For the first time in my life I understood why people committed crimes in the heat of passion.

It wouldn't take a genius to guess why I'd nearly lost control. Monica had enraged me because she'd managed to stumble across an agonizing truth in my life. One I'd never revealed to anyone except for Joelle.

When I was eight years old I'd found my mother's journal underneath a loose floorboard in a small room off my parent's bedroom that used to be my nursery. When I read it I discovered the one thing no child should ever know about her mother: She didn't love me.

After that terrible incident I'd pretty much decided to give up. Let my students play all day. *Animal House* was far better than *There Will Be Blood.* Trying to be a good teacher was the hardest thing I'd ever done, harder than quadratic equations, harder than trying to tie a cherry stem in a knot with my tongue, harder, in some ways, than having to give up tennis. My respect for Carl and other talented teachers like him deepened. I'd never be one of them.

The next week was a grueling repeat of all the school weeks that had come before them. Even though I tried to hide it, Carl had begun to notice how bedraggled I seemed at the end of each day. I fibbed and told him I was coming down with a cold.

Thank God next week was Thanksgiving holidays. I didn't know what I was going to do after they were over, but at least I would have several days to recover from the mayhem in my classroom.

Nineteen

Saturday morning, over Thanksgiving break, I was sprawled out on Carl's couch, wearing one of his old dress shirts.

"You're so damn sexy in my shirt," Carl said.

I fingered the top button of my shirt. "I'll show you how sexy I can be."

"Choose the locale," he said.

We'd already tried out almost every square foot of his apartment, including the top of the washing machine in the laundry room. A location that definitely had the Toni Lee seal of approval.

"Shower?"

"Meet you there in one minute. I'll bring the body wash."

I jumped up from the couch with a squeal and dashed in the direction of the bathroom. "Don't forget the rubber duck," I said over my shoulder.

We enjoyed a half-hour of sudsy, naked fun. Afterward Carl was toweling my hair dry on a stool in the kitchen, both of us smelling like an orange grove from the citrus body wash. I nibbled a bagel and talked about what movie we might want to see. I noticed Carl seemed distracted.

"Did you hear me?"

"I'm sorry. I was thinking about a problem I'm having in class."

"You?" I hopped up from the stool to face him. That was hard to believe. It was like hearing that Tiger Woods couldn't get the ball into the clown's mouth in miniature golf.

"Yes, me. I have a student named Rose Wyld who's failing my class. If she gets an F, that means she can't compete in the Miss Hall pageant. Her older sister's called me several times. The two of them even went in to see Dr. Lipton. He emcees the pageant every year and has the final say about who gets in."

"Did he back you up?" No telling with Lipton.

"He did side with me, but that didn't stop Rose from begging for extra credit work, nagging me every day, sometimes crying in class. I've tried to help her but she just won't buckle down and study for the tests."

"I'm so sorry." He looked so distressed; I wished I could smooth out the worried folds in his forehead.

"It happens. Some students just don't like to take responsibility for their own grades."

His cell phone buzzed. Carl picked it up from the kitchen counter, and as he listened to the person on the other end, he frowned.

"Not a problem. I'll take care of it right away," he said, clicking off the phone.

"What's wrong?"

"That was my friend, Ed Jensen, the truant officer. He's sick today, and there's a student he says needs immediate attention. I told him I'd check on her."

"Really?" I was a little disappointed that our holiday festivities were going to be curtailed. This wasn't the first time Carl had assisted the truant officer during off hours. The guy never seemed to be off-duty.

"Would you like to come with me?"

"Why not?" I'd yet to do a home visit with any of my students, although I knew many teachers considered it part of their jobs.

A half-hour later, we were driving through a rundown residential area chockablock with wood-splintered shotgun houses. Several lots were littered with stained mattresses, old clothes, and rusting refrigerators. Every now and then we'd see a rare, brave house with signs of civility: a tidy lawn, pansies encircling a mailbox, healthy potted plants on the porch. I hoped one of the better residences belonged to the kid we were checking on, but I doubted it.

Carl parked in front of a house that looked uninhabitable. The peeling siding revealed a rotting gray inner skin, and a bright orange sign pinned to the door said, "Unlawful to Occupy." The windows were black, as if someone had covered them up with tarpaper.

"Are you sure we're in the right place?"

Carl cut off the engine, and we both sat motionless, listening to it tick. "It's the address I have."

I knew there were some rundown neighborhoods surrounding Harriet Hall, but I'd only experienced them from behind the window of a moving car. I'd definitely never strolled around in one.

We got out of the car, and it was eerily quiet, no bird sounds, no shouts of children playing. Our shoes sounded loud on the pavement. I felt like we were being watched, but I didn't see anyone around. Then I noticed two men in their twenties lounging on a dilapidated porch on the house next door. Their jaws looked set in stone, their eyes blank as if no one lived behind them.

Carl must have noticed the men too because he slipped a protective arm around my waist. His shoulders broadened, like a toad puffing up to three times its size. He was sending the men a message: "Don't mess with us."

We crossed a weed-choked yard glittering with broken glass. I could feel the men's gaze crawling all over us. A cold drizzle dripped from the sky, stinging our faces. Just as we were about to descend the stone steps, *bang,* the front door opened.

A young woman wearing mismatched pajama tops and bottoms plodded out on the porch, holding a tin bucket. A vacant-eyed toddler, garbed in only a sagging diaper, hung onto her leg. The woman dumped the contents of the bucket off the side of the porch, and the smell of human waste rose up.

"Excuse me," Carl said. "I'm looking for Janey Jefferson. Someone said she might live here."

I tightly squeezed his arm and Carl said, "What's wrong?"

"Janey's my student." She'd been out of school for several days in a row. In order to keep up my ninety-five percent attendance rate, I hadn't reported her absences to the truancy office.

The woman scratched her belly and glared at us. "What do you want?"

"We're teachers from Harriet Hall," Carl said.

He climbed the steps to the house, and I trailed behind him.

"My sister be sixteen in two days," said the woman, her hair sticking out from her scalp in haphazard tufts. "She don't have to go to school if she don't want to."

"Do you think I could talk to her?" Carl said.

The woman considered his request for a moment. "You got five dollar?" she said.

I rummaged in my purse and opened my wallet. "Here's twenty," I said and handed her the money. She tucked it into her waistband.

"Come on," she said, motioning us to follow her.

I didn't want to go inside. The entrance looked like the dark maw of an animal. My shoes felt like they were made of concrete. Carl must've noticed my reluctance. "You want to wait in the car?"

I thought about the two men next door with the dead eyes.

"I'll come with you," I said quickly. Janey was my student, not Carl's. I needed to buck up.

We crossed the porch, sidestepping stacks of yellowed newspapers, empty Domino's Pizza boxes, and Taco Bell wrappers. The screen door slapped behind us, loud as a gunshot. The front room was cloaked in gloom and reeked of rotting food and an ominous chemical smell. A stack of ketchup-stained plastic plates rested on an eviscerated couch.

What was Janey doing in this terrible place?

We zigzagged our way around holes in the floorboard and pieces of broken furniture until we reached a back bedroom, windowless and dark. Inside a figure was curled up on a bare mattress and clinging to a pastel blue sweater.

"She sleep a lot," Janey's sister said. "Janey, get up. You got company."

Janey didn't respond; she lay so still I was terrified she might be unconscious or even dead. I couldn't move, couldn't breathe. The woman kicked her lightly on the shin. "Your teacher here, girl. Get up."

I found my voice. "Janey. It's me, Ms. Wells."

Janey's eyes flew open, and she slowly lifted up her head.

"Mr. Rutherford and I came by to check on you, and see why you haven't been in school."

I glanced at Carl for guidance. A current of disquiet passed between us. I'm sure we were both thinking the same thing: Grab Janey and run.

"Would you like to have a little lunch with us?" Carl said.

Janey rose to her feet with great effort like a creaky old lady.

"If you going, you need to be back at the house in an hour," said her sister. Her voice was raspy as if she did a lot of yelling. She picked up the listless toddler and hefted him on her hip. "Need you to look after Deon."

Janey, who usually couldn't stay quiet for more than a few seconds, had yet to say a word. She slipped her skinny arms into the cardigan sweater she'd been holding. Mother of pearl buttons marched down the front; it looked like something an older woman would wear.

"Is that your grandmother's sweater?" I said.

Where was Beulah Jefferson, and why she'd let her granddaughter stay in this house of horrors?

When Janey didn't immediately answer, her sister said, "Our granny passed almost two weeks ago."

"I'm so sorry." I hugged Janey's bony frame but she didn't hug back. It was like embracing a hat stand. Maybe she was mad at me for allowing her absences to go on so long without finding out the reason. How long had she been out? I thought it might have been at least a week. I'd called her house once but I hadn't gotten an answer.

* * *

When we arrived at my condo, I asked Janey if she wanted to watch television. She obediently sat in front of my flatscreen, staring at the images, still not uttering a word. While she was in her TV trance, Carl and I conferred in my kitchen.

I knew most of my students were poor, but up until then I hadn't understood what poverty really was. I'd conveniently airbrushed out the filth, the stench, and the choking hopelessness.

"I've never experienced anything like that house before," I said to Carl. I couldn't shake the grimness of that scene. It had nested into my pores, fouled the air in my lungs.

"Wish I could say the same," Carl said. He, of course, already knew all about poverty; he'd been in the thick of his students' lives for years, while I'd been loitering on the sidelines.

"Should we call DFACS? Someone needs to snatch that toddler away from Janey's sister. He can't be getting proper care."

"I've dealt with cases like this before. Certainly we'll report it to DFACS, but that doesn't mean anything will be done. We're going to have to hound them."

"It's a condemned house. People can't live in condemned houses, especially babies."

"Sadly they do it all the time."

"Well then, if I have to, I'll pay for them to rent an apartment." Not that I had the money, but somehow I'd have to raise it.

Carl laid a heavy hand on my shoulder. "I know you want to help, but you can't just throw money at the problem. Who would sign the lease? And when Janey's sister trashes the apartment or turns it into a drug den, who's going to be liable for those damages? You?"

"I don't know," I said, my voice thin with frustration. "I just don't want Janey or that little boy living like animals. Worse than animals."

"I understand your frustration, but we have to go through certain channels."

"Janey can't go back."

"I agree. But we may have to take her to a temporary shelter."

"No! She's already too traumatized. I've never seen her like that before. So lifeless. If worse comes to worse, she'll have to stay here with me."

"Sorry, babe. That's not a viable solution. Teachers can't take in their students. Against policy."

While I was wallowing in feelings of helplessness, Carl lured Janey into the kitchen and spoke gently to her. It took a half-hour or so, but she started to open up to him. All the perkiness was drained from her voice. She was mostly monosyllabic and monotone, but at least she was talking again.

In halting sentences, Janey told us that after her grandma died, her sister Tameka and her boyfriend Flea sold everything in the apartment. The only thing Janey was allowed to keep was Ms. Jefferson's sweater. She said she hadn't been going to school because her sister made her watch Deon while Tameka went out to score crystal meth. In exchange for babysitting duties, Janey got a roof over her head—albeit a leaking roof—and food.

"Mostly canned ravioli," Janey said, her eyes dull as mud. "That was Thanksgiving dinner. It was cold because we ain't got a stove to fix it on."

I winced.

Carl continued to quiz her, and discovered she had an older cousin named Minnie in Beech City, South Carolina, thirty miles away. She'd seen Minnie at her grandmother's funeral and the cousin had offered to take her in. Janey chose to go with Tameka, mainly because she didn't want to switch schools. She hadn't any idea of what she was getting into.

"Minnie's probably changed her mind by now," Janey said. "She's already got three of her own."

The pizza we'd ordered arrived, and while Janey was eating, Carl called the cousin, who said the offer was still good.

"So long as Janey doesn't mind sleeping on the fold-out sofa," Carl said after he hung up the phone.

Better than a filthy mattress on the floor of a condemned house, I thought. As soon as Janey was finished eating, we drove her to South Carolina.

Minnie's modest living room was strewn with Legos and Matchbox cars and smelled of cabbage, but both Carl and I got a good vibe from it. Minnie enveloped Janey in her fleshy arms and kept repeating, "Bless your bones."

I tucked my phone number into Janey's blue jean pocket and told her to call if there were any problems. Before leaving I hugged her again, but she still didn't return the embrace. Was it possible she sensed how terribly I'd let her down?

On the way home Carl said, "Glad Janey had that cousin. I hate leaving kids at shelters. Now if only she can get Deon too."

We'd told Minnie the situation, and she said she'd also be willing to take on the toddler.

I was deeply ashamed of my negligence. Janey was like a completely different person and it was my fault. Would she ever go back to being the bubbly girl I remembered?

"You were so good with Janey," I said to Carl. "A student whisperer. Thanks so much."

"Thanks to *you*. You were the one who sent the report to the truant office."

Wrong, I thought as he turned out of Minnie's subdivision. In reality, I was a terribly negligent person, not fit to kiss Carl's boots, much less his lips.

I hated myself for lying to him. Another teacher must have reported her absences, maybe her art or P.E. teacher. Thank God *someone* did.

I'd always known it was wrong to be slack about keeping up with my students' attendance, but I hadn't fully understood how much it could hurt them. I vowed that from now on, when any of my kids were absent, I was going to find out why, even if I had to make a home visit myself.

Not only that, I was not going to give up on teaching these kids, no matter how badly they acted. It might take weeks or months before they accepted the changes in our classroom, and I would probably get extremely frustrated, but I had to persevere. No matter what.

Twenty

After the Janey episode, I had an overwhelming need to confess my sins to Joelle. I wanted to tell her the whole sordid story: my arrangement with Dr. Lipton, the countless ways I'd deceived Carl, and the five-million dollar deal with my aunt.

Unfortunately, even though I left her several messages, Joelle didn't return my calls. In fact, I had to write on her Facebook timeline three times before she got in touch. It was almost as if she was avoiding me. Was it possible she thought I wouldn't fit into her new, glittering circle of friends?

I immediately chided myself for not giving Joelle enough credit. Our friendship was one of the few things in life I'd always felt certain about.

It took me over a week but I finally caught Joelle on her cell and pinned her down to a lunch date. Monday was a teachers' workday, and because I didn't have any students, I was able to leave campus for lunch.

"How about Sybil's?" Joelle said.

Sybil's Café was in Savoy Center, Rose Hill's most affluent shopping destination. The clientele consisted almost exclusively of perfumed and expertly coiffed women, most with a collection of shopping bags at their feet. The cuisine was uninspired—a variety of limp and skimpy salads—and the service so lackadaisical your tongue would shrivel up before you'd ever get a water refill. But you didn't go to Sybil's for food or the service; you went there to be seen.

"Sure," I said, wanting to be agreeable. "Sybil's it is."
I'd just have to remember to eat a big breakfast.

When I arrived to meet Joelle, the prosperous jewel-box shops of
Savoy Center were dripping in tinsel and holly for the holidays, and
the parking lot was filled with luxury vehicles. I parked my
motorcycle between an Escalade and a silver BMW X6 and headed
to the restaurant.

A scrawny blonde woman stood near the entrance of Sybil's,
flagging me down. I had to get close before I realized the walking
skeleton with cotton-white hair was Joelle.

She lightly touched cheeks with me. Usually we hugged. Was
cheek-bussing going to be our new greeting?

"Hi there," I said. "Gosh, you look..."

Emaciated. Malnourished. Like someone who'd been
subsisting on lichen and berries.

"You look...hungry. I am too. I could eat a cow." Sadly I was at
the wrong restaurant for that.

"What do you think?" Joelle patted her hair, which looked like
it could be spun into a cone and sold as cotton candy. She was also
wearing a new string of pearls. I suspected they'd be gritty against
my teeth, indicating they were the real deal.

"Blonde, very blonde. But I've always liked your red hair." Not
that bright red was her natural color either. Nature had given her
dark brown hair, but Joelle was too lively of a person for such a
plain-Jane color.

"Trey has a weakness for blondes. It's a small concession to
make him happy. He's been doing so much for me. Did you know
he's been paying my house payment and most of my bills for the
last couple of months? He doesn't want me to work so many long
hours anymore."

"Seems like you're getting serious pretty quickly," I said warily.

"That's the way it happens when two people are right for each
other," Joelle said, fingering her pearls. "They just know."

"So what does your family say about him?"

"They like him fine." She didn't meet my eye which meant she was lying. Trey was too soft for the men in Joelle's family, who were all tall and strapping and spent their weekends doing manly stuff like hunting wild boar or chopping firewood.

"Any day now, I'm expecting him to pop the question."

"Oh?" I said softly.

"Is that all you're going to say?" she said. "Just 'oh?' I've never been so happy in my life. Would it kill you to share that with me? I've always celebrated all your tennis triumphs."

I wasn't used to Joelle being so snappish with me, and, contrary to what she claimed, she didn't look happy. I also knew she didn't want to hear one word against Trey or her possible marriage to him. "Of course, I'm thrilled for you," I said.

Joelle seemed satisfied with my comment and rewarded me with an arm squeeze.

The hostess appeared, and Joelle chatted her up; she was obviously a regular at the restaurant. We were shown to a prime white cloth table outside; the restaurant had outdoor heaters but it was also a fairly balmy day for December. Joelle followed her, moving stiffly and slowly.

"What's with the robot walk?" I said.

"Bikini Bootcamp classes," Joelle said, slowly lowering herself into a chair.

"It's only December."

"Never too soon to start."

When we were seated, she flapped a napkin over her dress. "Let's order a bottle of Chardonnay. My treat."

"I can't drink. I have to go back to work after this."

"Come on. I feel like celebrating. It's not like they're going to make you take a breath test when you return."

"I'm drinking very little these days."

"Oh yeah? What's going on? Are you taking a round of antibiotics? Did you take home a little souvenir from one of your one-night stands?"

"No!"

She lowered her voice to a whisper. "Don't tell me you're pregnant."

"Of course not."

I explained that I'd been seeing someone for a while as well, and he'd filled up such a hole in my life, I didn't feel the need to get sloshed on a regular basis.

"Define 'a while,'" she said. "Three days? A week? An hour?"

"Several months."

"Seriously? Why haven't you told me?" Joelle was conversing with me, but her gaze tracked two smartly dressed women who were entering a clothing store called Spoiled Rotten.

"We haven't been talking as much as we used to. We've both been so busy."

"If Toni Lee Wells is sticking with one guy, he must be the second coming of Ryan Reynolds."

"He's more like the second coming of Eric Benet. But sexier."

"Eric Benet?" She frowned. "Halle Berry's ex-hubby? Are you saying your new boyfriend is black?"

"Yes."

"So he's a fling?"

"No. I really care about him, but unfortunately there is a problem I wanted to discuss with you."

"Oh, honey. I'll bet there's a whole passel of problems," Joelle said. Her phone chirped out the song "Uptown Girl." Checking it, she said, "Baby's just pulled up in the parking lot."

"Baby's coming?"

Poof! There went my plans to have a heart-to-heart with Joelle. Maybe it was just as well; we hadn't gotten off to a stellar start.

"Yes, and don't pull a face. Y'all are going to have to get along if you're both going to be in my wedding party."

"You want Baby to be your bridesmaid?" I accidentally upended the saltshaker with my elbow. "After the way she's treated you over the years?"

Joelle flicked her wrist. "That history is so ancient the dinosaurs don't even remember it. Not to mention she's apologized over and over. Donnie will probably be Trey's best man so it makes sense, you know."

"Who will be your maid of honor?" I said, suddenly dreading the answer.

Since we'd been friends, Joelle had talked about her dream wedding at least a hundred times. The details were constantly being fleshed out: Chocolate fountain or champagne fountain? Horse-drawn carriage or limo? Dove release or Chihuahua release? (Joelle had a flair for the bizarre, or at least she used to before she met Trey.)

One aspect had never changed: I'd be her maid of honor. (No doubt wearing a flashy animal print dress.) Were things different now? Had Baby managed to usurp years of friendship in just a few short months?

The ground rumbled; drinking glasses shook. Baby had arrived. She gave me a cursory acknowledgement. She and Joelle immediately launched into an animated discussion of a dinner party they'd attended, where the hostess had served a cheap wine.

"Crane Lake," Baby said, eyes round with horror. "And she didn't even try to hide the bottle."

I didn't comment, thinking on the rare occasions I bought wine, Crane Lake was all I could afford.

Ten minutes passed, and the waitress had yet to honor us with a visit. I announced I had to return to school. Joelle didn't offer a word of protest, and Baby said, "Oh, the life of a career girl. Busy, busy." No doubt she was glad to be rid of me.

I got up from my seat, and plodded to my motorcycle, thinking Joelle might end up being an even worse snob than the people who used to dismiss her at Rose Hill Prep.

"Toni Lee!" Joelle called out. "Wait."

When she caught up with me, she said, "I need to make something clear. If Trey and I do get married, you'll be my maid of honor. Not Baby."

"Are you sure?" I glanced back at the table where Baby still sat, admiring her long, white teeth in a compact mirror.

"Of course," Joelle said, sounding like her old self. "You're my best bud, and you always will be. I apologize I've been out of touch lately. This is the first time I've ever been in love and it's making me a little soft in the head. Forgive me?"

"Of course."

I doubted very much she was genuinely in love with Trey. Far as I knew, love didn't turn a person into a jittery, walking skeleton. Somehow I was going to have to make her see that Trey might not be the best man for her.

The next day I was sitting in my empty classroom, contently nibbling on a pimento cheese sandwich, when I received an unwelcome phone call: It was Trey.

"I'm planning to ask for Joelle's hand tomorrow night." His voice sounded nasal over the phone. "And I'd like your blessing. I know your opinion is important to her."

Unfortunately that was no longer true. Joelle was far too indoctrinated in the cult of Trey for my opinion to hold any weight.

"What if I refuse to give my blessing?"

Silence. Then he said, "I don't know...Is there any way I could convince you?"

Should have guessed Trey was the literal type. I balled up my lunch bag and tossed it in the trash.

"Kidding," I said, even though I wasn't.

"I've brought home several rings on approval from the jeweler but I still haven't chosen one," Trey said. "Baby says a cushion cut, but I'm not sure."

A cushion cut! Joelle would no more want a cushion cut than she'd want a burlap wedding dress and a dandelion bouquet. Since she was eighteen, she knew exactly what shape diamond she wanted: a marquise. Thought it would make her fingers look skinny.

"No cushion cut. Might as well give her a lug nut."

"I'm glad I called. Say, would you mind coming over and taking a look at what I've chosen?"

He was asking me to choose the weapon for Joelle's destruction. Still, if I went, it would give me the chance to get to know Trey a little better. I thought of the saying, "It's best to keep your friends close and your enemies even closer." Also it was a convenient night for me to go; Carl was playing poker with Doc.

Trey's house was a boxy two-story brick Colonial surrounded by a hedge so well-manicured it looked like it had been tended with pinking shears. An American flag flapped on a pole, a brass lion head knocker graced the door, and a black Mercedes was parked in the drive.

Respectable but dull. Couldn't he at least have a whimsical bumper sticker on his car that said, "Visualize Whirled Peas" or "What would Scooby Do?" Then maybe I wouldn't think he was the wrong guy for Joelle.

When I rang the bell, Trey answered the door still in his work clothes, a stiff white dress shirt with monogrammed cuffs, dark slacks, and wing tips. Very natty looking. My guess was he took all his clothes to the dry cleaner, even his boxers.

"Thanks for coming. I appreciate your help."

I followed him into his living room, which had been decorated with a nautical motif. Pillows needlepointed with anchors. Compass rug. Liberal use of the colors red and blue. Probably made Joelle queasy every time she stepped inside. She got seasick watching reruns of *The Love Boat*.

"Can I offer you a drink?" Trey said.

"Nothing for me, thank you."

I parked myself on a striped chair and studied a shadowbox that featured various boating knots.

"You sure? I have Cristal. Joelle said you were a fan. True?"

Very true. Last Christmas I'd gotten a taste and loved it so much I told Joelle I'd name my first-born Cristal, even if it was a boy.

"I'll have a tiny glass."

He went into the kitchen and brought back a flute so overfilled with champagne it was sloshing over the sides. I eagerly grabbed it, reminding myself not to be swayed by grossly overpriced yet delicious champagne.

When I finished my first glass, he offered me a second, and as tempted as I was, I refused. I had to drive home.

"Maybe it's time you showed me the rings," I said.

He laughed. "We were having so much fun I almost forgot."

Fun was stretching it, but my Cristal buzz softened the edges of everything, even Trey.

After a moment, he returned with a large blue velvet box from Wooten's, the most prestigious jeweler in Rose Hill. They ran commercials that said, "When it's a Wooten ring, the answer is always yes."

I opened the padded box, and the brilliance of the rings' stones practically blinded me. They were so stunning I was tempted to marry Trey myself.

My gaze scanned the row of shimmering pretties, lingering on the last one on the left. "They're all beautiful, but this is the one she'll love the most." I pointed to a marquise big as a searchlight. Joelle could thank me later when she'd have to sell it after the inevitable divorce.

"I appreciate your help. I would have hated to make a mistake."

It did seem important to him to get Joelle the right ring, but I was still convinced he was the wrong guy for her and not even the Hope diamond could change that.

"You're welcome." I stood to leave.

He jumped up from his seat. "By the way, I was talking to Kirk recently. He had a great time with you the other night. I know he wouldn't mind taking you out to dinner sometime. Maybe we could double date."

"That's sweet, but I'm involved with someone right now...Thanks so much for the Cristal."

I made my way across the Berber carpet to the door, and Trey followed close on my heels. "Joelle mentioned you had a boyfriend. Calvin something?"

"His name is Carl."

"Is it getting hot and heavy?"

"Could be," I said mysteriously, even though I thought his question was exceedingly nosy.

"Black guy, right?"

"Yes. Why do you ask?"

"Just curious." He laughed. "Donnie told me a funny joke the other day. What's the difference between a black man and a park bench?"

I held up my palm. "I don't want to hear it."

"A park bench can support a family of four." He cuffed me on the arm. "Pretty funny, huh?"

"It's not one bit funny." Whatever points Trey had scored with the champagne were destroyed by that joke.

"Don't you have a sense of humor?"

"Not when it comes to racist jokes."

He waved away my comment. "I'm hardly a racist. I have plenty of black people working for me. Rosa, our housekeeper growing up, was like a second mama to me and my brothers. But let's be realistic; it's not like I'm going to ask her daughter out. And she probably wouldn't want to go out with me. Blacks are more racist than whites."

I hitched my purse on my shoulder and said, "Good night, Trey."

"Let me pass on a little advice to you." His jowls jiggled slightly as he spoke. "You're a good-looking girl. Nice catch. But once it gets around that you've been keeping company with a black man...It's bound to put some people off. They might think you're...well...sullied."

For a moment I was too stunned to come up with a reply.

"I'm leaving. Wouldn't want to give you cooties. Better throw away my champagne flute just in case. Also get someone to fumigate the chair I was sitting in."

"Now, Toni Lee. This has been such a nice visit. Do we have to part on an unpleasant note?"

"I don't think we have a choice, Trey. You just marginalized someone I deeply care about."

"Have it your way then...One more thing, though. Joelle tells me you're going to be a member of our wedding party, which is fine by me. But your friend, unfortunately, won't be welcome. Unless of course, you think he'd like to help out with the valet parking."

My mouth fell open.

"That was a joke! Well...at least the part about the parking."

I paused at the front door. "Have you discussed this with Joelle?"

He nodded. "She's in full accord."

Twenty One

I marched up to Joelle's mustard-colored stucco home and banged on the door so hard the Christmas wreath nearly fell off. I was huffing and puffing, breath streaming from my mouth like steam from an iron. Joelle appeared at the door, wearing a leopard-spotted warm-up suit. At least at home she was still true to spots and stripes.

"Did Trey call you? He said he might. What did the rings look like? Tell me everything." She dragged me into her living room. More animal prints there: Zebra wall hanging, snakeskin lamp shades, tiger drapes.

"The rings are beautiful. I told him to get you the biggest one, of course. A marquise cut. But there's something else—"

"How many carats? I know it's supposed to be a surprise but I'm dying to know."

"Three maybe?"

Joelle shrieked. "Oh my God. Wait until I tell Baby. Three? Are you sure?"

"Maybe. It's not like I'm a jeweler. Will you listen for a minute, please?"

Joelle fanned her overheated face. "Sorry. Go ahead."

"Trey told me that you and he agreed Carl shouldn't be invited to the wedding."

"Carl?"

"My boyfriend!"

Silence. Then a long drawn-out exhale of air.

"That Trey." Joelle sounded like a mother whose child has

been caught red-handed in the cookie jar. "I wish he wouldn't have brought that up."

"It's true, then?"

"Don't start freaking out on me, Toni Lee."

I whirled away from her. "What do you expect? This isn't *you*. You aren't a racist. What's happened to you?"

"Hear me out, please."

"I just can't believe—"

"Sit. Listen."

I begrudgingly sat on the edge of a furry club chair; my body was vibrating like a tuning fork.

Joelle sat across from me, kneading her thighs. "You know I'd be perfectly happy to have your boyfriend at the wedding, but the truth is, some people, like Trey's father, are offended by interracial relationships."

"But—"

Joelle held up a hand, heavy with a new topaz ring. "This is my wedding day, and to be honest, I want people to be focusing on the bride, not you and your date. Call me selfish, but that's how I feel. Can you try and understand?"

I couldn't speak. Did I even know her anymore? What had Trey done to her?

"Toni Lee?" Her tone was soft, contrite. "Why are we stressing over this? I won't be getting married for months. I bet you and Carl won't even be together by then."

"Yes we will."

"You can't know that."

"I do. I tried to explain when we had lunch. I've never felt like this about any guy before."

"Try to be honest with yourself. Couldn't your relationship with Carl possibly be a bid for attention?"

"It is not! I would never do that to Carl."

"Really? Because, according to Trey, you were making out with Kirk after my dinner party."

God Almighty. It seemed as if everyone knew about that.

"Okay. I backslid briefly. But at the last minute my strong feelings for Carl won out, and I did not go home with Kirk."

"Why do this? Why go crazy over some black guy when there were so many other guys before him you could have fallen for?"

That question was easy to answer. There were countless things to admire about Carl: He knew I loved candy corn and left me small packages of it in unexpected places. Once he'd left a trail of candy corn that led to the bedroom. On several occasions he watched horror movies with me, even though he sometimes had to cover his eyes during decapitations or other gory parts. But beyond all that, he possessed one singular quality that set him apart from anyone else I'd ever gone out with.

"Carl Rutherford is one of the best people I've ever met in my life. The genuine article. But even more important than that, he makes *me* want to be a better person."

Sappy as it sounded, it was true. From the first day I'd met him, it was as if Carl hadn't seen the person I was, but the person I'd always secretly longed to be.

"Hate to tell ya this, but you might not feel the same when you discover how hard it's going to be to date a black guy in this town," Joelle said.

"Not everyone in Rose Hill is like Trey. Who incidentally is such a huge racist he makes the Klan look like little kids running around in white sheets."

Joelle entangled her fingers in her bleached hair; I was surprised it didn't break off in handfuls. "I realize he might not be as tolerant as some, but you have to understand, that's the way Trey was brought up."

"That's your excuse for him? It's okay for him to hate because his parents practice hate?"

"Of course not, but—"

"No buts. Your boyfriend has a worm living inside of him that he has to constantly feed. It makes him extremely toxic and if you marry him, he'll infect you too. Sweetie, I know you've always wanted to marry a guy like Trey, but is it worth it? To marry some awful guy just so you can be a member of the country club and drive a car as big as a tank?"

Joelle's face got blotchy. "How can you possibly understand? Up until recently you have always had whatever you wanted. Luxury condo, Porsche, everything. Now you think I should dump my fiancé, who has made me incredibly happy, just because he doesn't want to upset his parents by having your boyfriend at his wedding? Honestly, could you be more selfish?"

I looked at Joelle with her gaunt cheeks and ruined hair. A hunger glittered in her eyes, like she wanted to chop Trey up into hundreds of pieces, devour every one, and still lick her lips, craving more. At the age of twenty-two, I didn't claim to know everything about love, but I was pretty sure what Joelle and Trey shared wasn't it.

"I'm afraid for you, Joelle," I said as gently as I could muster. "I think you'll be miserable with Trey."

"You're just jealous. You're used to having me all to yourself and now that you have to share me with others, you don't like it."

"Joelle—"

"Just go. And since you have such a low opinion of Trey, maybe you shouldn't come to the wedding."

Not that I wanted to be there. It'd be like watching Joelle drive her Toyota Corolla into the Savannah River.

I was reluctant to crash Carl's guys' night out, but I couldn't stop myself. After leaving Joelle, I immediately drove over to Doc's, where the poker game was being held. I just wanted to lay eyes on Carl for a minute; he'd be the anti-venom for my poisonous evening.

I'd been to Doc's house before. A week earlier, Carl and I had attended a Christmas party there. Unfortunately all the small brick homes on Doc's street looked alike. Then I remembered the Budweiser tree Doc had constructed out of longneck bottles and PVC tubes. I drove slowly down the street until I spotted the tree.

Doc's house was dark, and no cars were parked in the driveway. Was it possible the game had ended early, or the location had changed? My motor idled as I texted Carl: "Call me."

Hours later and Carl still hadn't returned my text. I stuffed my face with holiday candy corn and watched *Santa Claws, Santa Slay* and *Silent Night, Deadly Night*. I kept thinking about a bottle of Marilyn Merlot wine I had in the rack. I could have chugged it like spring water, but decided to abstain.

At some point I fell asleep and woke up with a start at three a.m., remembering I still hadn't heard from Carl. Had something happened? Was he lying in a ditch crying my name?

I checked my phone and found a text from him. It came at midnight, an hour after I'd fallen asleep.

"Sorry, babe. Didn't see your message until now. Late poker night at Doc's. Lost my shirt."

I had to read it three times before it sunk in and it was still hard to believe: Carl lied to me.

What's worse, he'd been incredibly smooth about it: The casual tone. The inclusion of supporting details. All the marks of an experienced fibber, which begged the question, what else had he lied about?

A little voice in my head said, "It's not as if you've been completely honest with Carl," but I immediately squelched it. This was about him, not me! Plus I knew why he'd lied to me. As far as I was concerned, men lied about their whereabouts for only two reasons.

1. They wanted to get drunk at a sports bar with their buddies.

2. They wanted to get frisky with another woman.

Carl had not been at a sports bar. He was one of those rare guys who'd never once uttered the phrase, "How about them Dawgs?"

I pitched the phone across the sofa, stumbled into the bedroom, and belly-flopped onto the mattress. Not that I could possibly fall back to sleep.

Maybe there's an explanation, I thought. My mind was too busy tallying up past hurts to think of one. First my family—especially my mom—had turned on me, then Lois, then Joelle, and now Carl. It was as if I'd been surrounded by fakes my entire life. Was it any wonder that I'd turned out to be one myself?

Twenty Two

Used to be when I had a bad night's sleep on a school night, the next morning I could pass out the fun gadgets, don dark shades, and zone out while the students frittered the day away. No more. No matter how tired I was, I had to teach. It was a promise I'd made myself after the incident with Janey. Lately I'd set such a high standard that every day I felt like I was channeling Socrates.

To top it off, a new student named Darnell showed up. Unfortunately I was in no mood to acclimate a greenhorn into the classroom fold.

"Are you sure you're in the right place?" I said when he introduced himself. Usually I received reams of paperwork on new special education students.

"Yes, ma'am," he said.

Darnell was dressed in geeky high-waisted jeans and a spotless white t-shirt. The letter D was carved into his buzzcut at the back of his scalp. He handed me a schedule; everything was in order.

"Welcome to our class. I'm Ms. Wells."

"Nice to meet you, ma'am," he said. I was impressed by his politeness. I didn't get a lot of that at Harriet Hall, and hoped the rest of the students wouldn't corrupt him as the day progressed.

Darnell kept to himself throughout the morning classes. At lunch he asked if he could stay in the room with me. "I don't know anyone at this school," he said forlornly.

I usually didn't allow students in the classroom during lunch. Those precious fifteen minutes were the only time during my day where I didn't feel like I was simultaneously juggling plates and whistling Dixie. But Darnell looked so pitiful, I made an exception.

I also knew it had to be hard for him to transfer to a new school in the middle of the year. At Harriet Hall it happened all the time. The students were like carnies, living with an aunt for one year, a grandmother for the next. Their family situations were reflected in the way they talked. Instead of saying, "I live with my auntie," they'd say, "I stay with my auntie." Next week they might be staying with someone else.

After lunch, I led the class in a game about banking terms. It wasn't going well. The kids were as resistant as ever. Darnell didn't participate, but that wasn't surprising since he hadn't been exposed to the material. At one point he raised his hand and said, "May I be excused?"

"You need to use the restroom?" I said.

"No."

"Where did you want to go?"

"Out. I don't like this game."

He probably felt intimidated, thinking he was already behind.

"Just sit tight for a couple of minutes, we're almost done."

He stood. "Can I have a pass?"

"No sir," I said.

In a flash, his entire personality changed, jaw tightening, fists balling. It was as if a Ninja warrior had jumped into his skin.

"This game is for babies."

The class laughed nervously, and I gave him a deadly look. The kid obviously wanted attention, and I wasn't going to give it to him.

"Sit down, Darnell. We'll discuss this after class."

"You want to see me after class?" His question was a challenge.

I nodded and commenced with the game.

"You gonna screw me after class?" His lips twisted in a lurid way, and he bucked his narrow hips back and forth.

This time no one laughed. Even they knew Darnell had gone too far. The students were quiet, their bodies rigid, waiting for my response. I felt shaky inside, like I'd swallowed a dozen goldfish. I didn't want Darnell to know he'd gotten to me.

"The game is over for now," I said evenly. "Please take out your textbooks and read pages three hundred to three-ten. Answer the questions at the end of the section."

It'd been a while since I'd assigned busy work but the situation seemed to call for it. I needed a diversion.

Darnell upended a desk. "Who cares about the questions!" It sounded like an explosion when it hit the ground.

"Please leave this classroom." I was unable to keep the tremor out of my voice.

He ducked his head and came at me like a human cannonball. He was so fast I had no time to duck out of the way. Darnell butted into my midsection and slammed me against the cinderblock. A sharp pain bayoneted the back of my head, and his fist loomed above me. Down it came in slow motion; in seconds, my face would bloom into a bloody pulp. Then someone grabbed his wrist.

The class thronged him. Vernon held Darnell's arms back as he struggled to get loose. The boy spat out obscenities. Monica kicked his shins. The room rang with screams. Darnell wrenched loose of Vernon's grip and made a run for it. Vernon gave chase.

No," I said, calling him back in a weak voice. "Let him go."

Wetness trickled down my cheek. I touched it, and my fingers came back bright red.

"She's bleeding!" shrieked Monica. "Ms. Wells's bleeding. She gonna die. That bad boy killed her."

Gingerly I picked myself up from the floor, woozy with the smell and feel of my own blood. "Calm down. You're not going to get rid of me that easily."

My head cleared, and I held onto the wall to keep upright. The number one rule for every teacher was to never leave a class unsupervised. In a breathless voice, I told my students to collect their book bags and follow me over to Ms. Evans' class. A scramble ensued and as soon as they were packed up, I led them into the hall and knocked on the classroom next door. When Ms. Evans saw me, she said, "Blood? On the third floor? This is a first."

"Could you watch my class while I go to the nurse?"

"Someone should go with you," Ms. Evans said. "Just in case."

My kids bickered over who should accompany me to the nurse's office. "Vernon," I said. "The rest of you stay here."

Vernon and I left Ms. Evans' classroom and took the elevator to the main floor. I lurched my way to the nurse's station, still slightly dizzy and unsteady on my feet. The students and teachers we passed stopped short and gaped. I probably looked like Carrie with a bucket full of pig's blood dripping down her face. "I'm okay," I repeated several times, as if trying to convince myself.

Vernon's complexion was ashen; he held my arm tightly and kept saying, "That boy ain't right. Ain't right at all." His concern was touching and unexpected.

When we arrived at the nurse's office, I instructed Vernon to go back to Ms. Evans' classroom. The nurse, a woman in her fifties with an outdated poodle hairstyle, immediately sat me down on a metal stool and swabbed my wound with an antiseptic rub that stung. "You're lucky. The cut's not deep; you won't even need a stitch."

"Why so much blood?"

"That's how it is with head wounds. All those blood vessels in the scalp."

The nurse was very matter-of-fact. She probably had to be with all the nasty business she saw on a daily basis, like cigarette burns, black-and-blue marks, impetigo and other infections allowed to fester and spread. Harriet Hall had it all.

After I was cleaned up and bandaged, I staggered over to Dr. Lipton's office to report the assault. He immediately summoned Mule, the security guard, on his walkie-talkie and told him to look for Darnell just in case he was still on school property. Afterwards he said, "What did Nurse Maynard say about your injuries? Do you need to visit a doctor? "

"No. She said it was a fairly minor wound."

He smiled, revealing gold fillings in the back of his mouth. "Good."

"So what happens now?"

"Once we get our hands on him, the boy will be suspended."

"Do we need to call the police?" The smell of hair tonic filled my nostrils. Dr. Lipton's hair was slick with it.

"Let me worry about that. Right now you should go home and rest. In fact, there are only two days left before we dismiss for the Christmas holidays. No point in you coming back until after the first of the year. Don't worry about finding a substitute. I'll handle that."

I shook my head. "I need to be here tomorrow. It'll upset my students if I don't show up. They'll think I'm badly hurt."

He plucked at the fabric of his pinstriped suit. "I'll send someone from guidance to speak with your students. And I'm not *suggesting* you take those days off. I'm telling you."

Twenty Three

When I got home I swallowed a sedative and immediately climbed under my down comforter and constructed a fortress of pillows around me. All I wanted to do was hide from the world for a short while. Maybe until the next Ice Age.

I woke to the sound of knocking. Too groggy to get up, I burrowed even deeper beneath my covers. The knocking ceased, and my front door opened. Heavy footsteps sounded down the hall and stopped.

"I have a full can of wasp killer," I said. "And I'm not afraid to spray it."

"It's just me. I used my key."

Carl. My mood momentarily perked up as it always did at the sound of his voice. Until I remembered he was one of the reasons I was hiding.

"Go away," I said from beneath the covers. "I'm not feeling well."

"Come out, come out wherever you are." He pulled away the comforter. I resisted and we engaged in a brief tug-of-war. Carl easily won.

He winced when my face was revealed and sat on the bed next to me. "You're all banged up. What happened?" In a rote voice I filled him in on the Darnell drama in my classroom. I decided not to say anything about his lie to me. I didn't have the energy for a big, emotional scene which would surely climax with me screaming, "Whose bed have your Reeboks been under?"

"Why didn't you call me?" he said.

Because you've shaken my belief in humanity, I thought.

"Have you spoken to the police?" Carl said.

"Dr. Lipton said he'd handle that for me."

"That's not how it works. *You* have to talk to the police. You're the one who has to press charges. "

"Then why did Dr. Lipton say he could do it for me?"

"Because if you press charges it'll make the newspaper, and teacher assaults are terrible publicity for a school. It's to Lipton's advantage to hush them up. Rumor has it there have been three other teacher assaults this year at Harriet Hall, and none were reported to the police."

Three assaults were three too many, yet if I insisted on pressing charges, Dr. Lipton would do what he always does when I displeased him: Threaten my job. After coming this far, I had no intention of getting sacked.

"I just want to forget about the whole nightmare."

Carl cocked his head, a genuinely puzzled look on his face. "That doesn't sound like the Toni Lee I know."

I gave him a narrow-eyed look. Do we ever really know a person?

"I bet I can guess the reason for your reluctance. You're worried about the student, aren't you? Even though he hurt you, you don't want to see him go to jail."

Boy. Did he have me wrong.

"Look at it this way," he continued. "If he assaults one teacher and gets away with it, he'll assault another. You really need to talk to the cops."

The nerve of him telling me the right thing to do. Big phony.

"I don't want to press charges," I said through my teeth.

"But, babe—"

"Don't you 'babe' me, you...cheater."

Damn. Hadn't meant to blurt that out.

"What?" he said, looking genuinely stunned. I had to give it to him; the guy was smooth as whipped butter.

"You lied to me about poker last night. I drove by Doc's and the house was all dark. No cars anywhere."

Carl's mouth opened and closed several times. It was like watching a goldfish in an aquarium.

"Well...?"

"It's true," Carl finally said. "I've been hiding something from you. For a while."

A while? I wasn't sure I was ready to hear his confession. It was even worse than I thought.

"What I'm about to tell you must be kept absolutely confidential. I *was* with Doc, but we weren't playing poker."

"What were you doing?"

"A few teachers from Harriet Hall have been meeting for several months, trying to figure out a way to get rid of Dr. Lipton. We're positive he's urging certain faculty members to falsify grades and attendance. He also may be asking some teachers to manipulate mid-year testing results. We'd like to find out who he's managed to corrupt."

A wave of queasiness nearly knocked me backwards. Carl wouldn't have to look very far.

"We want to bring Dr. Lipton down before he's appointed superintendent, but so far he's been untouchable."

I couldn't remember a time when I'd been so disgusted with myself. My shame was so great I said something I shouldn't have.

"If it will help, I'll report Darnell."

"Thank God. Last year a teacher almost died from an assault. She's still in a coma and might never recover."

I remembered my father mentioning rumors about assaults at the school, but I hadn't wanted to believe it.

Carl climbed into bed with me and started to kiss me with extreme passion. I wasn't surprised. He seemed to get most turned on when I was good, not naughty. Here was the truly kinky part: His belief that I was a good person turned me on too. Why couldn't I be the kind of woman he thought I was?

After he'd ever-so-slowly undressed me, and it was time for

the main event, he said, "I have something to tell you."

I wanted to say, "Not now, cowboy," but his tone was too serious, the look in his eye too solemn.

"Do you know why I could never cheat on you?"

"No."

"Because I love you, Toni Lee. I want to spend the rest of my life with you."

As his words sunk in, the room grew too warm, the blood rushing through my ears too loud. I couldn't speak; my throat was too dry. It wasn't that I didn't love him, I did. I loved him so much I could have Facebooked, Tweeted and Instagramed it. I wanted it tattooed on my bicep, spray-painted across the front of my pink house. I could have paraded down Main Street in a sandwich sign saying, "I love Carl."

But while my "I love you" was genuine, his "I love you" was intended for a woman who only existed in his imagination. He didn't love me; he loved the person I was pretending to be.

Carl was poised over me, his arms tensed. I had to say something. The guy was just hanging there, waiting.

Confess, I urged myself. Tell him every single one of your dirty little secrets: your arrangement with Lipton, the five million dollars. Everything. Spew it out.

But then I imagined him rolling off the bed and walking out of my life for good. The image terrified me worse than any horror movie I'd ever watched. I honestly didn't know if I could survive another loss in my life. So instead, I swallowed hard, gazed into his eyes, and said the first thing that came to mind: "Give it to me, babe."

Twenty Four

The next morning we stood in my narrow galley kitchen, sipping coffee and acting overly polite to each other. That's what happens when one person bares his soul, and the other person acts like a heartless sex fiend and says, "Give it to me." I could tell he was wounded, and I ached for him.

"I don't feel like going to school today," Carl said.

"That's not like you."

"It's Rose Wyld again. She just won't let up."

I was relieved he'd brought up a safe topic.

"Is she still nagging you about her grade?"

"Constantly. Yesterday she got nasty with me, cursing me out. I had to write her up."

"I'm sorry." Carl never wrote up students; he preferred to handle his own discipline issues.

"I hated to do it. Rose's such a troubled young woman. Her mother used to prostitute herself for drugs, and her older sister took her in. She's led a very sad life, and the Miss Harriet Hall pageant has been such an obsession with her. I think she expects it to fix something inside of her."

I felt an unexpected twinge of recognition. Hadn't I been that way with tennis tournaments, always thinking if only I could win the next tournament, I'd feel better about myself? My frequent victories never changed a thing within me, but I never stopped believing they would.

Of course, it was the same with the five million dollars. Didn't I also think that having so much money would make up for the other deficits in my life? Like losing my ability to play competitive tennis, the lack of a close family, always feeling I wasn't worthy of love. After all, if your own mother didn't love you, who else would?

"Toni Lee," Carl said.

"Sorry. Zoned out for a minute."

"I was just asking you when you were going to talk to Lipton."

Oh yes, the promise I'd made in a moment of weakness. There'd be no getting out of it.

"I'll go see him this afternoon. After the Christmas assembly."

I stood outside of Lipton's office, trying to get up the nerve to speak. His door was open, and he was huddled over a stack of paperwork. I cleared my throat to alert him to my presence.

He glanced up, an impatient expression on his face. "What are you doing here? I thought I told you to stay home."

"I just stopped by to talk with you...Got a minute?"

"For you I have more than a minute."

When I closed the door he said, "You can leave it open."

"I think this might be a closed-door kind of conversation."

"You've got my attention. Have a seat."

"I'll stand, thank you." I refused to sit in that tiny wing chair with the cut-off legs. Today was not the day to feel like a Lilliputian. I needed to channel my inner Gulliver.

Dr. Lipton, on the other hand, appeared to be channeling Tom Wolfe. He wore a white suit with a polka-dot tie and matching handkerchief poking out of his breast pocket. "What's on your mind?"

"This morning I logged into the special education computer files to see if I could find information on Darnell, my attacker."

It was a very sad story. Darnell had never had a real family; he'd been in seven different foster homes since he was a toddler.

"And?"

"Did you know he came straight from the Youth Detention Center? He served a year for another teacher assault. Sounds like a pastime of his."

Dr. Lipton leaned back slightly in his chair, the leather creaking. "No need to worry about that thug. He's been suspended."

"And arrested? You told me you reported him to the police."

"I did indeed. I assume they picked him up."

"I guess they'll get in touch with me to press charges."

"Not necessarily. I gave them the incident report; that's all they need."

Dr. Lipton had obviously been counting on my ignorance of police procedure. Had I not talked to Carl, I would have assumed he was telling me the truth.

"Who's the officer you spoke to? I'd like to call and see if they were able to find Darnell. I want to make sure he doesn't assault any more teachers."

He smiled. "Why don't you let me handle all of that?"

I threw my shoulders back, readying myself for the upcoming confrontation. "You didn't report it, did you?"

"Now where did you get a crazy idea like that?"

"If you'd just give me the name of the officer—"

"I said I'd handle it," he said, his chest expanding. "Where's your trust? I can't have teachers on my team who don't trust their leaders. Understand?"

"I am a team player," I said hotly. "Don't forget I'm going to be helping you with mid-year testing. That's a really big deal. I could get in all kinds of trouble if I got caught."

He paused for a moment. Then, in a low, deep voice he said, "There are others who could assist. You're not the only one."

"I'm not trying to be difficult. I'm worried Darnell will come back and hurt me again. You'd think you'd want your teachers to be safe, especially after what happened last year. I don't understand why you're letting all these other assaults happen and—"

"What other assaults?"

Damn. I'd said more than I intended. Quickly I tried to

recover. "I meant *my* assault...Someone should have informed me about Darnell's history."

The hard set of Lipton's jaw told me it was too late. "Who have you been talking to?"

"No one."

"I don't believe you."

"Why would I lie?"

His fingers tapped out a rapid rhythm on the varnished surface of the desk. "I've had enemies in every one of my schools. I also happen to know that right here at Harriet Hall, there are vengeful teachers who are jealous of my professional accomplishments and whose primary aim is to bring me down and spread lies. I always find out who they are and deal with them accordingly. So why don't you save me the trouble and tell me who you've been talking to?"

I put on my best poker face. "No one."

He studied me for a moment with his unwavering gaze. How had I ever found him to be charismatic? Now he just seemed like a hoodlum.

"It's that boyfriend of yours, isn't it? Rutherford."

Panic, cold and sharp, shot up my spine. I ordered myself not to flinch or blink.

"Carl and I rarely talk shop."

Silence. Lipton's stare was a probe, searching for the slightest opening.

"All the same. It's not a good idea for you to fraternize with him anymore. End it."

"What?" I said, stunned. "Now you're telling me who to date?"

"I believe your relationship with Mr. Rutherford is interfering with your job performance, therefore it's reasonable for me to ask you to stop seeing him. It'll also renew my trust in you."

"And if I don't?"

"Failure to comply with a supervisor's instructions is always grounds for dismissal. Especially for an untenured teacher."

I took a couple of short, fast breaths, feeling like a bear

hopelessly caught in a steel trap. When would it ever stop?

"Quit looking at me like I'm the big bad wolf," Dr. Lipton said. "I'll let you in on a secret. Dr. Scott's wife is ill, and he wants to retire sometime after mid-year testing. If all goes as planned, the Board will appoint me as the new superintendent. Then you can date the Pope for all I care. In return, I'll make sure you keep your job and even transfer you to a much cushier school...Sound like a fair exchange?"

I wanted to tell him he'd gone too far, that I would never give up Carl, not even for a month, just to keep my job. Then I wanted to leave his office, phone the police, and report Darnell. Afterward I'd pay a visit to the superintendent and tell him about all the insanity going on at Harriet Hall.

I didn't do any of those things. I was too scared to lose my inheritance for good and to have to make it on my own for the rest of my life. I thought about Daddy. He couldn't do it, and I wasn't sure if I could either. Yes, I'd come far in the last few months, but obviously not far enough. There was a big part of me that was weak and pathetic and I knew it.

"I'll have to think about it."

"How long?'

"I don't know. I'm upset right now."

"You have until tomorrow to make your decision."

"Fine." I stood.

"Ms. Wells, you might not believe this, but everything I do springs from my love of this school. When Harriet Hall gets bad press, people think, 'No wonder. It's that black project school.' Until I took over as principal, there was talk of closing it down or restructuring it. I was the one who stopped that from happening, who changed things, who brought pride back to the institution. A couple of negative newspaper articles and all my hard work goes up in smoke. Can't you understand that?"

I did, but I also knew that pride was worthless when you cheated to obtain it. Just as worthless as my Rookie Teacher of the Year nomination.

"Is that all?"

"Yes. And I trust that you will make the right decision. Remember. It's only for a month."

Twenty Five

I fled to the ladies' room, dropped to my knees on the cold ceramic tiles, and threw up my lunch into the toilet. What had happened in the last few minutes had sickened me more than any alcohol. I was every bit as immoral as Dr. Lipton. What kind of person was I to meekly agree to ignore Darnell's assault and to consider dumping my boyfriend?

Before going home, I stopped by my classroom. It was planning period and the substitute, a middle-aged black man with a gray Van dyke beard, said he was relieved to see me. Apparently a rumor was flying around campus that I was seriously injured or even dead. My students had been wringing their hands all day long, and according to him, even Monica had shed a few tears. Lipton must not have kept his promise to send someone from guidance to speak to my class.

I stayed until the next period started so I could reassure my kids, and give them each a Christmas gift bag I'd put together earlier and stored in the closet. First to arrive in class was Monica, who stopped short when she saw me.

"You alive?" she asked, thick eyebrows jumping. She was dry-eyed now but her eyes were still puffy from her earlier tears. I was moved but tried not to show it.

"Care to take my pulse?" I offered her my wrist.

"Nah." She gave me one of the quickest hugs on record. "I'll take your word for it, cracka."

Most of my students were more demonstrative than Monica, throwing their arms around me or patting my shoulder, as if proving to themselves that Ms. Wells was really there and not lying stiff and waxy in some morgue. I was also presented with a homemade card—a crude drawing of me with big Texas hair and long pin-like legs with the caption "World's Best Teacher." The incident with Darnell seemed to have changed the classroom dynamics for the better.

"You looking forward to Christmas vacation?" I said to Vernon as I gave him his goody bag.

Vernon shrugged his broad shoulders.

"You don't seem excited," I said.

"Too cold where I stay. Meemaw can't afford to keep the heat going all the time. And sometimes I don't get no lunch."

Carl once told me many Hall students dreaded school holidays because they missed the amenities the school provided, like free meals, a climate-controlled building, and a structured schedule. So many kids had chaotic home lives that, in comparison, their hours spent at the high school seemed like the Ritz.

"Sorry, Vernon," I said, feeling helpless. "Maybe there's some kind of meal or recreational programs going on over the holidays. I'll look into it and let you know."

Unfortunately there was only so much a teacher could do to help her students. You couldn't begin to fix everything in their lives no matter how much you wished you could. But I would do my best.

On the way home from school, an idea occurred to me, one that might soften the blow when I made my confessions to Carl. As soon as I pulled up to my house, I texted him and asked him to come over after school. There was something important I had to discuss with him.

While I waited, I went inside and rehearsed what I was going to say. He arrived an hour or so later.

"You okay? You seem kind of—"

"Can we sit for a minute?" He looked a little green-faced, as if he'd eaten bad shellfish.

Maybe he was still upset about last night, and my failure to return his "I love you." Maybe further worries about Rose were plaguing him.

I took a seat on the couch in my living room and patted the cushion beside me. Carl ignored the invitation and remained standing, towering over me. It took him a few seconds to speak.

"Ed, the truant officer, dropped by my room after school. We were discussing Janey's case, and he told me something very upsetting."

I flinched, knowing what was next. The incident with Janey was coming back to nip at my heels.

"He said he never received a notice about her absences from you," Carl continued. "In fact, the paperwork came from Janey's P.E. teacher. He also tells me he's never gotten a single excessive absence notice from you, which is highly unusual. What gives?"

My insides quivered; the betrayed look in his eye made me want to leap out the window.

"Well?" he said.

I twisted my hands in my lap. "I have something to tell you. That's why I called you over today. Please listen with an open mind."

My confession came out in a great rush of words. I told him everything: my bargain with Aunt Cornelia and the five million dollars, the dishonorable things I'd done and was planning to do for Dr. Lipton to keep my job, and why I couldn't report Darnell to the police.

I kept expecting him to interrupt me and tell me what he thought about me, but no insults were forthcoming. Carl's expression was unreadable.

Then I told him the part that might buy me some redemption. After talking to Vernon, I came up with a great idea. Didn't know why I hadn't considered it before, but it made so much sense.

"I've made an important decision today. I'm going to earmark half of my inheritance to help Harriet Hall students."

After a few seconds of silence, I got a response: "That's generous of you."

Carl's words were complimentary but his tone was cold.

"Maybe you'll give me some ideas about the best way to spend 2.5 million dollars."

I said the amount out loud for a reason. I wanted Carl to think about how much money it was, and all the good work that could be done with it. Maybe, just maybe, it could negate some of my dishonorable deeds.

"I'm sorry." His voice was so soft I had to strain to hear him. "But it isn't enough."

"What do you mean?"

Carl threw up his hands. "There isn't enough money in this world to make up for what you're doing. You saw what happened to Janey because of your laxness. What if her P.E. teacher hadn't reported her? She'd still be at her sister's house. Maybe she'd even be hooked on meth by now."

"No," I said, refusing to consider that possibility. "I would have eventually checked on her."

"It might have been too late. But that's only the beginning. You're also trading other teachers' safety for five million dollars. What if Darnell enrolls in another school and assaults someone else? Maybe this time he'll put a teacher in the hospital or even kill one. Would that be worth five million dollars to you?"

"Of course not, but—"

"But what?"

I opened my mouth, wishing some saving words would spring out. It didn't happen; there were no saving words.

"Thought so," Carl said.

"I can't do anything about Darnell. But Dr. Lipton will be leaving Harriet Hall after mid-year testing in January. After he does, I can stop falsifying my attendance records and grades."

Carl drew back, startled. "What do you mean, January? Lipton's not due to leave until the end of the year."

"He told me Dr. Scott's taking early retirement because of his wife's illness."

A wild look entered his eyes. "You didn't tell him anything about poker nights, did you?"

"No! What kind of person do you think I am?"

He was silent, too polite to answer the question honestly.

"Speaking of Lipton, you need to be careful. He's suspicious of you. He even told me I needed to break up with you if I wanted to keep my job."

Carl stiffened. "And how did you respond to that?"

I couldn't answer, couldn't bear to tell him that I hadn't yet made up my mind.

"I'm curious," Carl said, blinking rapidly. "What wouldn't you do for five million dollars? Where do you draw the line?"

"It's just until after mid-year testing. Then you and I—"

"I'm sorry, Toni Lee. There is no you and I anymore," he said quietly.

I watched him stride out of the room, my heart leaping in his direction. I wanted to chase after him, but I'd just make a fool of myself. The guy was done with me. He'd seen who I really was, with all my warts and blackheads, and decided he wanted nothing to do with me. Who could blame him?

Twenty Six

The morning after Carl dumped me I couldn't get out of bed. I was afraid to, terrified of myself and what kind of wild stunts I might pull if I were up and walking around. Chug Johnny Walker Black straight out of the bottle. Drink and dial every man in my address book. Spend the little bit of money I had on a decadent weekend at the Ritz Carlton in Atlanta.

Early that morning Lipton texted me with a question mark. I texted back: "It's over."

Later on in the afternoon my phone buzzed. For a second, my heart pulsed with hopefulness. *Carl, Carl, Carl!*

But it wasn't him. It was Jenny Simmons, reminding me of my promise to donate one of my old tennis racquets to the silent auction at the Spinsters' Ball, and could I please bring it over immediately. She called me a couple of times earlier in the week but I'd forgotten all about it.

"I'm feeling ill. Could I drop it off tomorrow?"

"The ball is tonight," she said brusquely. "I need it by seven p.m."

Around six-thirty I willed myself off the mattress. My whole body ached from lying in bed for hours. I padded to the bathroom and flung open the medicine cabinet seeking my Goody's Powder. My eye caught a prescription bottle of painkillers I'd gotten after a root canal in July. I hadn't taken a single pill because the label said in bold letters, "Do not mix with alcohol," and back then alcohol was like oxygen to me. In any case, if I ever needed a pill to blot out all my pain, mental and physical, it was now. I rattled out two pills into my palm and dry swallowed them.

The night was cold and starless, and the air was sharp with the smell of sulfur from the paper mill on the South side of town. I drove my Porsche to the Club, the site of the Spinsters' Ball. I got out of my car, and the muffled sound of the band drifted from the main ballroom.

A half dozen couples were filing into the building lit with gold fairy lights. The men strutted in tuxes, and the women floated in jewel-toned gowns that shimmered under the halogen streetlights.

I could feel the painkillers kicking in. A swell of wooziness pitched me forward, and I nearly stumbled. The pills were stronger that I thought. Best to drop off the racquet and get home as soon as possible.

I made my way to the entrance, occasionally careening, as if on the deck of a sailboat in rough waters.

Once inside I crab-walked past the coat check gal and the fifteen-foot Christmas tree festooned with hundreds of gold and silver balls and bows. "Jingle Bell Rock" played in the lobby.

On the way to the ballroom, Baby's huge face, big as the moon, zoomed into focus.

"Where's Jenny?" I waved my tennis racquet about.

"You trying to kill flies with that thing?" She looked me up and down. "What's wrong? Are you high *again*?"

"Meh," I said.

Damn. The pills were kicking my butt all over the place. Needed to find Jenny. I dragged a hand along my cheek. Face melting.

Took a step. Someone pulled the floor out from under me. *Bam.* On the ground.

"Toni Lee!"

Joelle stood over me. White-faced and far too skinny. Looked like she was being eaten up from the inside.

"She's plastered," Baby said. "Worse than Lois's funeral. If anyone's wearing a hat they'd better hang on to it."

Joelle's face came in closer. She wore an expression of concern. "Is this about your boyfriend?"

How could she possibly know about my split with Carl? I hadn't told a soul except for Lipton. Hadn't bothered to change my Facebook status to single.

"I saw it on the news earlier," she said. "Did you have any idea he was capable of something like that?"

I struggled to my feet. What was she talking about?

Trey manacled my arm, holding me upright.

"Time for somebody to go home. I'll get Toni Lee a cab. You and Baby go on in. I know you two promised to help supervise refreshments."

"Are you sure?" Joelle said. "She's pretty wasted. Maybe I should—"

"You have an obligation, Joelle," Trey said sternly. "I'll take good care of her."

Baby tugged on Joelle's arm. "Come on. Let's get out of here before she blows."

"But she's upset," Joelle said. "I can't just—"

"Go!" Trey said, as if he was addressing a golden retriever.

That's all it took. Joelle scurried off. Over her shoulder she said, "I'll call you later."

Stop, I wanted to yell. What were you saying about Carl? But she was gone, and Trey was dragging me down the hall, his fingers pressed cruelly into the tender underside of my arm.

I felt a swirl of cool air, and we were outside. The smell of grease and old garbage curled from a nearby dumpster. Clouds floated out of my mouth.

Trey's gray eyes bored into me, hard and cold like diamonds.

"What did I tell you about your boyfriend from the hood? What do you think of him now that he's shown who he really is?"

Before I could respond, he grabbed my shoulders and shoved me against the building. My skull banged against the bricks. He forced his tongue into my mouth, and squeezed my breasts as if checking for ripeness. I struggled to get loose from his grip. Finally he let go of me

"I was right." He wiped his lips with the back of his hand. "You are sullied."

He straightened his black bowtie and said, "Stay away from Joelle. Don't call her, and don't stop by to see her. She's going to be my wife, and doesn't need to hang around white trash like you."

I wanted to spit in his face but my mouth was too dry from the pain medication. He pinched my breast once more before going back inside. I remained flattened against the wall, wondering what Joelle and Trey had been talking about.

A door opened, and I cringed, thinking it might be Trey again. Instead it was someone in a white uniform.

"Toni Lee," said a familiar female voice. "Are you out here?"

"Yes." It came out more like "yeth." I was relieved to see Henry; maybe she could tell me what was going on with Carl.

She slowly approached me, head cocked, lips pursed in disappointment. "I saw Mr. Winston drag you out here. Are you drunk? You look terrible."

"Bad night." One of my shoes fell off, and I was trying to slip it back onto my foot.

"Is this about Carl? Are you upset because of what happened?"

"What is it?"

"You really don't know?" Now that she was closer I could see hollow, dark smudges beneath each eye. Whatever it was, it had to be awful. I'd never seen Henry look so stricken.

She let out a protracted exhale of air. "Carl's in jail."

"What?" I shook my head in denial. The movement stirred up everything in my skull.

"This morning a female student accused him of making sexual advances. She burst into his classroom and said he took her virginity in the field house. The whole floor heard her. Security was called; they interviewed the girl, and the girl's sister also confirmed the accusations. After that the police took my son away."

"Who?" Although I could make a pretty good guess.

"Someone named Rose Wyld."

I shook my head again, even though it made me dizzy. "She's lying."

"You don't think I know that? You don't have tell me what kind of man my son is."

"Gotta get him out." I fumbled with my bag, wanting to give her money, anything I had. I'd sell my soul, my body, my bone marrow. A couple of quarters spilled out. Some lint. An unwrapped Werther's caramel.

"His younger brother Mitt is working on bail money as we speak. He should be out by tomorrow morning."

I was listing to the left, and Henry uprighted me with a gentle shove to my shoulder. "I wish I could take you home, but we're too busy. This is one of the club's biggest events, and if I didn't show up tonight I'd have been fired. Come on. You need to sleep this off for a while."

She led me to the ladies' locker room and told me to lie down on the chaise lounge inside. I wanted to protest—how could I sleep while Carl was incarcerated?—but the painkillers in my system overruled my troubled mind. Reluctantly I stretched out on the chaise, and within moments I was asleep.

Later I woke up with a gasp. Where was I? Then it came back to me. I was at the Club and the Spinsters' Ball was going on above my head. The thump of the bass threatened to come through the ceiling. My mind was still muddy, but I wasn't as bad off as earlier. Henry had taken me down here and...

The memory came back like a slap across the face.

Carl.

Arrested.

Jail.

I forced myself up off the chaise. It'd been a humiliating night, and I was certainly the talk of the Spinsters' Ball. Someone might even call my aunt, but I couldn't think about that. Carl's troubles were foremost in my mind.

I left the locker room and headed to my car. I didn't want to go home, didn't trust myself there, what with a rack stocked with cheap wine and a closet full of party clothes. No telling what I might do to keep my pain at bay.

I drove ever so carefully to Tranquility Hall. My daddy was out of town as usual, on his annual holiday gambling junket to Atlantic City. Aunt Cornelia would be there. Not that she was a comfort, but she was all I had.

Twenty Seven

Tranquility Hall was dark and silent. Aunt Cornelia must have already turned in. I scribbled a note for her and left it by the teapot in the kitchen. Then I climbed the double-helix spiral staircase to the second floor where my childhood bedroom was located.

Daddy had changed nothing since I left. My mother had my bedroom professionally decorated before I was born. In the center of the room was a canopy bed with a lacquered gold-leaf finish headboard and billowy ivory curtains. They closed with the pull of a tasseled cord. Twin armoires stood like sentries on each side of the bed.

It was a room fit for a princess—in fact the material surrounding my bed looked as if it had been stolen from Princess Diana's taffeta wedding dress. Clearly my mother had been expecting a fairy-tale type of daughter and had been disappointed when she'd gotten me instead.

I'd never been comfortable in my bedroom. Many times when I was a kid I'd drag a Little Mermaid sleeping bag into the hallway and camp outside Daddy's bedroom.

But tonight the lilac-water scented linens looked especially inviting. I shed my clothes and crawled nude between the sheets, falling into a deep slumber.

Hours later I was jolted out of dreamland by my aunt's voice. "What's wrong with you? It's nearly noon and you're still in bed."

"Don't feel good." It was true; my eyelids weighed ten pounds each, and I felt boneless with exhaustion.

"I've gotten some calls. Is it true you were drunk last night?"

"Took painkillers I got from the dentist. Had no idea they had such a kick. You can see the bottle if you want."

I didn't care if she believed me or not. I was too exhausted.

Aunt Cornelia sniffed around my face. "I don't smell spirits." She pressed the palm of her hand on my forehead, her numerous rings cool against my skin. "You seem clammy. I'll check on you later."

Yes, later, I thought. When the thirteen-year cicadas return. Before I went back to sleep again, I texted Carl. Maybe he was out of jail by now.

I sunk into a foggy hibernation; hours passed without notice. Periodically I lurched to the bathroom, eyes closed, bumping into furniture, all in a dreamlike state. Now and then I heard Aunt Cornelia's voice, but it was faint and faraway like a distant train whistle.

I got caught up in a nightmare, trying to find Carl behind an endless series of silk curtains. I felt the covers being pulled away from my body. Desperately I grabbed them but they slipped through my fingers.

Aunt Cornelia stood over my bed, an apparition suspended in a haze of perfume. "Good. You're ready for your shower. After you're done, you're to come downstairs and eat something."

I curled into a fetal position. "No shower."

She tickled the sole of my foot. "Get in there now. I'm not leaving until you do. You've been sleeping for forty-eight hours."

Had it been that long? I checked my phone. No messages from Carl. I knew our relationship was over with, but it still seemed unnecessarily cruel to withhold information from me. I reluctantly abandoned my bed and crept to the bathroom. I showered, dressed, and went downstairs, my senses still muted.

My phone dinged. Someone had left me a voicemail.

"This is Henry. Got your number from Carl. He's home now, and we've secured one of the best attorneys in the state. Deena and Katherine came down from Atlanta to be with him. Sounds like they might be rethinking the divorce. It's best for everyone if you leave him alone."

The next few days I sat in the den at Tranquility Hall, watching TV. No horror movies. I'd lost my stomach for knife-wielding fiends. It didn't matter what was on; it was background noise.

One morning my Aunt Cornelia blocked my view of a Proactiv acne treatment infomercial.

"This isn't normal. What's the matter with you? You need to tell me."

"I'm tired. Teaching takes a lot out of a person." I craned my neck to see around her.

"This is more serious than being tired. You haven't talked to a soul since you've been here. I assume you're planning on going to Joelle's house for Christmas as usual?"

"Not this year. She'll be with her fiancé."

"What about that fellow of yours? Carl?"

I didn't respond.

"I asked you a question."

"We're taking a break," I muttered. Cornelia had no interest in Rose Hill news so she certainly hadn't heard about Carl's arrest.

"Now we're getting somewhere."

"What?"

"It's obvious you're suffering from a broken heart."

"No." My voice was as faint as a fly buzzing under a Mason jar. "Don't feel a thing."

"This lolling about won't helping matters." She clapped her hands together. "I'm sending my assistants home, and I'm taking the rest of the day off. It's Christmas Eve. You and I are going to celebrate the holidays."

I wouldn't have been more surprised if she'd suggested nude hang gliding.

"You always work during the holidays," I said.

"Not this year. Get your coat."

*   *   *

Our first stop was the mall. It was riotous with holiday decorations: multicolored lights blinking, tinsel twinkling, and strung ornaments twirling.

Cornelia lamented the lack of a Saks Fifth Avenue or a Nordstrom's in the Rose Hill Mall. "Dillard's will have to do," she said.

She picked out Christmas sweaters for us to wear, saying, "If we want to get into the spirit of the season, we need to dress the part." After the mall, we stopped at the grocery store for cookie making supplies.

When we got home, Aunt Cornelia put on Bing Crosby's "White Christmas" and suggested we don our new sweaters.

Her sweater was appliquéd with Rudolph. The nose lit up. My glittery snowman sweater was every bit as tacky. If you poked his stomach, it played, "Frosty the Snowman."

"Time to bake the cookies," she said.

At first, she seemed relaxed, singing along to the Christmas music, periodically saying, "Isn't this festive?" But as the task wore on, she got more intense about it. Batter had never been beaten so hard; dough had to do her bidding or risk being tossed in the garbage disposal. An hour into baking, she was barking orders at me. "More sprinkles on those cookies. Silver balls not gold. You call that a candy cane?"

I couldn't take it anymore. I pushed away a bowl of cookie dough. "Maybe you should do this yourself."

"What do you mean?" She swiped at her flour-dusted nose. "I'm doing this for *you*."

"Then we should stop. I feel like I'm being held prisoner in a cookie sweatshop."

I thought Cornelia was going to get mad. Instead she dropped the cookie cutter she was holding and said, "I'm sorry."

"Excuse me?" I wondered if I'd heard her correctly. My aunt was not one to casually throw around apologies.

"I didn't mean to get all worked up," she said. "I've always had trouble letting my hair down. Your mother used to make fun of me all the time. She was the only one who could loosen me up."

I had to stop myself from rolling my eyes. My daddy and my aunt were continually describing jolly versions of my mother. I didn't believe a word.

"You reminded me of Nina when you said the thing about the sweatshop. She always thought I worked too hard."

The topic of my mother made me want to flee the room. "I know you must miss her," I said quickly. I picked up a spoon and returned to beating the cookie dough.

"Especially this time of year, and not just because she died right after Christmas. Your mother was wild for Christmas. Decorating, parties, picking out the perfect gifts for everyone, the whole shebang. This house was lit up like Las Vegas during the holidays."

And now it's not even decorated anymore, I thought. Christmas at Tranquility Hall died with my mother. After she was gone, my aunt and Dad tried to celebrate for my sake. They hired people to decorate the house, bought me piles of toys, and instructed my nanny to take me to see Santa Claus, a one-time occurrence because I peed on his lap.

It was a relief for both of them when I started spending the holidays with Joelle's family. After that, except for buying me a few gifts, they'd given up on Christmas altogether.

"Once you were born, your mother got even more Christmas-crazy," Cornelia said. "She was like a little kid. Playing on the floor with you. Having the time of her life."

That story seemed about as probable as tales of unicorns and mermaids. Either my aunt was lying or my mother was a master at hiding her true feelings about me.

After the cookie-baking flop, I assumed Aunt Cornelia would give up trying to cheer me up, but later that evening, she announced we were watching a movie together. I wasn't used to her wanting to spend so much time with me. It was unnerving.

*   *   *

"We're watching *The Way We Were*. It's a favorite of mine. Have you ever seen it?"

"Is it in black and white?"

"Color, silly," she said. She dimmed the lights in the den and placed a jumbo box of Puffs on the coffee table. "You'll be needing tissues. It's a tear jerker."

Not me, I thought. If I couldn't cry over Carl, why would I cry over actors playing parts?

During the film Cornelia kept reaching for the tissues, dabbing at her eyes. She didn't cry quite enough to smear her mascara. The movie was entertaining. Robert Redford looked like an airbrushed version of Owen Wilson. Barbra Streisand was lithe and sexy. No sign of those caftans she'd worn in *Meet the Fockers*.

After the credits rolled, Cornelia scrutinized me and said, "I can't believe it. Not a single tear. Everyone cries during *The Way We Were*."

I shrugged.

"When's the last time you had a nice, long boo-hoo session?"

"I don't remember."

She plunked the tissue box on my lap. "Give it a try. You'll feel better. If I can cry now and then, so can you. Nothing to be ashamed of, so long as you don't make a spectacle of yourself."

"I'm not ashamed. I just can't."

"Why not?"

"My tear ducts have seized up."

"That doesn't make any sense."

"No. It's true. And..."

"What?"

"Never mind."

"Go on."

"My mother hated it when I cried." I surprised myself by saying that last bit; I plucked a tissue from the box and tore it into small pieces.

"Where did you get that notion?"

"I just know."

"That's nonsense. I've never heard of such a thing."

Was it my imagination or was she protesting too much? Whichever the case, I was tired of tiptoeing around the issue of my mother.

"I'm sorry, Aunt Cornelia. I know you loved your sister very much, but we both know she wasn't happy being my mother."

"Why would you say such a thing?"

I'd started down the path. Might as well spill all.

"I found her diary. She wrote she didn't love me and that I was a terrible child and she wished she'd never had me. She said that her life had been perfect until I came along."

There. I'd said it. I could still see my mother's cramped handwriting on the page. She'd used a fine point black marker. It was as if she'd wanted her words to be indelible. Sometimes her pen had even gouged holes in the paper.

Two spots of color burned in Cornelia's cheeks. "You're wrong. Nina loved you as much as any mother could love a child."

"Don't bother trying to deny it. I still have the diary. I can show it to you."

I knew it backward and forward; my mother's words had worn deep, painful grooves into my memory. I would never forget them.

Silence stretched between my aunt and me. What could she say now that I'd thrown the facts in her face?

She coughed a couple of times before she spoke. "I'm very sorry you found that diary. It should have been tossed in the garbage. There was no reason for you to have ever read it."

"But I did." It was a relief to speak of my mother's true feelings, to quit pretending I'd ever been a cherished daughter.

"Your mother wasn't herself when she kept that journal."

"Maybe you need to read it."

"I don't need to. I can imagine what it said. You have heard of post-partum depression, haven't you?"

"What?"

"PPD. It's frequently in the news. When you were a child there was much less known about it. People called it the baby blues. Your mother had a bad case. Wouldn't get out of bed for about over a month, refused to care for you. But over time, the depression lifted, and she was her old self again."

I thought about all the things my mother had written. The venomous tone. The word "hate" in big, block letters. How could they not be her real feelings?

"Why didn't you tell me about this before?"

"Your father and I never saw a reason to tell you about it. You were a baby when it happened. You couldn't have possibly remembered it. I don't know why you didn't come to me with this when you first found the diary."

"I was afraid."

"Why?"

"I don't know."

Actually I did know. First of all, Cornelia and Daddy adored my mother. Who was I to be badmouthing her? Certainly they'd be upset if I tainted her memory. There was also one another reason: I'd feared my mother had a very good reason not to like me. That I was not a lovable child.

After reading that diary, I'd drifted through my early elementary years, ducking my head, cowering in the back row, speaking in a near whisper. I was too shy to interact with others except for my best friend Joelle. My first tennis lessons changed all that. Suddenly I had something to feel good about. But then I got injured.

The PPD explanation wasn't enough for me. How could I be sure what came first, my mother's distaste for me or her depression? Maybe the former had caused the latter and even when my mother got better, she may have resented me. Regardless, there was nothing my aunt could say that would convince me my mother had loved me.

Twenty Eight

The day after Christmas, I called Doc, hoping he'd pass on a message to Carl. What I had to say wouldn't change anything between us, but I still wanted him to know it.

When I got Doc on the phone, we initially discussed Carl's legal troubles and how absurd it was that an upstanding guy like him been accused of sleeping with a student.

"There's not a male teacher in this world who doesn't worry about that kind of accusation," Doc said. "In most cases it's your word against the student's. Even if you're cleared of all charges, you still have a dark cloud hanging over your career."

Doc hadn't spoken with Carl since his arrest and wanted to know if I had any news. "I've tried to call him a few times but he hasn't gotten back with me," he said.

"I haven't heard from him either." I told Doc we'd broken up the day before his arrest.

"Sorry to hear that. You two made a sweet couple," Doc said.

"Thank you," I said softly. I went silent, gathering up my strength for what I was about to say next.

"Toni Lee. You there?"

"Yes, I'm sorry. Listen, there's something I need to tell you about what's going on with Dr. Lipton and me."

I told him I knew about the "poker games," but promised I'd never tell a soul. I went on to discuss my arrangement with Dr. Lipton concerning mid-year testing and how he threatened my job if I didn't go along.

"I agreed to help him cheat. But I've done a lot of thinking over the last few days and..."

I took a deep breath. *Could I say it?* If I did, there was no going back.

"Toni Lee?"

"I've changed my mind." The words flew out of my mouth in a great rush. "I'm not going to help Dr. Lipton cheat."

Doc was quiet for a minute. Finally he said, "Good for you. I'm proud of you."

"I won't be telling Dr. Lipton about my decision, of course. Otherwise he'll just recruit another teacher to help him."

"You do know what's going to happen when the test results come back and they aren't as high as Dr. Lipton expected, right?"

I leaned against the kitchen counter for support, still floored by the enormity of what I'd just done. "He'll fire me, but I don't care anymore...Anyway, I wanted you and the other teachers who meet for poker nights to be aware of my decision."

"Thanks. If we could just find one more teacher who Lipton has tried to strong-arm, we could get the superintendent to listen to us. Truth is, he and Lipton used to be fraternity brothers and the two of them are pretty tight. You don't know of any other teachers who are helping Lipton, do you?"

"No, sorry. There is one more thing though..."

"Yes?"

"If you do talk to Carl, will you tell him about my decision? I just wanted him to know that, in the end, I did the right thing."

"Sure thing. Be glad to."

When our conversation ended, I glanced out the window. The sky was winter white. A single crow perched on the bare branch of a dogwood tree. It was so quiet in my house I could hear the wind nudging against the windowpanes.

I'd done it.

I'd declared my intention to give up the money.

I didn't have to do it. Carl was lost to me for good. Unless they could find another teacher to finger Lipton, he was going to be the next superintendent. Some people would have simply proctored the tests and collected the money at the end of the year. No harm. No foul.

I sat motionless, awaiting a sickening feeling of regret but it never happened. Instead an unfamiliar feeling of freedom swept over me. I might be a pauper on the verge of losing my low-paying job, but I wasn't beholden to anyone. For the first time ever, I felt like my life belonged to me and me alone.

Twenty Nine

The holidays coughed up their last bit of tinsel, and I spent New Year's Eve with my aunt, drinking melon mocktails and watching the countdown in Times Square. We talked a little bit about my daddy; Cornelia claimed he was acting weird.

"How so?"

"He hasn't asked me for extra money in weeks."

"That's a good thing. Right?"

"Maybe. But also odd."

She wanted to talk about my mother more, but I pleaded with her to stop. I said it was something I'd have to figure out on my own. To my surprise, she listened to me. Maybe she sensed the conviction in my voice.

I almost told her I was going to get fired, but decided to wait. Maybe some kind of miracle would happen. Dr. Lipton would hit his head and lose his memory. Maybe the "poker players" would get enough evidence on him to get the principal sacked. One could only hope.

On January second, the long, tumultuous holiday break was over, and it was time to drag my sadder-but-wiser self back to school. I actually looked forward to seeing my students. Unfortunately the reunion was bound to be bittersweet, considering I was on my way out as their teacher. Mid-year testing was only a week away, and I'd been told results would come back within a month.

I also hated to think about Carl's absence from the halls of Harriet Hall. How was I going to endure it?

I arrived at the school ten minutes before the first bell and on the way to my room, I ran into a few of my colleagues. Everyone seemed a little sober and subdued, as if they'd been rudely roused from an eggnog and fruitcake daze and couldn't quite believe the party was over. I was stowing my purse in my supply closet when Mule Jordan, the security guard, stuck his bullet-shaped head into my room.

"You ready for the rabble?" I said with a smile. "Hopefully the students won't be too hyped up after the holidays."

Mule filled up the doorway. He was as broad-shouldered and muscular as a bull but his brown eyes were soft. His manner was courteous.

"Hate to be the bearer of bad news, ma'am, but Dr. Lipton has asked me to tell you to clean out your desk and escort you off school property. He says your services are no longer needed at Harriet Hall."

I blinked several times, confused. "I don't understand."

"Let me put it more bluntly. You've been dismissed, and you need to leave the grounds."

"Did I do something wrong? What did Dr. Lipton say?"

"Sorry, ma'am. He didn't tell me any of that."

"I'll just have to speak with him myself then." I headed toward the door.

Mule blocked my path, his chest wide as a baby grand piano. I'd always thought of him as a gentle giant but, at that moment, I could imagine him strong-arming me.

"Please start clearing out your desk, Ms. Wells. And I'll also be requiring your key."

I was completely befuddled. Lipton needed me. Why would he fire me? It made no sense. Mule shot me an impatient look so I promptly gathered up a few personal items from the desk and slipped my room key off the chain.

I grabbed my purse, a box of my stuff, and my motorcycle helmet and followed Mule down the stairs. When we reached the first-floor hallway, I saw Doc striding in our direction, wearing a striped sweater with plaid pants. He looked like a walking optical illusion. When he spotted us, he immediately turned and scuttled the other way.

"Doc. Where are you going?"

Instead of stopping he quickened his pace.

"I know you can hear me," I called after him.

Doc broke into a run.

"Traitor!" I yelled and started to sprint after him.

Mule trotted behind me and grabbed my arm before I could get far. "Ms. Wells. You're coming with me. And no more outbursts."

"But I—"

His grip got firmer, and I knew I wasn't going to be allowed to confront Doc. Mule was obviously experienced at excising Dr. Lipton's enemies. He guided me to the side door and out to the faculty parking lot. In the distance, the high-rise projects rose up like gray ghosts against a milky sky.

"You can't return to the campus for any reason," Mule said to me as I put on my helmet. "If you do, you'll be considered a trespasser."

He waited until I was on the bike and the motor was rumbling. Then he loped back to the main building. I gunned the engine and shot out of the Harriet Hall parking lot.

At home I paced my tiny condo, desperate to act, but not knowing what I could do. Lipton was protected by Mule; Doc was unreachable and obviously a spy for Lipton. I wondered what Doc had told Lipton about Carl's role in the poker game. Was Carl aware that his old friend Doc was a turncoat? I knew I wasn't supposed to contact Carl again but I didn't have a choice. I picked up my phone, my fingers flying as I texted him. "Call me," I typed. "Emergency."

A few minutes later my phone rang. I choked out a hello, expecting to hear Carl's familiar baritone. Instead the voice on the other end was high-pitched and extremely pissed off.

"Leave my husband alone," Ms. Sprague said. "He doesn't want to talk to you, he doesn't want texts from you, and he definitely doesn't ever want to see your skanky self again. In fact he hates the sight of you and wishes he'd never met you. You got that?"

"Ms. Sprague, I'm sorry to bother you, but I really need to—"

Click.

I stood motionless for a moment, reeling from her nasty comments, especially the part about Carl hating me. That didn't stop me from trying again. I pressed "Return Call." It rang several times, and then it was picked up.

"Listen, Deena. I *have* to speak with Carl. It's—"

WOOOOOOOOOOT!

My ears rang, and I threw down the phone, the battery popping out as it hit the floor. Ms. Sprague had blown a whistle directly into the phone receiver. I wandered around the house rubbing my stinging ear, wondering if she'd punctured my eardrum.

Now what? Carl didn't do Facebook, Twitter, or even Tumblr. He did have an email account, but he and I never emailed each other so I didn't know his address. Doc surely had it, but it's not like I was in a position to ask him. Then I remembered I'd recently received a group email from Doc. He was one of those people who was always sending out alarming warnings about computer viruses, phone scams, and other questionable information. Maybe Carl's email was on that list. Unless, of course, Doc had blind copied everyone.

I sat on my couch with my laptop and opened Doc's latest email. It cautioned against street gangs who were depositing a mixture of LSD and strychnine on elevator buttons. Unfortunately, the recipients were not disclosed. I also noticed I'd gotten an email from Harriet Hall High School, which wasn't unusual. The new secretary periodically sent out school news to everyone on faculty and staff. The subject line read: "Miss Harriet Hall contestants announced."

I frowned at the mention of the pageant; it, after all, was the primary cause of Carl's troubles. I scrolled through the list, not recognizing any of the names, until I got to the last one. *Rose Wyld.* That didn't make sense. I knew she didn't have the grades to be in the pageant, so why was she listed?

My doorbell rang, and when I peered out the peephole I had to squint to make sure I wasn't seeing a mirage. Joelle stood behind the door. I hadn't heard from her since the night of the Spinsters' Ball, even though she told me she'd call. I guessed Trey had ordered her not to.

I opened the door and could tell immediately that something was wrong. Her face was the color of eggshells, and she looked frail, as if the mildest of squalls could topple her over.

"Thanks for letting me in. If I were you, I'd have sicced my Doberman Pinscher on me."

"Lucky for you I don't have a Doberman Pinscher. Just a fake ficus, and it's pretty tame."

I ushered her into my living room. Neither of us spoke as we sat across from each other.

Joelle, eyes hazy with tears, broke the silence. "You were right. I should have listened to you."

She was inviting me to gloat, but I had no desire to do so. I was just relieved she'd come to her senses.

"It's over, I take it?"

Joelle nodded, shaky with tears. She fumbled in her purse for a tissue. "It all started when he refused to go to my family's for New Year's Eve."

The Posey family New Year's dinner was an annual holiday tradition, and up until this year, I was always invited. Joelle's brothers and cousins attended, and the table was covered with every Southern dish imaginable from collards to Johnny cakes to fried catfish. In the corner of the kitchen, a pony keg of PBR was set up, and old-school country music stars like George Jones and Loretta Lynn crooned from a scratchy seventies-era stereo. I looked forward to it every year.

"Trey's never liked my family," Joelle said. "I'd listen to him badmouth them and never said a word in their defense. Talk about being brainwashed."

More tears came, and she sniffed into a wad of tissue.

"He wanted me to go to his parents' house and have oyster stew and champagne. I probably would have blown off my family, except Jimbo and his wife were bringing their new baby. Well, I just had to see little Calvin."

"Of course." Joelle was mad for children; she'd make a great mother one day.

"I kept nagging Trey, saying we only had to stay for half an hour or so, and I guess he got tired of me asking, because he hit me." She gingerly lifted her sweater to reveal a lurid blue bruise on her belly.

"Oh my God."

She shuddered. "That's not the worst of it. Trey's used me for a punching bag before. No one knew. He pummeled me in places where the bruises wouldn't show. Afterwards he'd always apologize and buy me something. You saw all that jewelry I was getting. Well, my hide paid for every damn piece."

"I can't believe this," I said. But I could. Hadn't I gotten a taste of Trey's brutal nature?

"I kept hoping he'd stop after we were married or when he opened the new business in Atlanta and was feeling less stressed out. That's why I've been dodging you. I knew you'd figure out something was wrong, and I wasn't ready to let him go."

I remembered how stiff she'd been the day of our lunch. That jerk! I could kill him.

"I didn't tell anyone what was happening. Most times he'd just knock the wind out of me. Occasionally I'd have to lie down afterwards. Honestly I started getting used to the pain." Her eyes glazed over; her chin trembled. "But this last time was different. This time was the worst."

"Why?" I said, dreading the answer. Had he done some kind of permanent damage?

"I was pregnant. And I lost the baby."

I was so stunned for a moment I couldn't speak. "Oh, Joelle," I said finally. "I am so sorry. So very, very sorry." I hugged her fiercely.

She was crying. "It's my fault. I should have left him before it happened, but I didn't."

"It's okay," I kept repeating, but I knew it wouldn't be okay. Not for a long while.

Joelle spent the night with me in my bed and spoke of the baby she'd lost. She hadn't known the gender, but she'd felt certain that the child had been a girl.

"I dreamt about her," she whispered, hugging a pillow to her chest. "She had long, dark ringlets, and she wanted to be a ballet dancer. Her favorite color was orange."

I knew without asking that her name would be Lacey; Joelle had loved that name as long as I could remember.

"I'd already bought her something," Joelle said in a faltering voice. "Pink marabou slippers only a little bigger than my thumb, and zebra jammies."

Joelle continued with her story. After Trey hit her, she'd had a miscarriage within the hour. As soon as Joelle was able, she'd called the police and he'd been arrested. Unfortunately he was already out on bail.

"Do you think he'll try to retaliate in some way?" I said.

"Not if my brothers have anything to do with it. They had a come-to-Jesus chat with Trey. I don't think he'll be bothering me anymore."

Joelle's brothers would beat up anyone who looked at their sister cross-eyed. Trey was lucky he wasn't at the bottom of the Savannah River, communing with the catfish.

She kept apologizing for uninviting me to the wedding, for abandoning me at the Spinsters' Ball, and neglecting to check on me afterward.

"The only thing I cared about was being Ms. Trey Winston.

Can you ever forgive me? I don't blame you if you can't."

It was easy to forgive her. Not just because I loved her but also because we had so much in common. Up until a few days ago, I, too, had been obsessed with one thing: a five million dollar payday.

"Of course I forgive you."

I proceeded to tell her all of the events that had been going on in my life for the last few weeks, including my aunt's offer and how I'd been fired and wouldn't receive my inheritance. We also discussed my upset over Carl's predicament. There was something else I wanted to tell her—a secret I'd been harboring for a few days—but I decided it could wait for another time.

The next morning I woke up, feeling the warmth of another body snuggled up to me. For a millisecond I thought Carl was beside me in my bed. Then I heard Joelle's distinctive snore.

I left the bed and tiptoed around in the kitchen, preparing breakfast. Joelle came out of the bedroom cursing, which wasn't a cause for concern. That's the way she generally woke up, and I took it as a good sign. If she had a few f-words in her, she couldn't be too bad off. Still, I knew she had plenty of healing time ahead of her.

For Christmas Aunt Cornelia had given me a book on grief. It first spoke of the various stages a person had to suffer through before they healed from a loss. It was a roundabout journey. You might think you've conquered denial and graduated to anger, only to find yourself shoved back into shock. It seemed unfair, like a game of Sorry when someone landed on your space and made you start all over again.

Joelle slumped at the breakfast nook, and I presented her with a copy of the *Rose Hill Courier*, a cup of black coffee, and a short stack of buttermilk pancakes.

"I expect you to eat every bite, young lady. You're a stick."

She probed a pancake with her fork. "When did IHOP start delivering?"

"They don't. I made those pancakes."

"You cooked something? With your own two hands?"

"You bet."

Since I couldn't afford to eat out all the time and because Carl's cooking was often suspect, I'd learned how to make a few select dishes. I wouldn't be tackling paella or whipping up a béchamel sauce anytime soon. But with the help of Bisquick and Aunt Jemima, I could serve up a few flapjacks.

Joelle ventured a small bite. "Not half bad. Never thought I'd see the day." She took an even larger bite. "What are you up to today, now that you're not working?"

"Something very important."

I'd been obsessing over Rose Wyld, wondering how she'd been chosen as a candidate for Miss Harriet Hall. Dr. Lipton had final say on who got into the pageant. In light of Carl's arrest, it was possible the principal had decided not to count the F grade on Rose's transcript, but I suspected he may have done something even worse.

I planned to visit Rose and pressure her to change her mind about Carl. I didn't know if I could sway her, but I was going to give it my all. Over breakfast, I told Joelle what I intended to do.

"You shouldn't go by yourself," Joelle said. "I'll come with you."

Thirty

I'd gotten Rose Wyld's address from the Harriet Hall database. She lived a few blocks away from the school in an elderly bungalow with dingy yellow siding and crooked shutters. Burglar bars striped the front windows and a "Beware of Dog" sign was planted in the tiny yard. Joelle parked across the street, and we approached the house, frozen grass crunching beneath our feet. A cold front had blown into town overnight, and the temperature was only thirty degrees. The sun was out, but it might as well have been Jupiter for all the warmth it gave.

When I rang the doorbell, a dog let out a couple of deep-throated barks and heavy footsteps approached. The front door flung open and the smell of bacon drifted out. Inside, a scowling woman with several nose piercings loomed. Her teddy-bear patterned medical smock looked at odds with her ominous glare.

"Who are you?"

"May I speak with Rose for a moment, please?"

The scowl got darker. Hands planted on hips wide as a Volkswagen Beetle's bumper. "What for?"

"I'm an acquaintance of hers."

She gave me and Joelle a onceover. "Rose don't know any white folk. You people need to leave her be."

Sounded as if I wasn't the first to try and talk Rose out of her accusations. I wondered who else might have been around.

"Is she inside?" I inched toward the door. "It'll only take a sec."

"Didn't you hear me?" The woman was so close to me I could

smell a cool blast of peppermint on her breath. "She doesn't want to talk to you or anyone else."

"Please. It's a life-and-death matter."

"No." She shoved me so strenuously I nearly lost my footing. Then she slammed the door.

Joelle rushed to my side. "You okay?"

"Fine. Let's go back to the car."

When we reached Joelle's Toyota Corolla, I said, "Drive up a few yards away and let's wait a bit."

"What for?"

"That woman was wearing a medical smock. I have a feeling she's about to leave for work."

"Maybe she just got home. Hospital people keep odd hours. We could be sitting here until the streetlights come on."

"I don't think so. She looked too fresh for having just come off a shift. And I smelled toothpaste on her breath."

Joelle moved the car, and we waited inside with the heater blasting over our laps. We didn't talk much. My friend had been quiet most of the morning, and whenever she did speak she was short, which was understandable after all she'd been through. The fogged-up window squeaked as I wrote Carl's name in the condensation with my finger.

We spotted Rose's sister, bundled up in a yellow down jacket that made her look like Big Bird. She lumbered out the door and headed in the direction of the bus stop. When she was out of sight, I got out of the car.

Joelle cut off the engine. "How are you going to get Rose to answer the door?"

In the past I might have tried to bribe her by waving a twenty-dollar bill in front of the peephole, saying, "Andrew Jackson would like to have a word with you." If Andrew didn't sway her, I'd enlist the help of Benjamin Franklin. That sort of tactic now seemed cheesy and just plain wrong.

"I'm going to talk to her. I don't know exactly what I'll say but—"

"That's a terrible plan. Sounds like you haven't thought it through."

"Will you just trust me for once?" I said.

Joelle looked skeptical, but she didn't protest.

When we left the car the street was quiet except for a nearby train clacking across the rails. No one was out and about. It was too damn cold.

We returned to Rose's house. I knocked on the door, the wood frigid against my bare knuckles. There was the sound of footsteps, followed by a high, childlike voice: "Go away. I don't want to talk to you."

"It'll only take a minute," I shouted through the door.

I told her who I was, and why I was there. I asked if we could please talk about the situation for a minute. No pressure, just a little confab.

I heard the locks turning and gave Joelle a triumphant thumbs-up. I hadn't expected such an easy victory. The door swung open and a leggy, spotted shorthaired dog bounded out. It knocked me to the ground and pounced on my chest, snarling and spewing doggie breath, hot and rancid, into my face. I fully expected it to rip into my jugular, but at the last moment, its owner yanked the beast away.

Joelle rushed over to me and knelt beside me. "Are you all right?" She glanced up at Rose as she helped me up off the ground. "What the hell's wrong with you? Take that beast inside. She's pregnant, for God's sake!"

A shameful look crossed Rose's face. "I'm really sorry. I only meant for Brutus to scare her."

Brutus was still growling and snapping at the air inches away from my leg. Rose guided the dog inside, murmuring softly to it. When she closed the door, claws frantically scratched at the wood, and the creature let out a forlorn howl.

I shot Joelle an incredulous look. "How did you know?"

"The half-dozen pregnancy tests in the trash can were my first clue. Why didn't you tell me?"

"I wanted to, but I wasn't sure how you'd take it after everything that's happened."

Joelle refused to look at me.

"You're upset, aren't you? I was afraid of that. I'm really sorry."

"It's fine. You have to do what's best for you, but I hope you understand that I refuse to go with you."

"Go where?"

"You know where." She lowered her voice. "The clinic."

"What clinic? Wait. Did you think I was...? Good God, no. I'm *keeping* the baby."

Joelle's eyes brightened. "You are? I just thought...I mean, you've never shown even the tiniest interest in kids, and you and Carl aren't together anymore, so I figured—"

It was true I'd briefly considered other options and for all the reasons Joelle mentioned, but I knew I'd regret it always. It was time for me to take responsibility for my actions.

"I want this baby. More than anything."

Joelle reached out to touch my still-flat belly. "I'll be damned."

"So you're not upset?"

"Are you nuts? I'm thrilled. I can't believe it. I'm going to be a..." Her forehead bunched. "What am I going to be?"

"A godmother!"

She squealed and gave me a hug. "When are you going to tell Carl?"

"I don't know."

I was waffling over whether to tell him or not. He was a man of integrity, and would insist on owning up to his responsibility. Not that he'd marry me, but he'd definitely want to be involved and pay child support. That would mess things up with Deena, and I only wanted Carl to be happy. Having a baby with a woman he didn't love would make him miserable, and I'd already made him miserable enough.

"One baby lost but another baby found," Joelle said,

thoughtfully. "Sounds weird but it's almost like the universe is correcting itself...And, of course, you're going to need my help every step of the way."

The front door opened, and Rose came out carrying a mug, which was a shock. I assumed she was done with us.

"I brought you some herbal tea. My sister drinks it when she's feeling poorly. I hope the baby's okay."

"Thank you," I said, taking the warm mug.

"Who's the daddy?" she asked. Rose's voluptuous body was squeezed into a tight acrylic sweater and jeans. The combination of her womanly curves and her world-weary eyes made her look years older than sixteen. The only thing that gave her youth away was a soft pad of puppy fat clinging to her chin.

"Carl. I mean, Mr. Rutherford, but that's our secret." It was safe telling Rose. I couldn't imagine she'd be having any further conversations with Carl.

She pushed up the sleeve of her sweater and scratched a dry patch on her elbow. "That's too bad."

"It is. Because my baby's father will be in jail."

Rose flinched.

"But if Mr. Rutherford had sexual relations with you, that's where he belongs. Even though I love him very much, I'd be the first to say that."

Rose stared down at the stoop, the toe of her tennis shoe tracing a fissure in the concrete. At least she hadn't gone back inside yet; I took that as an invitation to say more. Just speak from the heart, I thought. Trust that the right words will come.

"On the other hand, if you're not telling the truth, and Mr. Rutherford goes to jail, it's going to hurt a lot of people. Not just Mr. Rutherford, but his mother, his brother, his daughter Katherine who's only five, and all his students who believed in him and trusted him. But out of all those people, there's one person who'll hurt more than anyone else. Any idea who that might be?"

She didn't answer, but I noticed a slight tightening in her cheek muscles.

"You, Rose. Because if you lied about Mr. Rutherford in order to be in the Miss Harriet Hall pageant and if you win, you'll never enjoy it. You'll always know you sacrificed people's happiness for it. That'll eat away at you for years, long after the pageant is over."

It occurred to me that I could have given myself the very same lecture. Hadn't I sacrificed people's happiness for money?

I waited for her to say something but she still didn't speak. I kept quiet for a few moments to let her mull over the matter and then I said this, "If you look me in the eye and tell me Mr. Rutherford seduced you, I'll accept that and be on my merry way. Does that sound fair to you?"

Rose lifted her head; she kept blinking as if she were on the verge of tears. She looked so pitiful I honestly thought a small miracle was going to occur, and she was going to take back her accusations against Carl. Rose parted her lips as if to speak, paused a moment, and then abruptly pivoted and bolted back inside the house.

"Damn. I honestly I thought you'd convinced her," Joelle said.

I kept looking longingly at the closed door, wishing it would open again, but nothing happened. I'd lost her for good.

Joelle gave me a look of awe. "You were good with her. How is it you changed so much and I haven't even noticed? My guess is you're a great teacher, and will also be a wonderful mother."

"Thank you." It was the nicest compliment she'd ever given me. "Let me just try one more thing."

I dug out a piece of paper and scribbled my phone number, address, and email on a card. "Just in case you change your mind," I wrote. Then I pushed it through the mail slot in the front door.

Later, I stopped by a florist to purchase a dozen red American Beauty roses and drove to Westwood Hills Cemetery, located only a few blocks from the Rose Hill Country Club.

I parked my Porsche and strolled along the meandering stone path that cut through the gravesites. It wasn't the best day to be outdoors. Fog slunk eerily around the headstones, and a damp coldness soaked through my wool coat. I ducked my head against the chill and continued to walk until I reached my mother's grave.

My father used to take me every January third, the anniversary of her death, and I hated to visit. I always feared my mom would do something supernatural like conjure up a breeze to toss pebbles in my face or summon hail from the heavens to pelt me on my head.

I gently laid the roses on her grave. "It's Toni Lee," I said softly.

I'd never talked to her before at her gravesite, but over the next half-hour, I made up for it. I told her about finding the diary, and how I'd always felt like I was somehow defective because she didn't love me. I also told her that lately I'd been feeling better about myself, which was bizarre. Except for the baby, my life was like a wrecked Cadillac, smoking at the bottom of a ravine.

"It'd be nice if you gave me a sign you loved me."

I knew my request was silly and unrealistic, but it didn't matter because I was talking to a granite stone.

"Maybe you could make it rain rose petals or have a bird alight on my shoulder? It doesn't even have to be that showy. I'd even take a house fly landing on my hand."

I sat on a stone bench beside her grave, waiting for at least ten minutes, shivering and watching my breath mingle with the fog.

Nothing happened, of course. I didn't know what I'd expected.

"Toni Lee?"

I looked up. My daddy stood at my mother's gravesite with his own bouquet of roses; his were yellow.

"When did you get home?" I said.

"Too late last night to call. Surprised to see you here."

I shrugged.

My daddy picked up a couple of twigs and leaves from my mother's grave and laid his flowers next to mine. "Corny told me about the diary. I'm really sorry. Wish you would have said something to me. I could have cleared this up a long time ago."

No, you couldn't, I thought. I'd have been even more skeptical of my father's reassurances than I was of Aunt Cornelia's. No one could really clear it up except for my mother, and she wasn't able to talk.

I spread my arms wide to hug him in his bulky ski jacket. "Glad you're back. Hope your trip to Atlantic City was fun. Did you lose much?"

"Not this trip. Corny said the two of you spent time together. Never known her to goof off during the holidays; she always thinks the planet would spin off its axis if she isn't around to hold it up. Maybe she's getting a little mellower in her dotage."

"Maybe."

Since Christmas Cornelia had seemed slightly less strident. Even her platinum pageboy wasn't cut quite as sharply.

"I'm glad I ran into you here. There's something I need to tell you. I'm making some changes in my life. The biggest one is....uh...well, I'm getting married."

"What? I didn't even know you were dating anyone. Who is it?"

My daddy stomped his feet to keep warm. "Her name's Maureen, and she's a blackjack dealer in Jersey."

"A dealer? Do you think that's a good idea? I mean, gambling's always been a problem for you and—"

He smiled. "Not anymore."

"Excuse me?"

"I've been going to Gambler's Anonymous. Haven't made a single bet in five weeks."

"Really?

"All thanks to you."

"Me? I don't understand. What do I have to do with it?"

"Just what you've been doing with your life. You quit acting like a fool. You're making a go of things without Corny's help. Hell, I figured if my daughter can do it, so can I. Tonight I'm giving Corny my notice, and then I'm going to unload that big dinosaur of a house and use the money to invest in a business of my own. Maybe my own tree removal business. I miss working outdoors and with my hands. Maureen's tired of the gaming life. She'll be moving down here."

"That's wonderful!" I kissed him on his cold cheek, his whiskers grazing my skin. "I can't wait to meet her."

Now was not the time to tell him I was knocked up *and* out of work. Didn't want ruin his moment of triumph.

"Want to know something strange? Ever since I made the decision to live life on better terms, I haven't hurt myself once. No trips, no spills, no shaving cuts."

I looked him over. It was the first time I'd seen him without a Band-Aid or a bruise. I was surprised I hadn't noticed earlier.

"Congratulations. I'm really happy for you, Daddy."

After I said goodbye to my father and left the cemetery, I decided it was time to have a serious sit-down with my aunt. I drove over to Tranquility Hall and once inside, I found her in her office, door open, pecking away at her computer. Usually she kept the plantation shutters closed, as if she feared the least trickle of sunlight or snatch of blue sky could break her concentration. Today the shutters were flung open and light poured in.

I peeked over her shoulder at the screen. Absent were the usual color-coded spreadsheets and pie charts; instead she was visiting a site called Mature Love Match.

A photograph of a silver-haired gentleman was on the screen. His profile was titled "Hubbell Looking for His Katie." Just like the main characters from *The Way We Were*. Looked as if Cornelia was surfing for a love connection.

"Aunt Cornelia."

She was so startled, her arms pinwheeled like a comedian in mid-pratfall. I was afraid she'd fall backwards in her chair but luckily she righted herself at the last minute.

"Didn't mean to scare you."

"I'm fine." She quickly minimized the internet page.

"Is this a bad time? I wanted to talk to you about something."

"No. I was just...I was in the middle of...You saw, didn't you?"

"There's nothing wrong with—"

"Shamelessly peddling myself on the internet?"

"I didn't know you were in the market." How funny that both Cornelia and Dad had been shot by Cupid's arrow.

She avoided my eyes, obviously embarrassed. "Recently I've been trying to delegate more tasks so that I might have time for a dinner date or two...What can I do for you?"

"I need to talk about our contract."

I thought it made sense to start with the first time Dr. Lipton had asked me to falsify records and go on from there, although I still wasn't sure if she'd believe me or not. After that, I recounted all my recent adventures, including my run-in with Darnell and my visit with Rose Wyld. I didn't leave anything out, not even the grossly unflattering parts, and Lord knows there were a slew of those. To her credit, Aunt Cornelia listened attentively and abstained from commenting.

"So you were fired?" she said.

"That's right."

She picked up her teacup and took a dainty sip. "You were fired, so technically you should kiss your inheritance goodbye."

"You got it," I said.

"On the other hand, you've turned into a responsible young woman, which was the reason I struck the bargain in the first place. Poetic justice almost demands that you get the money, especially since you were fired unfairly." She picked up a tube of silver hand cream from her desk and squirted a dime-sized dab on her palm. "What's an aunt to do?"

"Keep the money. I don't deserve it."

"Slow down, missy," she said sharply. "It's my decision, not yours."

"The truth is, I broke the contract in another way." I touched my belly. "I'm pregnant. I found out over Christmas break."

Aunt Cornelia opened her mouth, but nothing came out.

"And I'm not married. As you recall, our contract expressly prohibits bastardy."

"I'm going to be a great aunt?"

"That's right."

A horizontal line formed between her eyes. "Who's the daddy?"

"Aunt Cornelia!"

"Just getting all the facts. Does my brother know?"

"Not yet. I wanted to tell you first."

"And what does Carl say about all this?"

"I haven't told him. He's got too much on his plate right now." I told her about Carl's legal troubles. "Even if he is exonerated, he might get back with his ex-wife. I can't count on his involvement."

She sighed. "Raising a child on your own won't be easy. And you're still so young. Almost a baby yourself."

True, but I'd been through so much in the last few months I felt I'd aged at least a couple of decades. When I took the pregnancy test and saw the faint pink cross on the indicator stick, my mind quaked with fear: What if I'm a terrible parent? What if I crush or drop the child? And worst of all, what if, like my mother, I don't love my baby? Still, I couldn't imagine doing anything but keeping him or her.

"Well then. Now that my grandnephew or grandniece is on the way, I suppose I'll have to stay in Rose Hill a while longer."

"But you're always saying you don't like it here."

"It doesn't matter what *I* want. You can't do this all by yourself."

Maybe I could. Lately I'd been amazed by everything I was accomplishing.

"I appreciate the offer. But I don't want me or my baby to be a burden on you."

She touched my shoulder. "You've never been a burden to me, and I'm sorry if ever I made you feel that way."

Another apology from her? That was twice in a month. It was almost more than a niece could take.

"Quit looking at me like I've grown a horn in the middle of my head. I only say it because it's the truth...Now then, about our contract—"

"Yes?"

"You're right. You violated the terms of our agreement, so you won't be getting the money. Hate to be a hard case, but I didn't get to be where I am now by letting people off the hook. A deal's a deal. I wish it were different, I truly do. I'll be giving the baby some gifts here and there, but there will be no inheritance for you."

"I understand completely."

Now she was acting like the Aunt Cornelia I knew and used to fear. I'd already come to terms with the fact that my days of frivolous spending had come to a permanent end, and had decided that maybe that wasn't such a terrible fate after all.

After our discussion, Cornelia said there was something she wanted to show me in the solarium. The room was one of my favorites in Tranquility Hall. In a house gloomy with dark wood, musty alcoves, and the residue of dismal memories, the solarium was light-filled and cheery.

She pointed to a white rocking chair in one of the corners. "I gave that chair to your mama. She used to rock you to sleep there every night. I know she'd want you to have it now."

I'd seen it before but never paid it any mind. I tried to imagine my mother rocking me in it, but my brain rejected the image.

"Go on. Try it out," she urged.

I plunked down and started rocking gently back and forth. The motion of the chair and the sunlight burning off the earlier fog made me feel drowsy. In moments my limbs grew heavy, my head drooped, and without intending to, I sunk into a brief slumber. I woke to the sound of Cornelia singing. Her voice was soft, high and light. She stopped when I opened my eyes.

"What were you singing?"

"Just a song my mother used to sing when I was a child. Your mother also sang it to you. In that very rocking chair. Funny, I haven't thought about it in years."

"Would you sing it again?"

Her cheeks bloomed pink. "I'm not sure if I can even remember the words."

"Please?"

"I'll try."

A tiny turned up nose. Two cheeks just like a rose.
She's something Heaven has sent. This little girl of mine.
No one will ever know. Just what her coming has been.
She's all the world to me.

She got through it without once stumbling over lyrics. When she was finished, I stopped the motion of the rocking chair. I felt lightheaded.

"You okay? You look woozy."

Suddenly my nostrils filled with the scent of freshly washed cotton and peaches. I could feel the graze of sunlight on my scalp, and the soft cushion of arms. I could taste the sweet tang of milk.

"Toni Lee."

"I remember," I said softly.

"Remember what?"

"That song. I remember. My mother sang it to me."

"That's impossible. You were much too young."

Technically that was true, but the memory was vivid, as if it had only happened yesterday. I also recalled how I felt: safe in my mother's embrace, but more importantly, I sensed her love for me. It radiated from her skin; it trembled in her voice.

"She used to call me Tee-Lee, didn't she?" I said.

Her eyes widened. "I'd forgotten all about that nickname."

"So had I. Until now."

That's when I knew it. My mother, despite her bout with depression, had genuinely cared about me. It didn't make sense that I'd remember such a thing, and most people wouldn't believe it, but I knew that it was true. She loved me, she honestly did. It seemed I had finally gotten my sign.

Thirty One

The next day I checked my phone and found a video text message from someone called Rosie. The last time I'd gotten a video text from a stranger, it was of a well-endowed man pleasuring himself.

I was about to delete my newest text, thinking it surely referred to Rosie palm and her five sisters, but then I remembered...*Rose!*

I quickly clicked on the video. At first, it was difficult to figure out what I was seeing. It looked like two people in flesh-colored clothes, wrestling, but I eventually realized they were *not* wrestling. They were having *sex*...in a motel room. The female, sadly, was Rose and the male...

I squinted. Hard to make out. But when I saw a head full of slicked back curls, I figured it out.

"Should have guessed," I said as I closed the text.

Along with the video was a note. It said, "Check your email."

I looked. As promised, there was a new message.

Dear Ms. Wells,

I wanted to set things right, and they say a picture is worth a million words. Soon as I'm done writing this email I'm going to call that police lady and tell her I was lying about Mr. Rutherford.

You're not the only person who didn't believe my story. A bunch of his students have been calling me and coming by, saying they knew I wasn't telling the truth. It wasn't my idea to hurt Mr. Rutherford. Dr. Lipton called me into his office and asked me to accuse him of having sex with me. He said Mr. Rutherford was trying to get him fired, and if I helped bring him down, I'd be allowed to compete in the Harriet Hall pageant. He said if I didn't help him, I wouldn't graduate. I told Dr. Lipton that if I was going to do something awful like that to my teacher, I needed to do more than compete. I needed to win. He said fine, but he wanted to see me in private and make sure I had what it takes to be Miss Harriet Hall. He told me to meet him at a motel, and I knew exactly what he had on his mind.

When Dr. Lipton went to the bathroom, I set up my phone to film us. I wanted insurance in case he didn't keep his word.

I'm so sorry. You're right. No title is worth all this. I'm going to show the police this video too, because I don't want Dr. Lipton to be asking other girls for private meetings.

Your friend,
Rosie

P.S. Both my parents are doing time in state prison. It's a very sad thing for a kid to have her parents in jail. Now your baby won't have to go through that.

I was relieved that Carl was off the hook, but horrified for Rose. She'd experienced so many trials for someone so young. And Dr. Lipton! I always knew he was a creep, but statutory rape put him in an entirely different category. I, too, suspected he'd slept with other Miss Harriet Hall winners. No wonder he always wanted to be in charge of the pageant.

I composed an email in return.

Dear Rose,

You've done a very brave thing, and I'm extremely grateful. I'll be in touch with you soon. I want to help you get through this difficult time if you'll let me.

Love,
Ms. Wells

All day long I kept checking the *Rose Hill Courier* website to see if there were any new developments. At seven p.m. there was a breaking news notice: "Harriet Hall Student Changes Story. Principal Arrested." I scanned the article, looking for the most important part: "The district attorney has dropped all charges pending against teacher Carl Rutherford."

Immediately I called Joelle and Aunt Cornelia to let them know the news. I also did something I should have done ages ago. I drove to the police station and reported Darnell's assault to prevent him from harming any more teachers in the future.

Three days later I got a call from Harriet Hall. For a second my heart floated to my throat. *Carl?* But of course it wasn't him. The voice on the other line was male but unfamiliar.

"Toni Lee Wells? My name is Mr. Ames, and I'm the new interim principal at Harriet Hall. Several staff members have told me that you may have been unfairly dismissed. Could you come in Monday morning at nine a.m. to talk?"

I was so stunned it took me a second to reply. I'd never imagined I might be able to get my job back.

"Ms. Wells?"

"Yes, sorry. I'd love to."

After we hung up, I held the phone to my chest, daring to think that maybe I hadn't lost everything after all.

Thirty Two

Monday morning found me in Mr. Ames' office, twitching nervously in a straight-back chair. The interim principal had a sleek desk made of glass and silver tubing that had replaced Dr. Lipton's imposing Old World model. Sunlight slanted in windows free of suffocating drapes, and the place smelled of lemon cleaner. It felt like Dr. Lipton had been exorcised from the room.

Mr. Ames was a long-limbed, light-skinned black man with hair cut so tidily it looked like it had come from a spray-can. He wore a white shirt and a skinny black tie, his sleeves rolled up to the elbow.

After exchanging pleasantries, I immediately told Mr. Ames about the various sins I'd committed under Dr. Lipton's administration, including my dark days of being plugged into my iPhone when I should have been teaching. I didn't stall or stammer or try to minimize my transgressions.

After I finished with my story, the new principal pinched the skin between his eyes and leaned back in his chair. He was silent for so long I was convinced I'd meet the same fate as Dr. Lipton's desk. Finally he spoke.

"Ms. Wells. You were a first-year teacher working in a very challenging environment and you received no support from the administration. It's understandable you'd make some errors in judgment. I don't approve of the way you handled yourself initially, but it sounds as if you're now committed to becoming an effective educator."

Effective educator? A few months ago if someone had used those words to describe me, I'd have snorted wine through my nose. Now I genuinely liked the sound of it.

He stood and extended his hand to me. "Welcome back to Harriet Hall. If you'd like, you can go up and visit your students. I'm certain they're anxious to see you. They've been haunting this office, pestering me about your return."

After thanking him and leaving his office, I flew up both the staircases leading up to the third floor, two steps at a time, to my classroom. When I entered, the students were busy working on assignments, heads bent over their work, pencils scratching across paper. Vernon was sleeping and snoring loudly. The first person to notice me was Monica; she sprung up from her seat and hollered my name. In seconds, everyone in the class thronged me, squealing, hugging, and high-fiving.

"You back for good?" Monica said.

"That's right."

"Snap. I was hoping you'd stay away," Monica said.

"Okay then." I took a step toward the door. "See y'all later." I winked at the substitute, the same older black man who'd subbed for me after Darnell's assault.

Monica grabbed my arm and tugged me back. "Can't you take a joke, Ms. Wells?"

"You saying you missed me?"

"I don't miss no teachers." She ducked away from me, but we both knew she didn't mean it.

Later that day, I spoke with a couple of faculty members and found out what had gone down at Harriet Hall after I'd been fired. Once Lipton had been arrested, Ms. Evans, one of the participants in the poker game meetings, went to the superintendent and discussed her suspicions concerning Doc and his alliance with the corrupt principal. Doc had been put on unpaid leave until his hearing, and I'd definitely be asked to testify. As for Carl, nobody had any news.

*   *   *

My first week back at school flew by quickly. On Friday afternoon I stood by my window, passing a hand over my soon-to-be-burgeoning belly. On my desk was a bowl of leftover Christmas candy corn. It was the only vice I had left from those wild and wicked months right after my accident. By now the stores were probably stocking Valentine candy corn, which I'd probably skip. Who wanted to eat sweetheart candy when your one true sweetheart was lost to you forever?

After Valentine's Day came Easter candy corn in pastel shades of pink, green, and yellow. By then I'd look like I was smuggling a basketball underneath my blouse. After Easter candy corn was gone, there were several, bleak candy-corn-less months. In September, when harvest candy corn was shipped into stores, I'd be welcoming my new baby into the world.

I wondered how many candy corn seasons I'd go through before I'd be over Carl. Probably never, considering in a few months I'd have a fist-flailing memento of our brief time together.

"Toni Lee."

I whirled around, startled; Carl stood in my doorway. I stared, assuming he'd shimmer and disappear like a mirage. But he remained, sucking all the oxygen atoms out of the room.

"Mind if I come in?" Carl said.

"Please."

Since our breakup, I'd thought of him hundreds of times, but seeing him in person made me feel as if I might float up to the ceiling and bump my head on the acoustical tiles.

Carl dropped a package of pencils on my desk. "They were cleaning out Doc's office. These were lying around, ripe for the taking."

I smiled at his reference to our first encounter.

"Thank you."

"That Doc," Carl said softly. "Never would have guessed. And I always thought I was such a good judge of character."

I lowered my gaze. He was probably lumping me in with the Docs of the world. Carl had no clue about the role I'd played in his name being cleared. Nobody did, except for Joelle and Aunt Cornelia. Not that it made up for my other heinous crimes.

"Thank God for my brother bailing me out," Carl said. "I haven't always approved of the way Mitt makes his money, but I'll say this: His healthy bank account certainly came in handy when it was time to spring me from jail and hire an attorney. Maybe sometimes it's okay to receive a little help from the family."

Just not all the time, I thought.

We silently eyed each other, and an assortment of feelings passed through me—regret, sadness, and as usual, red-hot desire. Carl looked away first, gazing in the direction of the door. I panicked at the idea of his leaving. I might never see him again.

"Why are you here? Picking up your stuff?"

"I had a meeting with the new principal. Wanted to see if I could get my job back. Nice guy. Said he'd been hoping to hear from me. Looks like I'm returning to Harriet Hall."

"You're going to finish out the year?"

"Yes, ma'am."

That was a shocker. On one hand, it'd be thrilling to see him every day. On the other hand, bumping into him all the time would be like picking at a scab. How was I supposed to get over him?

"And then...?"

"Then what?"

"You'll get a job in Atlanta?"

"No. Deena and Katherine are moving back to Rose Hill after the year's out. Deena didn't care for all the traffic and the higher cost of living."

"Is Deena going to be working here too?"

I tried to hide my horror at the notion. Visions of Carl and Deena nuzzling each other at faculty meetings bludgeoned my brain.

"No. She's hoping to get a position as a principal at an elementary school."

Sounded as if they'd worked out their differences. Good for them; awful for me. Also, if Carl stayed on at Harriet Hall indefinitely, what was I going to do? Could I tent my growing tummy under muumuus and drop waist dresses for the rest of the year? And what about next year?

I'd definitely have to change schools after the baby was born, which was a shame because I wanted to stay right where I was. Harriet Hall High School could be a burr in my shoe, but I'd grown to love it.

"You must be happy about the change in plans," I said.

He nodded. "I've been missing my sweet girl."

I flashed a smile, counterfeit with brightness. "And Ms. Sprague, of course."

"Say what?"

Was he gonna make me say it again?

"I'm sure you'll also miss...Deena while she finishes up the school year in Atlanta."

A corner of his mouth jerked downward. "Why would I miss Deena?"

"Aren't you two back together?"

"Where did you get that crazy idea?"

"Your mother said something about it. And when I called you over the holidays, Ms. Sprague answered. She told me to leave her husband alone."

Carl rubbed his temple. "That was wishful thinking on my mother's part. As for the phone, Katherine stuck my phone in her Barbies' case. Deena must have answered it, and leaped at the opportunity to give you grief."

My stomach fluttered. If Carl and Deena weren't reuniting, did that mean there was a chance for us?

"Deena and I will never get back together," Carl said. "I'm not the kind of guy that makes the same mistake twice."

Had he guessed what I was thinking? Of course he didn't want me back. Not after I'd lied and pretended to be someone I wasn't. No doubt I was as big a disappointment as Deena.

"So why did you call me?"

His hands were in the pockets of his gray wool slacks, jingling change.

"It wasn't important."

"Oh...Although..."

"Yes?"

He lowered his lashes. "I wish you'd gotten through."

"You do?" I said, completely astonished.

"Yeah."

"After everything I've done?"

"I did a lot of thinking over the holidays. When I was sitting in that cell, I would have done practically anything for bail money. If I'd been you, maybe I would have helped Dr. Lipton for the five million dollars too. That's a lot of money."

"You wouldn't have done it," I said, with no doubts whatsoever. "You're a better person than I am."

"Well, you were going to give half of that money away."

"Not my original plan."

Carl waved away my comment. "But after I broke up with you, instead of holding it against me, you went out and did something amazing." He grazed my arm with his fingertips. "I know you talked Rose into changing her story."

"How did you find out?

He ignored my question, saying, "Then I discovered you made the decision not to help Lipton with mid-year testing, thereby forfeiting five million dollars."

"I don't understand. Who told—?"

"I promised not to reveal my source. But I'll give you a hint...It's someone who doesn't skimp on the perfume."

Aunt Cornelia! I should have guessed. She couldn't help but meddle in my life. And maybe that wasn't such a terrible thing. Carl no longer seemed angry with me.

Carl inhaled deeply, his broad chest filling with air. "So...I'm thinking that, maybe, just maybe..."

"Yes?"

His voice dropped to a near whisper. "This breakup of ours was a mistake."

I could barely breathe or talk. Had I heard him correctly?

"In fact, I'd go a giant step further and say we might want to consider taking things to another level. Remember when I said I loved you and wanted to spend the rest of my life with you?"

I'd never forget it. It was the last time we'd been together, and I'd screwed it all up by saying, "Give it to me, baby." He'd given it to me all right. My little shrimp cocktail was doing backflips in my uterus as we spoke.

"I decided that if I ever had another chance with you, I needed to back up my words with action." Carl reached into his pocket and withdrew a small green box. Then he dropped to one knee.

I felt myself get dizzy again. He was proposing for real, and this time, I had no doubts about what my answer would be. I was weak with happiness, but the feeling passed as quickly as it came. Suddenly I understood why he was proposing. Aunt Cornelia must have told him I was pregnant.

I turned away from him. "I'm so sorry, but I can't accept that ring."

"You can't?" To his credit, he made an effort to sound upset.

"You don't really want to marry me. You're only asking because of what Aunt Cornelia told you."

And frankly, this time my aunt had gone too far. So much for changing into a tolerable person.

"Told me what?"

"Don't pretend."

"I have no idea what you're talking about."

"That must have been one quickie trip to the jeweler. Probably went through the drive-thru."

"I'm confused."

I whirled around to face him. "When did you get the ring? Today?"

He bit his bottom lip. "I have a confession to make."

Finally, I thought. The man was Honest Abe; he couldn't help but tell the truth.

"I bought the ring a couple of weeks ago. I was going to give it to you the night I told you I loved you. But when you didn't say it back..." He slowly stood, a pained look in his eyes. "I decided it would have to wait."

"Let me get this straight. You were going to propose that night after I was assaulted?"

He nodded.

"Hold on...You really don't know, do you?" Maybe Cornelia hadn't told him everything after all.

"About what?"

I swallowed. "Here's the thing. I'm..."

"Yes?"

"We..."

What if he wasn't happy with the news? He already had one child. Maybe that was all he wanted.

"Go on."

"You and I...We're expecting."

"Expecting what?"

"A lizard. What do you think? A baby, Carl. We're expecting a baby. I'm pregnant."

"A baby?"

"That's right."

"You and me? A baby?"

I wondered if this was all too much too soon. Maybe he'd fear I was trying to trap him, and he'd go back to not trusting me again. Wasn't it the oldest, most hackneyed tale in the book? Boy dumps girl, girl shows up on doorstep with a bun in the oven.

"Listen. If you want to take the ring back, I certainly—"

"Are you crazy?" Carl tenderly put his hands on the sides of my face. "I just can't believe it." He glanced down at my midsection. "Pregnant?"

"That's what the pink line said."

His eyes looked shinier than usual. Was he going to cry?

"Wait," he said. "Let me do this right." He knelt on one knee again and pried open the box. Inside was a simple oval-shaped diamond solitaire. "Toni Lee Wells. Love of my life. Will you marry me?"

I paused. "There's something I have to tell you before I answer."

"What now?"

I swallowed before I spoke. Now that there were no more secrets coming between us, I could say what I should have said the last night we were together.

"I love you, Carl."

"Does that mean yes?" Carl said.

I was too overcome to speak, so I nodded.

Yes to him. Yes to love. Yes to the baby, and yes to getting married. The feeling was too big to be contained in my body; it was fighting to get out.

And that's when it happened. I felt something wet and unfamiliar pearling up in my eyes. Could it be? Yes, it was! *Tears.* I barely recognized them, it'd been so long. They were the first ones I'd cried since I'd read my mother's diary. Looked as if I hadn't forgotten how to weep after all. Carl wrapped his arms around me and held me to his chest as I leaked almost fifteen years' worth of waterworks all over his white dress shirt.

Carl followed me home from work, and even that brief period of separation made me ache for him. He must have felt the same way. As soon as he parked and got out of his car, he grabbed me around the waist, gently bent me backwards, and kissed me deeply. It reminded me of the photo of the sailor kissing the girl in Times Square on VJ Day.

The sky was so big and endlessly blue, I thought about the Dixie Chicks song "Wide Open Spaces." We sprinted up my walk, a current of anticipation flying between us like sparks from a car battery. I stopped short when I saw an envelope shoved in my door.

I almost ignored it, but my curiosity won me over. I grabbed it.

"Can't you look at that later?" His hand caressed the small of my back, raising goose eggs all over my body. I could scarcely wait to consummate our engagement.

"It'll only take a sec."

"Okay," he said, nibbling on my ear.

I'd never torn open an envelope so quickly; inside was a card on my aunt's letterhead.

If you marry him before the baby's born, it isn't bastardy. Something to consider.

Aunt Cornelia

P.S. I hope to endorse this on your wedding day.

P.S.S. I'm proud of you, and I know your mama would be too.

Folded inside was a check made out for five million dollars. I nearly cried again when I thought about how many Harriet Hall students were going to benefit from the money. As for the distribution of the funds, I knew exactly what I was going to do: I'd reserve a portion for a down payment on a modest three-bedroom house and a college fund for the baby, but the bulk would go to the school. I was almost certain Carl would agree with me. With our two salaries combined, our family would have enough for the essentials and a little leftover for occasional niceties, like a honeymoon, maybe in one of the romantic little inns in Charleston.

After all, hadn't a steady stream of unearned money kept me from growing up? My life had only become meaningful when I had to make my own way.

"What's that all about?" Carl said, pointing at the note.

I smiled mysteriously. "I'll tell you later. Let's just say this: We shouldn't waste too much time planning our wedding."

Karin Gillespie

Karin Gillespie is national bestselling author of five novels and a humor columnist for *Augusta* Magazine. Her nonfiction writing had been in the *New York Times*, *The Writer* and *Romantic Times*. She maintains a website and blog at Karingillespie.net. Sign up for her newsletter on her website, follow her on Twitter or connect with her on Facebook.

Don't Miss Karin Gillespie's Bottom Dollar Series

BET YOUR BOTTOM DOLLAR
Karin Gillespie

A Bottom Dollar Novel (#1)

Welcome to the Bottom Dollar Emporium in Cayboo Creek, South Carolina, where everything from coconut mallow cookies to Clabber Girl Baking Powder costs a dollar but the coffee and gossip are free. For the Bottom Dollar gals, work time is sisterhood time.

When news gets out that a corporate dollar store is coming to town, the women are thrown into a tizzy, hoping to save their beloved store as well their friendships. Meanwhile the manager is canoodling with the town's wealthiest bachelor and their romance unearths some startling family secrets.

The first in a series, *Bet Your Bottom Dollar* serves up a heaping portion of small town Southern life and introduces readers to a cast of eccentric characters. Pull up a wicker chair, set out a tall glass of Cheer Wine, and immerse yourself in the adventures of a group of women who the *Atlanta Journal Constitution* calls, "...the kind of steel magnolias who would make Scarlett O'Hara envious."

Available at booksellers nationwide and online

Visit www.henerypress.com for details

A DOLLAR SHORT

Karin Gillespie

A Bottom Dollar Novel (#2)

It isn't every day a movie star steals your husband. When that day comes for Chiffon Butrell of Cayboo Creek South Carolina, she looks to the Bottom Dollar Girls to help her out of one fine mess.

Husband Lonnie has run out to Hollywood and holes up with famous star Janie-Lynn Lauren. He's left behind Chiffon, her three children and a very tiny bank account. Chiffon breaks her ankle and has to rely on her estranged sister Chenille to lend a hand.

When the tabloid media gets wind of her husband's torrid romance, sleepy Cayboo Creek lands on the star map. Under the glare of camera lights, the two sisters must put aside longtime grievances to forge a newfound relationship. Meanwhile the rest of the gang is cooking up a questionable scheme to raise money for the senior center.

The Bottom Dollar Girls are back and in fine form in this hilarious sequel to *Bet Your Bottom Dollar*.

Available at booksellers nationwide and online

Visit www.henerypress.com for details

DOLLAR DAZE

Karin Gillespie

A Bottom Dollar Novel (#3)

Cupid is running rampant in Cayboo Creek, South Carolina, and all the Bottom Dollar Girls have been struck dizzy with his arrows. When high school heartthrob Brewster Clark returns to town, both Birdie and Mavis are angling for his affections, threatening their long-term friendship.

Ever-so-proper Gracie Tobias meets Rusty the dreamy doctor of her dreams but soon discovers he's actually a blue-collar duct doctor. Will their wildly different social positions drive a wedge between them? Meanwhile Elizabeth is trying to put the sizzle back to her marriage. Not even octogenarian Attalee is immune to love's siren call. She gets engaged to beau Dooley and plans a wild bachelorette party and steamy honeymoon.

Traveling love's rocky road keeps the Bottom Dollar Girls asking, "Is it ever too late for moons and Junes?" Through much laughter and a few tears the girls discover that the answer is a resounding no.

Available at booksellers nationwide and online

Visit www.henerypress.com for details

Henery Press Books

And finally, before you go...
Here are a few other books
you might enjoy:

THE BREAKUP DOCTOR

Phoebe Fox

The Breakup Doctor Series (#1)

Call Brook Ogden a matchmaker-in-reverse. Let others bring people together; Brook, licensed mental health counselor, picks up the pieces after things come apart. When her own therapy practice collapses, she maintains perfect control: landing on her feet with a weekly advice-to-the-lovelorn column and a successful consulting service as the Breakup Doctor: on call to help you shape up after you breakup.

Then her relationship suddenly crumbles and Brook finds herself engaging in almost every bad-breakup behavior she preaches against. And worse, she starts a rebound relationship with the most inappropriate of men: a dangerously sexy bartender with anger-management issues—who also happens to be a former patient.

As her increasingly out-of-control behavior lands her at rock-bottom, Brook realizes you can't always handle a messy breakup neatly—and that sometimes you can't pull yourself together until you let yourself fall apart.

Available at booksellers nationwide and online

Visit www.henerypress.com for details

WAKE-UP CALL

Amy Avanzino

The Wake-Up Series (#1)

Sarah Winslow wakes up with a terrible hangover... and a kid in her boyfriend's bed. She makes the horrifying discovery that, due to a head injury, it's not a hangover. She's got memory loss. Overnight, five years have disappeared, and she's no longer the hard-living, fast-track, ad executive party girl she thinks she is. Now, she's the unemployed, pudgy, married, stay-at-home-mom of three kids under five, including twins.

As she slowly pieces together the mystery of how her dreams and aspirations could have disintegrated so completely in five short years, she finds herself utterly failing to manage this life she can't imagine choosing. When Sarah meets the man of her dreams, she realizes she's got to make a choice: Does she follow her bliss and "do-over" her life? Or does the Sarah she's forgotten hold the answers to how she got here... and how she can stay?

Available at booksellers nationwide and online

Visit www.henerypress.com for details

DOUBLE WHAMMY

Gretchen Archer

A Davis Way Crime Caper (#1)

Davis Way thinks she's hit the jackpot when she lands a job as the fifth wheel on an elite security team at the fabulous Bellissimo Resort and Casino in Biloxi, Mississippi. But once there, she runs straight into her ex-ex husband, a rigged slot machine, her evil twin, and a trail of dead bodies. Davis learns the truth and it does not set her free—in fact, it lands her in the pokey.

Buried under a mistaken identity, unable to seek help from her family, her hot streak runs cold until her landlord Bradley Cole steps in. Make that her landlord, lawyer, and love interest. With his help, Davis must win this high stakes game before her luck runs out.

Available at booksellers nationwide and online

Visit www.henerypress.com for details

Made in the USA
Lexington, KY
29 August 2016